An Innovative Murder for the Season

by Deborah DR Kralich

An Innovative Murder for the Season

A Lt. Sinclair Plate in Sand Waves Mystery

I

Copyright 2015
TX0008216719

Deborah DR Kralich

Published by Ruskras Corner
The United States of America

A note about the Houston/Galveston area. To make room for the fictional colony of Sand Waves and other fictional areas in this series, the map of the area was extensively redrawn, the distance between the cities lengthened and the Gulf of Mexico pushed back, creating new land areas. The geographical areas indicated in this book are completely fictional and are not to be construed as to represent any real communities, areas, streets, or neighborhoods or otherwise existing entities.

An Innovative Murder for the Season, A Lt. Plate in Sand Waves Mystery
ISBN 978-1-942-542-03-2
First in a series
All cover designs, artwork, photography by Deborah DR Kralich, copyright 2015
Text excerpt from *3748 A.D. The Return of the Cat* copyright 2015 by Carl S. Kralich, used with permission.

An Innovative Murder for the Season

Cast of Characters

Janey- A transplant from the Midwest, the elite Command Designed Colony of Sand Waves, Texas has become too hot for her and she longs for cooler climates.

Randy- Janey's husband, his failed career haunts him and he is torn between two women, knows he has to choose, and fears he will make the wrong choice with terrible consequences.

Arthur- Randy's father, his success as a minister does not dull the pain of feeling betrayed by his own father and rejected by his son, years after being abandoned by his wife.

Aerial- Once the child bride of Arthur's father, Marcus. After nearly 25 happy years of marriage, she is now a grief stricken middle-aged widow. Dedicated to her store, her only consolation is true love.

Marcus- Dying two years ago, his widow only a year older than his son, a dramatic change in his life just before his death has unforeseen consequences beyond the grave.

Misha- A refugee, sharp beyond her years, she is

playing a dangerous game that could wind up getting her fired or even killed.

Laurel- A daughter of Texas, she has fallen on hard times and hopes by catching the eye of a prominent established man, her luck will change.

Mark- A congressman, both his political and social positions run counter to what his constituents expect, leaving him vulnerable to blackmail.

Eileen- A minority resident of a command designed colony, she has come to understand it was designed to keep people like her out. But her powerful lover wants her there.

Daphne- Also a resident of this colony, she thrives in the booming economic atmosphere but she isn't above a little trickery to accomplish her goals. A flirtatious cop feels inclined to warn her against murder.

Monica- Not only a resident, she takes credit for all the colony's successes, and demands everyone pay her homage. If they don't, she has no qualms about ruining them.

JW- Visiting from West Texas, this rich rancher

has more financial dealings in mind than just buying an elaborate display for Christmas in an artsy specialist store.

Deidre- JW's wife, she intends to stand by her man no matter what happens or what he might do. But another woman threatens her territory and Deidre has to fight for her position.

Mack- A rare working person in this colony of elites, he has his eye out for a special woman, and hopes to find her in Sand Waves, regardless of the consequences.

Plate- A Sand Waves police officer, his official duties frequently conflict with the social implications of living, loving and working in a colony full of people who are beautiful, rich, famous and murderers.

The Detached Robbers- After a Texas crime spree, a specialty store in Sand Waves is their next destination. If Officer Plate has his way, it will be their final destination.

& Innovations of the Season- the unique store where all are trapped in a weekend full of love, intrigue and terror. See store layout in diagrams on pages 388, 390.

November 1982

Prologue

The covering was pulled back and a gloved hand flipped a switch.

The witch came to life.

Spotlights glared, focused on her.

She was not an ugly witch, but not a beautiful witch either.

Her carved features were full of angles and her eyes were sinisterly wide with anticipation as she bent towards her cauldron.

The cauldron, 42 inches tall and 50 inches in diameter, emitted smoky steam that smelled falsely of incense.

A cat resting beside the witch had seemed to be a finishing touch to the display.

But the kitty was alive and he jumped off the platform as soon as the witch began to move, staring suspiciously at the intruder, who was maneuvering a dolly awkwardly to get it closer.

The dolly was not empty.

It held a lifeless human form.

The witch gripped her giant spoon with both hands, her black satin sleeves lightly brushing the edge of the cauldron as her arms moved the spoon back and forth.

She was bent over slightly.

But not so much that her traditional black witch's hat did not still point upwards.

She was a short witch, about 5 feet tall. Surrounding her was a variety of ghouls and scary creatures, all gazing in anticipation at the pot.

Traditional Halloween music blared on before her arms could make a complete motion.

The kitty fled.

Hurriedly, the gloved hands quickly flipped the switch back and all noise and light ceased.

The witch became an inanimate statue again.

Light was not a problem but sound was.

The witch's arms were now where they needed to be.

It was much darker but a little dim light came through a cloudy skylight some 20 feet above.

Struggling a little bit, the gloved hands reached down to the floor and grabbed the dead body off the dolly.

Aided by the lever-operated manual lift on the dolly, and pulling by its jacket, under the arms, the gloved hands managed to force it headfirst into the cauldron.

Pushing it down into the empty circular space just like forcing an oversized quilt into a washing machine slightly too small for it.

The body was now halfway down.

The legs had to be grabbed and pushed around the huge utensil, as if the spoon was the agitator in the center of the washer.

The gloved hands forced the still supple body down far enough so that for anyone to see it they would have to step up on the platform, stand beside the witch, and look down into the cauldron.

Satisfied the job was finished, the covering was carefully replaced and the gloved hands withdrew, feeling cautiously, in the dim light, along a thinly paneled dividing wall until reaching the hollow door that led to the other side where bright colorful lights glistened and festive music of a Christian celebration, rather than a pagan holiday, played joyously.

Little blood had escaped the body until it had been moved.

The now bloodstained dolly was maneuvered among a large section of boxed Christmas trees surrounded by displayed decorated examples.

The gloves had blood on them now as well.

After passing through that door, the owner of the gloves ripped them off and stuffed them into a briefcase that had been hidden within a promotion of luggage offered for sale.

Now bare hands snapped the briefcase shut and scrambled its combination lock.

Hugging the side wall during the short walk to the back, head down, the person forged towards escape.

Exiting the building through an unlocked overhead door, the person safely deposited the briefcase in a modern and expensively distinctive vehicle, sitting down in the driver's seat, and flipping on the radio.

So many unforeseen complications.

And the radio's message held news of even more.

Latest on the brutal execution murders at a Houston retail establishment.

Late this Friday afternoon, a continuation of the series of robberies of detached retail stores turned deadly.

Three people inside the Fashions 80's Trends and Classics Store were shot execution style during the course of the robbery.

Two clerks and a customer are dead. It is not known what caused the incident, fifth in a string of armed robberies with the same MO, to turn deadly.

Witnesses found the bodies hours after the culprits had escaped. Police are calling this set of criminals, and it is known that there are least two perpetrating these events, the Detached Robbers.

This is primarily because every establishment they have struck has been a small to moderate independent establishment, detached from any other dwelling, with a moderate to large parking lot surrounding the building.

While most retail establishments in modern times are located either in an enclosed shopping mall or a strip center with several other businesses, there are still numerous stores in old single family dwellings that have become commercialized.

In a few restricted areas, new buildings are still being built for single purposes despite the marketing wisdom of the 1980s being that a cluster location is better for business.

The Detached Robbers must believe clusters of businesses pose too much of a hazard, for they are targeting only detached buildings, finding a vulnerable entry place, usually in the back or on the roof.

In other news- Massive flooding is forecast this afternoon in the greater Houston area.

Take precautions in areas that normally flood, more rain is forecast... for more details-

Throughout these announcements, the bare hands had

clutched the steering wheel with a death grip, but now a set of fingers reached and switched off the radio.

In just a flash of time the forecast of pouring rain and massive flooding became reality.

The engine had never been started.

There was nowhere both safe and dry to go.

Except back inside.

Was it safer to leave the briefcase in the vehicle or carry it back inside?

Gloves could probably be explained away but a .357 caliber revolver was a ticket to the electric chair or rather, the new 1980s method of execution just come to Texas, lethal injection.

The gun was a dilemma.

If another weapon was going to be needed, there was a much better choice available.

This gun needed to be hidden where, if found, it would not be for hours, preferably days, weeks or months.

No decision was made until the last minute when a strong grasp of the case's handle dragged it back out of the car.

An umbrella was clutched by its handle as well.

The car door was slammed shut and the carrier of the briefcase and umbrella started around to the front of building.

Upon entering the building, the solution to the problem of the gun was instantly solved.

There was a perfect place to hide it.

Chapter 1

"Forecasts are there's going to be massive flooding tonight. Better close early, send everybody home while you still can."

The officer of the law, a member of the Sand Waves Police Department, leaned against the horizontal counter that faced the front doors of the specialty store, Luxuries and Innovations of the Season, one of the few businesses allowed to occupy the precious real estate in the Command Designed Colony called Sand Waves, located south of Houston.

The counter held a cash register at one end and a glass display shelf at the other. Bright and occasionally blinking Christmas lights covered everything.

The store manager, an attractive slim brunette woman in her mid 20s, felt mild anxiety as some of the lights clinked and the counter groaned when the policemen's body pressed against them.

Although he was slim, he looked solid.

Probably weighs 185 at least, thought Janey. *No more than 5 feet 11, he has to watch it.*

Almost subconsciously, she favorably compared herself to him, at only three inches less in height and 124 pounds, and declared herself the victor. But that judgment was only around the periphery of her mind as she was having to cope with the store owner on the premises, employees, incoming merchandise, this cop, and weather worries, at the same time as she was trying to cheerfully and politely wait on a customer.

"I hate it that I missed your Halloween displays this

year," said the customer. "I guess it is too late to see them."

People came from all over the area to view the elaborate animatronic displays at the store, different for each season.

"I am sorry, ma'am," said Janey. "Our Halloween displays are put away promptly the first day of November. The only holiday we don't have a grace period for them, so to speak."

"I heard they were spectacular this year. I hope they didn't all sell? I hear the Witch's Display was priced at five figures this year like the Christmas displays are."

"No, they did not all sell," said Janey.

Actually none of them sold this year, she thought, *and if I took the trouble to take you back to the warehouse to see them in storage you would most likely be just looking for your own entertainment, not seriously interested.*

Like most people these days.

"What a relief! Then they are still available? *The Witch Stirring her Cauldron,* I mean. I really wanted to see that one. I heard it was spectacular."

"Well." Janey hesitated. She could be wrong.

This could be a serious buyer.

The Witch Stirring her Cauldron, referred to by everybody in the store as the Witch's Display, was one of her favorite artistic endeavors. She had designed it herself without any assistance from the other store workers who doubled as display artists. It was her idea to have the odor of incense rise from the cauldron instead of steam.

"Out of season displays are stored in a portion of the building we use for a warehouse." Then, at the risk of antagonizing the customer, she changed her tone from accommodating to unfriendly. "IF you are SERIOUS about buying one I could page the owner who could take you back to where they are stored-"

"Oh, no, no." The woman jumped at the tone change and mention of the owner whom she pictured as masculine and intimidating. She hastily pushed money forward for the purchase she had made. "I haven't got room for anything like these displays. I'm just glad- well, I'll try to get here next year in time to see the Halloween decorations. You will put the Witch's Display back out?"

I was right, a gawker only, Janey thought as she finished ringing up the woman's meager purchase.

"Of course, the witch will return. She was very very popular with the crowds. Will that be all?"

Janey was giving change when the police officer interrupted the transaction, chattering something about crime.

She glanced at him, annoyed, and tuned him out audibly, but seeing his face for the first time.

His dark glasses indicated he did not favor the bright Christmas lights showering every display, shelf edge and draped across the walls and ceiling of the store.

And not only was he straining the counter with his weight against it, scraping the plastic Christmas lights against the glass, also his admonishment made her lose count. With the constant instrumental Christmas music playing over the loudspeakers, it was hard enough to count change without someone chattering in her ear.

She was well aware of the weather forecast.

She drew the money back away from the customer, who was now staring blankly at the officer, and started over.

"Eight, nine, ten and ten makes twenty. Sorry." Pressing the bills into the customer's hand, Janey was also annoyed at the cash register.

Despite her slamming it shut with her knee, the drawer bounced back open. Her hands now free, she whammed it shut the second time.

It clicked noisily and a little bell sounded. White numbers cleared themselves inside the little window at the top and up popped $00.00 once again.

"Thank you and come back," she called to the customer's back as she left.

The customer fetched her umbrella from the collection of wet dripping modern day water repelling parasols, piled by the front door.

She opened her umbrella as she walked the short distance from the umbrellas to the front door of the store, holding it in front of her like a shield as she crossed the threshold as soon as the door automatically drew back, and flinching as she exited into the pouring rain.

It was custom for everyone to leave their umbrellas at the front of the store to avoid hassling with them while shopping.

Theft was not a worry. For umbrellas, at least, the honor system was respected. The clientèle of this store did not have to steal umbrellas. For those who disdained the complimentary advertising umbrellas that were frequently a perk added to luxury purchases, there were several boutiques in the area that sold them for between $7.00 and

$25.00, petty change for most of Sand Waves' 25,000 residents.

Janey observed the still numerous umbrellas left, trying to mentally count customers still shopping, hoping her annoyance with her constabulary visitor had not gotten through to the Witch's Display fan.

Meanwhile, the police officer was still talking away about crime, the weather and the dangers of flooding, and of getting trapped if the store stayed open too long.

"Yes, Officer," she said snappily. "I'm well aware of the problem. The store is in the process of closing. As soon as these last few customers check out I will be asking permission from the owner about putting out the closed sign. I have already given instructions the music volume be lowered and that the back lights be dimmed, and the animatronic displays to be turned off, to signal that we are about to be closed."

Other customers began coming forward to the register as the lights were slowly faded from the back of the store towards the front. The instrumental Christmas music that had been playing to get customers in the spirit was turned way down. Soon there was a short line.

"Have I got time to get a few more of these crystal ornaments?" called a customer from the center of the store.

"Yes, go ahead," Janey called.

Having rung up the purchase of the next person in line, she was jerking as hard as she could on the cash register handle, trying to get it to pull down and open the drawer so she could deposit the customer's money.

"Soon we're going to have a new cash register that is

automatic, like in the grocery stores," she told the customer apologetically.

The customer scowled. "I hope you are not going to that barcode system like Kroger's. They don't want to mark anything anymore. And the prices the barcodes ring up don't match the advertised price half the time."

"No, ma'am. The owner thinks the barcode system cannot possibly work out. We are getting an automated register that is like a huge adding machine, with a touch keypad that electronically adds, and supposedly subtracts too," said Janey, struggling to get the register to pop out a receipt. "Like the ones they have at Weingarten's."

"Well, I won't ever be shopping at places where those bar codes are used to disguise the real price," said the woman, grabbing her elementary school age daughter by the hand and heading for the door.

The child gazed backwards at the animatronic displays, even gazing through the large front windowed wall until she couldn't see them anymore.

The register handle finally loosened and came down causing the cash drawer to pop open and hit Janey in the thigh.

"Ouch!" said Janey, looking down for a moment, as the pain flashed by. When she looked up, the customer was no longer visible. The police officer was still there.

"She didn't take her receipt," Janey said to him, forgetting for a moment who he was.

She thought for a second she knew him.

"Are we acquainted, ma'am?" asked the police officer as if he had read her thoughts. But he did not remove his dark glasses to let her clearly see his face.

He must have vision glare sensitivity, thought Janey, inadvertently reverting back to her days as an optometrist assistant before her marriage, helping people select eyeglass frames. She automatically surveyed his visible facial features. Straight nose. Medium ears. Blondish/brownish hair, blondish/reddish mustache.

The latter, rather flamboyant.

Her next thought was, *Oh, yeah. I know who he is.*

"No sir, we are not acquainted," said Janey abruptly. She turned her back on him as the next customer came up.

In the foreground, as she rang up the next customer's purchase, she saw Misha come forward with a basket of ornaments to be used on the display in progress, which was no more than a table of components sitting in front of the short cubicle referred to as the manager's office, although it was not an office and no manager used it.

Its opening faced the counter and it had no door.

Misha was a slim, short, dark haired, and dark skinned Asian. She should have been pretty but somehow the arrangement of her facial features gave her perpetual tenseness. Even when she laughed, which was rare, her expression never relaxed.

Misha was obviously preparing to punch out, using the unfinished display table as a stepping stone to the manager's office. She dropped the basket on the table and quickly bounced up the small step into the square 8-by-8 feet cubicle framed by three 48 inch tall walls and a fourth wall which was actually the outer wall of the store.

The employee punch cards were hanging on one

short wall next to the time clock. Employee purses and other personal items were also kept there, in a small short cabinet with mini-lockers on the other side. The open entrance to this space almost completely took up the cubicle wall facing the counter, while directly above the short cubical on the back wall, an oil portrait of a distinguished gray haired man looked down on the entire lobby area.

Unintimidated by the dominating portrait, Misha held her card above the time clock slot, killing minutes before inserting it because if the clock time read more than seven minutes past the quarter hour, she got another quarter hour's pay.

Misha had worked at the store several months and was well versed in the punch clock system.

The clock read six minutes past 7 PM.

As she stood there, tapping her fingers against the metal clock, she pulled a small transistor radio from her pocket and placed the earphone in her ear, gazing down at it in her hands as she switched the dial to try to find a station.

"You're not supposed to have that here," Janey called to her. "Sorry, sir," she said to the current customer as she handed him his package. "Come back soon." Then to the policeman, hoping to get rid of him, she said, "I think there is only one more customer not in line, and she's coming now to check out. The store owner is here on the premises and, as soon as I get a chance, I'll ask her if we can close early."

"I'm also concerned about all of you employees here," said the police officer. "I know you continue to work in the store a considerable time after it is closed and customers leave. There are other reasons, too. As I said, more than flooding may be going on I'm afraid."

"Have a good weekend and please come back," Janey said to the final customer at the counter, thinking what a blessing it was that none of these customers had been making any major purchases. Everybody was just buying a few little decorative odds and ends.

"Says on the radio- flash flood watch in effect all over the greater Houston area," said Misha, loudly from the manager's office.

"We're not exactly in the greater Houston area." Janey frowned. She didn't need Misha to start backing up the police officer.

"Sand Waves is close enough to Houston that a dangerous forecast for Houston needs to be taken seriously here," said the policeman, loudly in Misha's direction, but still bodily glued to the counter beside Janey.

You really think she has any influence on me? Janey thought contemptuously.

"You forget, boss lady, some of us live in Houston," said Misha, twisting the sound piece, which looked more like a hearing aid than a music device, and repositioning it in her ear. "We can't all afford to live in the Command Designed Colony, the holy ground of Sand Waves."

Her punch card already poised above the slot, now twisting her body rhythmically to the music, Misha raised the 9-by-3 card higher, then started it down.

"Misha, DON'T clock out YET!" Janey commanded, yelling, knowing when one of Misha's ears was occupied with her music, only the other was available to interpret words. And English was her second language.

The click of the punch clock was irreversible. It could only be stopped in advance.

Misha halted in mid-movement and glared.

Janey did have the power to fire her.

Misha put her purse back into her employee mini-locker and her card back in the display.

"I may need you to stay a little bit longer. I know it's Friday. But I'm not sure if we have any more customers in the back and I cannot leave the register to go check. I'm sorry, Misha. You can go as soon as we get everybody out. But you have to pull out your earplug and cut the radio off. Do not punch out."

"I get so sick of hearing Christmas music over and over again." But she did take out the earplug, frowning, then making an ugly funny face and mimicking off key as she swung her hips. "Jingle bells, jingle bells jingle bells…"

"How can you ever get tired of Christmas music? I love it. I can hear it all year long." Laurel came up to the front of the store carrying some boxes from the shipment of ornaments that had just arrived.

A deliveryman accompanied her and pulled a clipboard out of a briefcase.

He pushed the clipboard before Janey for her to sign.

"I didn't see you come in," said Janey, not really looking at him this time either. "You are supposed to check in with me here first."

"When I came in, you were very busy," said the delivery man.

As she rapidly wrote her signature, the delivery man

said. "I'll just unload the rest of the shipment in the back and be on my way. If that's okay?"

"Fine," said Janey, handing the clipboard back, barely glancing at him. From under the register she pulled out the additional paperwork she was going to need to do for the shipment. More delays.

"Need any help there?" The policeman called to the deliveryman. "I can help you unload."

Janey looked up from her paperwork, leaned on the counter with both hands and tried to find the words to politely ask the police officer what the hell was he doing there still, and would he please go away and leave everybody alone? But all she could think of to say was, "Officer, do you want a job here?"

The deliveryman, his back already to all of them, turned in mid-stride and twisted around, staring at the dark glasses of the police officer.

"No thanks, Officer," he called. "Just a bunch of lightweight Christmas ornaments." He turned back around and strode towards the back of the store.

"Delivery men are looking younger every day," said Misha, sarcastically.

"He doesn't look any younger than you, Misha. He doesn't look young at all to me," said Laurel, missing the sarcasm, as she pulled her box cutter and hairbrush out of her pocket at the same time, brushing her wavy auburn hair away from her blue eyes. The hair fell back against her forehead contrasting pleasantly with her creamy white skin color.

The police officer straightened up.

He stared contemplatively after the delivery man as the latter disappeared down the aisle. At the same time he answered Janey, "you could do with a bit of part-time security perhaps? I never get tired of hearing Christmas music either. For some reason I don't get to hear it as often as I used to."

Misha grimaced. "I hear it all year long. I will be hearing in my sleep through next November. I'm not Christian, you know. I am Taoist."

The customer purchasing the crystal ornaments finally made it to the register.

The police officer tipped his hat to her.

"Hope you don't have far to travel, ma'am," he said.

"Oh, I live right here in Sand Waves, in the Flower Dune Colony," said the woman. But hopes for a fast transaction faded as she pulled out her checkbook and started to write.

In the seven sections referred to as colonies, homes were separated by size and price. Flower Dune was an example of a colony consisting of homes in the $80,000s and $90,000s. Knowing where a person lived in Sand Waves could accurately predict their gross income 90 percent of the time.

"We don't need any security. The owner would never agree to that type of an expense. I was really just joking," said Janey in total exasperation.

"How much?" asked the customer, coming to the numeration section of the check.

"Thirty six, twenty nine," said Janey, as she pounded the cash register to get it to function properly.

She pulled out the handwritten ledger on which she had to record every check the store accepted.

"That's a beautiful old antique register," said the customer, as she slowly and methodically wrote the check. "My father had one like it in his store that he had before World War II."

"I can truly believe that," said Janey.

"Can I write this check for a little over and get some cash?"

"No ma'am, that is against store policy. We do not give cash back. Please make the check for the exact amount." Janey hesitated. "I'll need a driver's license and credit card or other form of ID with a number on it."

Finished with writing the check, the woman fished in her purse to find the identification that Janey needed.

Janey wrote the driver's license number and the credit card number on the check, carefully inspecting to make sure the written numbers matched the numerical amount of the check, seeing the woman's address preprinted on the check matched her address on her driver's license, and looking at the expiration date, the customer's birthday in 1986, four years hence.

Good, and she looks at least somewhat like her driver's license photo, thought Janey, also aware that the police officer was looking over the check as well, surreptitiously out of the corner of his eye.

"Thank you," she said, handing the receipt to the customer. She could find nothing wrong with the check, no reason to deny it. She pulled out her ballpoint pen to write details of the check in the handwritten red ledger.

"There's been some bad checks going around. They always want to write it over the amount of purchase and get cash back," said the police officer, as the customer walked away. "They have been in moderate amounts like that."

"She had a local address. Everything matched. The check number was high," said Janey to the police officer, defensively. She gritted her teeth, hoping the woman had not heard him.

"Did you know that some banks are allowing customers to start their checks with any number they want, so a high check number is no longer an assurance that the account has been active and legitimate for a while?" asked the police officer.

"No sir, I didn't know that," Janey stamped the check with the store endorsement that read 'For Deposit Only.' She glanced around as she put the check in the register. "MISHA!" she yelled. "PUT the radio AWAY! I don't personally care if you listen to music but you'd better hide that transistor from Aerial or she'll get a cat fit. You know she is here, somewhere in the back."

"I hope the streets don't all flood," said Laurel, still coping with the new delivery boxes. "I'm looking forward to a peaceful evening at home with my cat."

"If you can get there," said Misha, slowly going over to help her.

Misha was the teenage daughter of immigrants who had fled the fall of Saigon. Laurel, near 30, was a native Texan who, if she could have afforded the fees, would have qualified to join the Pioneers of Texas Group.

The commonality among them was that they were on

the lowest level of the employee hierarchy at the store.

They, along with Janey, were display artists. But as there were no lower level employees, they had to do everything asked of them.

Famous not only for its artistic décor, the store's cumbersome name was usually shortened in dialogue to "Innovations".

The store had gained notoriety beyond Sand Waves, even beyond the Houston area, because of its life size holiday theme display animations. Using animation technology perfected by the great American amusement parks in the 1960s, the store featured exquisite sculptures of famous characters associated with holidays, costumed in beautiful period clothing and engaged in holiday activities.

Customers could count on seeing at least three intricate and different displays each holiday season that were so thrilling they brought the viewer an experience that was frequently characterized as unique and enthralling.

At least two, usually three, of the characters would be interacting in animated movement with accompanying music.

There were exceptions like the newest store display, titled *Gunfighter Victorious over the Wolf*, commonly referred to as the Cowboy Display. It was a bargain at $11,000. This was a stationary display that blended the fairytale of Little Red Riding Hood with the western theme that was one of the prevailing cultures in the area.

Little Red Riding Hood stood at one end and a traditionally dressed cowboy, cigarette between his teeth, stood holding a smoking gun at the other end. He wore a yellow western shirt, blue denim jeans, a cowboy hat, cowboy boots and had a double holster to have a gun on each hip. His right hand held one of the guns, which was rigged to emit puffs of smoke, as was the plastic cigarette. Both electronic features were actually part of the cowboy and could not be removed.

A cheap toy gun was his backup weapon, placed in the holster on his left side, the side which faced the front of the display. Music played was an old western instrumental song.

Between the cowboy and Little Red Riding Hood was the fallen wolf. To avoid distressing very small children, this display was located near the back left side of the store and was elevated almost twice as high as the others. This also had the effect of the wolf being very hard to see from floor level.

There was no blood on the wolf either. So parents could reassure overly curious children, who frequently climbed on the display after spotting the tempting toy gun in the holster, that the animal was just asleep.

In front of the restrooms, the top of the Cowboy Display was visible from all areas of the store due to its extra height and the fact that all merchandise aisles in the store were only 5 feet tall so as not to completely block views of the displays from any place in the store.

Most displays were elevated between two and three feet with little steps on one side for employees to gain access.

Climbing on the displays by customers was forbidden by warning signs. But that did not stop people who were determined. Some teenagers took it as a challenge.

Small children just wanted to be a part of it all.

Occasionally an adult had to be asked to leave the store for attempting to become one with the art.

But those people were exceptions.

Most came just to look.

Until the recent recession, most patrons had made a modest purchase just in gratitude for the experience of being in the store.

Lately many people came and looked, and bought nothing.

The police officer was among the latter.

A clap of thunder sounded above all the music.

"I've got to go," said the police officer, "but I wanted to mention one more thing." And here he raised his voice so everyone could hear him clearly. "I was hoping I could convince you to close early without alarming you. I'm sure all of you had heard on the news about the armed robberies of small specialty stores, standing alone, not in a mall or strip center, but with a parking lot all the way around the building like this one, giving the robbers easy access to multiple points of entrance. I don't know if you've heard the news today that a couple of hours ago another robbery took place a little south of Houston, closer than ever to Sand Waves."

Janey, Misha, and Laurel stopped what they were doing and stared at the policeman.

"And this time they didn't just rob," he continued. "Everyone in the store, two clerks and a customer, were shot dead. Killed execution style."

Chapter 2

All three women stood still and gaped silently at the law enforcement officer. No customers were at the front in time to hear this appalling announcement.

He tipped his hat again, meeting the eyes of each of the women in turn. He did not lower his voice. "I'll be on my way. That's really why I stopped by. Just to make sure everything was okay here. Fortunately we've only got two boutiques, a bridal shop, a bookstore, three drugstores, and this place, here in Sand Waves that fit the geographical pattern. We will be watching out for all of you until the city or county lawmen get these guys."

The three women continued to stare silently as he walked out the door. Almost as soon as he left, a very wet customer entered, depositing yet another umbrella on the pile.

"Why is it so dark in here?" she asked.

"We may be closing early, ma'am," said Misha.

"What do you have for Thanksgiving?" asked the customer.

"Yes, we have a Cowboy Display," said Misha, pointing in that direction. "I was assigned to design it for the Thanksgiving."

The customer went off in that direction.

"Go tell Randy to turn the bright lights back on," said Janey. The dimmed florescent lights had previously enhanced the glow of the incandescent Christmas decorations but now the toned down lighting seemed spooky to Janey. And she wanted the customer to be able to see everything.

"We're not going home early?" Misha scowled.

"It's only 7 o'clock, two hours till closing. There's no way Aerial is going to let us go home early. She can't afford to. Business has been slow so far this year. And Misha, we have been over this, the Cowboy Display does not represent Thanksgiving. Aerial had already ordered all the special parts before she realized what you had actually come up with and it was too late to change it."

"How was I supposed to know that? I am Vietnamese. Remember? When my parents first brought me to America, I heard so many stories all at once, including the big bad wolf story and the Thanksgiving story. And we watched the cowboy movies on afternoon TV. I thought they all were connected."

"Did I hear somebody say my name?" Aerial fluttered into sight. Unlike the younger women, who wore tight blue jeans with a loose fitting smock, Aerial was dressed in a lightweight chiffon dress, totally out of season, which would have looked formal if it had not been slightly above her knees.

No one would have cast her as the owner of an establishment like Luxuries and Innovations of the Season.

Aerial fingered the brooch on her shoulder that held the scallop edging on her chiffon dress in place. She looked at Janey expectantly. "How is it going? Are you ringing up lots of sales?"

"That customer was asking about Thanksgiving," said Janey. "I told you we should have made another Thanksgiving Display after that one sold year before last and what Misha designed turned out not to be appropriate."

"But there's no demand for Thanksgiving displays," protested Aerial. "Frequently I have to sell them at a loss. If only Thanksgiving was further from Christmas on the calendar, I could give it floor space. Christmas is so much more profitable."

"Aerial," said Laurel. "They say we are about to have a pretty bad situation outside."

"What?" Aerial looked around the store in such a way that it was obvious she had not heard any news and had no idea what they were talking about. Her mind was still on the problem of Thanksgiving and how doing justice to it intruded on Christmas revenues.

"Aerial, it's raining hard," said Laurel. "We're under a flash flood watch. And there's no letup in sight. If we could just close a little earlier tonight- and there's been murders."

Aerial was greatly relieved to the point of enrapture at this statement. She mentally dismissed the Thanksgiving problem. "Oh thank heavens! Oh thank goodness! What a relief! What a load off! Thank goodness!"

"Aerial," said Janey. "Have you lost your mind? Did you hear what Laurel just said? The last time we had this kind of rains you and Marcus had water in your home and Randy and I had over an inch in ours. What you think thanking heaven for?"

Aerial was slightly disconcerted at the mention of the name Marcus but she let her anxiety flow in that direction for only a second. Then her fears turned back to the present.

"Oh, my dear, you don't know, I mean I thought we had lost our appeal." She gestured around the store. "Just look at this small crowd tonight. And when you take into account that at least a third of our people come here only to see the entertainment displays. And many of them now don't ever buy anything- I was beginning to think that this year, my first full year without Marcus- but thank goodness it must be the rain! Or murders also, did you say? But the rain! The rain! Of course! Thank heavens!"

"Really, Aerial," said Janey. "If you cared so about finances, if you cared anything at all about profit, you could just charge a small admission to see the displays. Or better yet, expand. The future is in costumes. I noticed yesterday the male rack is thinned out. We've established a good clientèle. Or we could expand into a full time department store, maybe with the drugstore inside. The planners of this colony didn't allow for enough drugstores to serve the needs of the residents. If you would just stock over-the-counter medications, something people need. People don't need all this holiday paraphernalia. Do away with these costly displays or put them in a separate section of the store and charge admission to see them. Like that toy museum does."

Janey stopped, out of words at last. Everyone looked at Aerial expectantly, wondering if the long diatribe had any effect on her at all. She felt carefully her stiff hairstyle as if fearing it had collapsed.

Aerial's coiffed auburn hair was about the same color as Laurel's but its solidity in hues gave it an artificial quality as opposed to the natural beauty of Laurel's hair. Janey's long straight brown hair was in dull contrast.

"You know you don't mean a word of what you're

saying, Janey," said Aerial.

"I do too, Aerial."

"I don't have anywhere to put anything like medications," said Aerial. "The store is full to the brim with merchandise."

"The center right section of the back wall is totally blank," said Janey. "You could put a rack there."

"As a display artist, Janey, you know the value of negative space," said Aerial.

"I am also acquainted with negative cash flow," said Janey.

"I'll have you know that I have a couple coming in today who are considering purchasing a display for their ranch," said Aerial. And her next statement contained a fib. "The display they are considering is one of the animated. It's the $25,000 *Santa finds Baby Jesus and the Cookies*. If we could just sell one high priced display a year it would solve all our financial troubles. We've always managed to do that until the last two years. It's that this recession has made the wealthy a little more cautious about what they buy."

Aerial actually did not know what the potential display customers were interested in. She was hoping it was not a Thanksgiving scene.

"But why take that gamble?" Janey asked. "One more year without a high priced display sale and we're going to be in trouble too deep to get out of. We're playing Russian roulette every year. There are just so many Texas oilman and rich ranchers."

"But you don't understand, Janey," said Aerial

defensively. "This is tradition. I owe it to Marcus to carry on."

"Aerial, Marcus was my husband's grandfather. I cared as much for him as any granddaughter. But he is dead and keeping up these outdated traditions he started at the expense of the company is not going to bring him back."

"Janey!" Laurel hissed, seriously angry. "How can you talk to her like that?"

"Oh my goodness, what am I ever going to do?" Aerial became distraught. "How am I ever going to cope with all this? With you girls bickering and trying to run this business by myself? Why did Marcus have to die so suddenly so young?"

"Marcus was 69. He wasn't young," said Janey.

"Why are you trying to hurt me, Janey? I'm only 51, too young to be a widow. And Marcus didn't have to die at 69. He could have lived another 10 or 15 years. He could have been 85. I know several 85-year-olds in good health. He might not have been all that young in years but when he died, I still needed him. He was still loved and still a vital part of all that we built. We conceived and created this holiday theme store together when we first married 25 years ago. We built it from an artistic idea to a paying reality. We designed the displays ourselves at first and then hired different artists like you and Misha and Laurel to help us create and celebrate all the joys of Christmas."

Aerial paused, tears coming to her eyes. But she remembered where she was and looked around anxiously to see if there were any customers watching. No one was in sight except her three employees.

"We never made much money, until they started this Command Designed Colony idea and built Sand Waves 12 years ago. It was almost like winning the lottery when we were approved to be one of the few stores, one of the few nonresidential structures even, allowed in Sand Waves. All the good we've done, promoting Christmas, has paid off and maybe business did slow down but everything was wonderful until Marcus died."

Janey stepped from behind the register, walked over to Aerial and embraced her. She was afraid Aerial was going to have a teary breakdown right in the middle of the lobby. "I'm sorry, Aerial. I'm taking things out on you that you can't help. Plus my head is killing me."

"My dear, why don't you come with me and I will get you some aspirin? Misha can handle things alone. Can't you, Misha? Laurel, you need to go back and work on the unfinished display."

"Sure, if it gets busy I will just call you over the loudspeaker." Misha walked to the register, picked up the loudspeaker microphone, and tapped it. It made a loud raspy boom all over the store.

Laurel went back to the unfinished display she was working on.

Three mannequins of varying heights waited. They were to be dressed as angels carrying presents.

The gift boxes were not ready yet. She grabbed some merchandise at random to substitute so that she could position the angels' arms and see what else would be needed.

Unseen by the others, tears slipped down her cheeks.

Chapter 3

Misha watched all of them leave, then carefully and surreptitiously glanced at the single customer still in view.

Satisfied that the customer was engrossed with her shopping, and Laurel was involved with the unfinished display, she reached and quietly, deftly pulled down the cash register handle so that it made no noise.

The drawer bounced open easily and softly, stopping at the touch of her hand.

Careful to make no noise, she lifted up the tray containing the money.

From under the tray she pulled out several large denomination bills.

That the old cash register kept no record of what was rung up was no secret at the store. The little role of register tape in the interior that should have recorded duplicates of all the transactions did not work, had not worked for years.

Misha looked around, still making sure that no one was watching, rolled the bills into a cigarette sized bundle and took the transistor out of her pocket.

She opened the back of it and slipped the money inside, with quickly working fingers that indicated she had done this often before.

She was safely at ease and waiting to serve when the next customer then approached with a small purchase.

"Cash, check, or charge?" said Misha, noting that this was not the customer they had just seen a few moments ago.

More people might be in the store than they realized.

"Oh, I think I have cash for this," said the customer. "Do you sell cigarettes here?"

Misha opened the register without punching any numbers.

She immediately began wrapping the fragile ornaments in tissue paper.

"Sixteen, forty five. No ma'am, we don't sell tobacco products."

The customer handed her a $20 bill.

"Out of twenty? Okay, fifty, a dollar, seventeen, eighteen, nineteen, twenty, thank you! Oh, did you need a receipt? It might take a moment. This register's being cranky. It is really old."

"No, that's okay," said the customer, a little huffily. "You people don't take returns anyway."

"All sales are final," said Misha politely. "Thank you and come back."

Without a word, the customer turned and walked out. Misha slipped the $20 bill into her pocket.

Within minutes of each other Janey and Laurel both returned to the lobby area.

"That customer was not the one we had seen earlier," said Misha to Janey.

"And here comes someone new," said Laurel.

A single woman entered the store, nervously setting her umbrella down.

She felt defensive from the beginning although no one could possibly know why she was there.

She looked around to see if any of the employees were black.

She did note the Asian girl, obviously an employee.

She knew none of the customers were likely to be

Asian.

Even an Asian employee gave her a little surprise.

Seeing the Christmas displays brought her no comfort despite the festive Christmas holidays she had once celebrated in Georgia during her childhood.

She hardly saw them at all for what they were.

Instead, she saw them as potential hiding places for the man she was planning to meet.

They did not usually meet at a location in Sand Waves.

It was too dangerous.

But she had insisted on a meeting. It had been over two months since she had seen him.

She had her satchel case draped across her chest, its long strap cutting her breasts in half and digging into one shoulder, while the case rested between her other arm and side. It was a soft fake leather and she dug her elbow into it as she walked past the counter.

She began searching through the store, looking for a person rather than merchandise.

He is not here yet, she thought, pretending to stare at *Santa finds Baby Jesus and the Cookies.*

Then she really saw the display for what it was.

Santa, holding a plate of cookies, rose and knelt on one knee in front of the Christ Child's manger which was watched over by animals.

Viewing this were several child mannequins, boxes of cookies at their feet, with their backs to the audience.

Santa did this repeated motion every seven minutes.

The display, on a round platform, was located to the

left in the store.

From the outside it was visible from a huge window on the left side of the outer wall.

A short aisle approached it on the other side and behind it was the Cowboy Display.

Customers still had plenty of space to walk completely around it on the inside.

Right behind the manger where various animals stood, a complete view of the front door could be had.

The newcomer maneuvered herself, pretending to be looking for the price tag.

She jumped a little when she found it.

Cost of this display was $25,000.

Pretending she could not read it, she slipped down among the animals in such a way that she felt she could not be seen by a casual observer, hiding behind a large sheep.

From where she stationed herself she was able to see every customer that entered.

She stiffened at each new face.

So far every face had disappointed her.

By the time she had taken up her position amongst the display, two more people had arrived who also had less than positive, yet very different reactions, to the festive décor.

Chapter 4

A middle-aged man, wearing a brown business suit with a narrow tie and white shirt, looked around in disgust.

Other customers might have taken him for an art critic passing judgment on the artistic merit of the displays, his review being entirely negative.

The man, although 50, looked to be in good physical shape. This was the result not of good genetics but of a strong self-discipline.

Somehow he radiated that self-discipline to others making most of them extremely uncomfortable.

He carried a briefcase in such a way that it was easy to tell he was more comfortable carrying a book. The briefcase was dark brown and rather shabby, a little dusty as if he had just pulled it out of the closet after several years of non-use.

Beside him, as far as the trait of self-discipline went, could be considered his female counterpart. She was also trim and svelte, and although she was wearing a long sleeved jacket and skirt that went below her knees, and a tight fitting blouse under the jacket that made the ensemble appear almost a uniform, when she walked her muscles moved like she was a soldier.

That she worked out most every day of her life was taken for granted by everyone who set eyes on her.

Yet despite their similar controlled appearances, there were incongruities between these two people that made them an unlikely couple.

She looked to be between 35 and 40, and while her tailored suit spelled businesswoman, she embellished it with jewelry that could only be considered gaudy, even in Sand Waves.

She also carried a briefcase, but hers was not a simple brown briefcase, rather it matched her suit in color, light gray, and had her name prominently featured on the front via an expensive engraved plaque that read 'Monica Moon'.

"Don't look now, Janey, but your cheerful, happy-go-lucky father-in-law is here. And he has got a friend with him." Laurel went into the manager's office and opened her mini-locker and extracted her purse and took it with her when she went back to working on the angels.

Janey saw that indeed Arthur and Monica had entered the store.

"I see you got your briefcase, Arthur. This is business? Miss Moon, isn't it? Should I get Aerial?" Janey approached them.

"Janey," said Arthur. "I'm glad you remember Miss Moon. Monica, you do remember my daughter-in-law, Janey? Randy's wife."

"Certainly. She visited your church one Sunday when I was there."

"One of the few times I've been able to get my son to come to church."

He moved to embrace Janey.

Janey kissed him formally on the cheek.

"You know I would come every week if Randy would."

"Yes, my dear. I know it is my son and not you. But this is not the time or place for discussing our family problems."

"So what are you two doing here? Not to see Randy or myself? Aerial?"

"No, not to see you, my dear, although it's always a pleasure."

"We do," said Monica, "have some very important business to discuss with Mrs. Marcus Harriman."

"I don't think I've ever heard Aerial call herself that," said Janey.

"She did before the '70s," said Arthur. "She was happy to call herself that when she first married my father."

"Would you be so kind as to tell her we are here?" Monica asked formally.

"Yes," said Arthur. "Please, Janey"

At that moment several more customers came into the store, shaking off their wet raincoats, and leaving their umbrellas by the door.

Misha remained at the cash register as Janey went off to find Aerial.

Behaving very much unlike a customer, Monica Moon was eyeing the place with a professional and critical eye as Arthur watched her with obvious admiration.

"Arthur, the store is so large and in such a prime location in Sand Waves. There are so many possibilities for this property with or without the building. When I first estimated a selling price of $350,000, I was assuming this was a mom and pop type establishment. I'll certainly have to revise my estimate."

"It began as a mom and pop. With my father and Aerial. But as the area began to grow and prosper, it did too. It's only been in the last two or three years profits have been down."

"But of course, the recession and the drastic increase in electricity explains that. The electric bills for this place must be astronomical. I see the airconditioner is on full blast. Still, are you sure you want to liquidate this? I understand you haven't any obligation on your personal finances at this time."

Monica's innocent sounding tone belied that she had already decided the fate of Innovations.

She needed Arthur to think it was his decision.

"Monica, I don't feel money can be a consideration here. Look around you. The commercialization of Christmas carried to its extreme. I just can't find the word to express the revulsion I feel at these gross displays. Sleeping Beauty and the Prince! What has that got to do with Christmas?"

This year, for the Christmas season, the most prominent scene at the front right of the store, where it was visible outside through the front windows and to everyone in the front interior lobby, was *The Prince's Embrace.*

Arrayed on an exquisite antique white French Provincial bed, Sleeping Beauty was movingly awakened by her six foot tall prince.

Breathtakingly life-like, Sleeping Beauty actually opened her eyes, rose from her bed, turned her head.

The prince reached forward to embrace his love as she rose from the bed, their figures coming within inches of each other before he drew back and she fell back down.

The three fairy godmothers all held presents for children and the second motion of the display was for the fairy godmothers to appear to be flying about. Actually wires simply moved them up and down so that they appeared to hover over the three stationary child mannequins in the foreground.

Surrounding them was a background of star lights and silver Christmas trees, lit with pink and blue Christmas lights and decorated with pink and blue star ornaments on an elliptical shaped platform.

The effect was breathtaking.

The construction cost of the display, retailing at $32,000, was actually a little over $18,000, yielding a nice profit when it sold.

But it had not sold yet.

It was going on three years old.

Plans were to redo it if it did not sell this year.

The Christmas décor would be stripped off, the festive color filled trees to be replaced with dark generic forest green. The presents ripped from the fairy godmothers' hands and replaced with hearts, turning it into a Valentine's Day display. The children mannequins' costumes would be changed from holiday attire to cupid costumes.

Fortunately, the costumes of Sleeping Beauty and the Prince were more fairytale-like and less holiday-like and would not need altering. Neither would the action or special effects, save the music.

The price would have to be reduced considerably.

Unaware of those plans, Arthur was still reacting to the mixing of Christmas and children's fantasy stories.

"The message is that nothing is real," he complained. "And the context! Why he is almost in bed with her. With little flying godmothers handing Christmas presents to children. Disgusting! Why it betrays the whole meaning of Christmas. So artificial! So plastic! It's dreadful. Why I can better abide the pornographic bookstores and massage parlors in Houston than all this."

"So, you want to do away with the store altogether?" Monica was continuing to speak with Arthur. Her tone was hopeful.

"Ideally. At least, get the Harriman name out of it."

"And how is your stepmother going to respond to this?"

"Please, my dear. I am not in the habit of referring to Aerial as my stepmother. I'm almost as old as she. She was just the- the young girl my father became infatuated with after my mother died."

Monica failed to point out that there was almost a 15 year age difference between the two of them.

And she intended to marry him.

She had dropped enough unmistakable hints to this effect that Arthur could not possibly think otherwise.

"Weren't they married 25 years? Surely she deserves more status than that," said Monica.

"My father was not a man to ever divorce. He paid for his mistakes like a man. Besides- ah- he never quite got over his- well, infatuation for her."

"You mean they were happy together?"

"I didn't say that. They may have gotten along and- and- retained, let's say, their romantic enthusiasm for one another- but that does not mean they were happy."

"Oh, of course not." Monica laughed. She reached

into her briefcase, took out a cigarette and a lighter.

Arthur was not amused. "There is much more to marriage than love, fidelity, and compatibility."

"What?" Monica lit her cigarette.

"A shared faith. A desire to serve God together. And as far as what Aerial thinks about this place? Well, I have the right to my share of my father's estate. I can force a sale. I have fooled around too long as it is. It has been two years since my father died."

"She could buy you out," said Monica, drawing a deep breath and letting the smoke out slowly.

"I happen to know that she does not have the capital. All my father left her with was the part ownership of the store and their home. He refused to buy life insurance."

"Then, I'll sell my home to keep the store," said Aerial, coming up behind them, holding her head up high. "And please extinguish your cigarette. This is a no smoking establishment. By Sand Waves Colony Federation Board ordinance."

Aerial pointed to a sign on the manager's office short wall.

"You couldn't get enough money, Aerial, out of that old house, even if it is technically inside Sand Waves," said Arthur.

When Sand Waves was conceived, a few older homes had to be taken in its borders. The owners, some residents since the beginning of the 20th century, had refused to sell.

Now, most of those people had passed on and the houses had sold. Marcus and Aerial had bought one of those before he died.

"Now I'm sure something can be worked out if you'll just let me handle the real estate details. As an heir, you have the right to demand your share of the estate in cash if you want it." Monica looked around for a place to extinguish her cigarette. She had seen a police car parked outside and was not going risk a fine.

"And who are you? And what business is it of yours?" asked Aerial.

"This is Miss Moon," said Arthur. "She is a friend and member of my congregation. She also happens to be a prominent real estate broker in Sand Waves."

"Ms. Moon. We don't use the title 'Miss' anymore, Arthur," she corrected him, and then addressed Aerial, "Reverend Harriman is interested in listing this property with us."

"Never! This store is not for sale. Arthur, have you no decency? Are you even human?"

"Please, please, Ms. Harriman," Monica began.

"Mrs. Harriman- I'll have no one call me Ms."

"Monica, you are being a bit inconsistent. You used old fashion titles for some people and for yourself-"

"Arthur, for myself, what I do may be different in many ways." Monica turned to her companion with more familiarity than she intended to.

"If you would just leave, Miss Moon. That would take care of the problem," said Aerial.

"Monica, go look around a little bit. I'll join you shortly."

"I don't want her here. Arthur, she needs to leave. I know she is your- your lady friend-"

"My relationship with Monica is complicated but I don't-"

"I don't care what you are doing with her. Just get her out of my store!"

"Aerial, we don't want a scene in front of customers. Can we go to your office and talk privately?"

"Yes, I guess that would be best. Let's go to the back offices. We don't use that space for much except storage. But we can find room to sit and talk somewhere."

As Aerial and Arthur went down one aisle to the back of the store, a thin, dark attractive man, came up another aisle and stood before Janey.

She looked at him with disapproval.

"Randy, you are dressed too casually for your position here," she said. "And too light for the season."

"It's 80 degrees outside," said Randy. "There is nothing wrong with my clothes."

Janey thought about starting an argument but decided to drop it. "Your father is here," Janey told him.

"Where? I don't see him."

"He went with Aerial. He brought that real estate agent your father has been seeing."

"Monica Moon. That woman. She's a leech."

"He wants his share of the estate. You can't blame him. I wish you felt the same way about your share."

"I happen to care for the store. You know that. And besides knowing him, he'll take the money and build some religious statue in a park somewhere. If Ms. Monica Moon doesn't get it all away from him first."

"You don't understand your father."

"And you do?"

"Yes, I do."

"That's what I said- you do."

"I thought it was a question. He's a fine preacher. A fine man. He certainly managed to accomplish more than you ever have."

"Just because he gets his name in the paper every once in a while."

"He's a well known man of the Word."

"The trouble is, most of the words are his own. And I've never been impressed by his words."

"And we all know you are a man of action," said Janey sarcastically.

Randy was angry and embarrassed although there was no one that could have heard them.

He feared losing control.

"Especially after a drink or two," said Janey.

"This is too much. I've gotten drunk twice in my life. The first time was at our wedding. When I married you."

"The consequences were a hell of a lot worse the second time."

"I don't know about that."

"You wrecked your career, lost your job, all in one drunken episode, ten seconds of idiocy and now look what we do for living. We sell plastic trees and little glass balls."

She held up an ornament and gripped it so tightly that it burst in her hand.

At that moment some customers passed them, forcing a stop to the argument. Randy went towards the restrooms, scowling at the thoughts going through his head. He passed the woman using the Santa Display to hide without noticing her.

She looked through him as well, still watching the door.

Laurel took a moment's break from her work.

"It is time for me to be off," she told Janey.

"I've already told Misha she can't go home yet. Suddenly we have a lot more customers. You just can't leave."

Angrily Laurel turned and went all the way around the Santa Display, running into Randy at the crossing.

She caught his arm in a somewhat comforting gesture but he never slowed his stride. The action, far from comforting Randy, distressed him. He went beyond her without comment, and quickly entered the men's room.

Laurel stood between the Santa and Cowboy displays for a moment.

She had a barely imperceptible reaction to an item out of place.

After debating whether to climb up on the display, she simply pushed it out of sight.

This is somebody else's problem now, she thought. *Everybody expects too much out of me.*

When she was sure no one was looking, Laurel turned toward the back of the store.

The long narrow simple display of Christmas caroling mannequins stood against the back wall opposite the ends of the aisles.

She no more saw them than they saw her as she passed quickly by.

Chapter 5

At that moment entered the epitome of the long tall Texan.

Wearing a cowboy hat that made him look taller than he was, he even bore a strong, if superficial, resemblance to the cowboy mannequin in the display.

He walked through the door, his companion trailing behind him.

He stood still and looked all around, taking everything in.

He failed to remove his cowboy hat upon entering as did the short young woman who stood deferentially behind.

She was dark complexioned with dark brown eyes and dark brown wavy hair.

She was petite and dressed in obviously very expensive clothing.

As the front doors closed automatically behind them, they stood in the lobby in the manner of royalty expecting a reception.

No one paid any attention.

Still, they stood there for at least a minute before going arm-in-arm to Janey's counter.

Misha had relinquished her spot at the register back to Janey and gone back to work on the unfinished display.

The man tipped his hat and set his stylish expensive leather briefcase on the counter. "Good afternoon, ma'am."

"Good evening, may I help you?"

"Why you are correct. It is almost nine." The man tipped his hat again. "I am JW Smith and this is my wife, Deidre."

"How do you do?" said Janey, mildly confused at this formal introduction.

"I believe we were expected, ma'am."

"I don't understand," said Janey, her mind occupied with the previous conversation with her father-in-law.

"Mrs. Harriman is expecting us."

"I am Mrs. Harriman," said Janey, not thinking.

"I believe we spoke on the phone earlier, Mrs. Harriman," said JW, in an annoyed tone of voice.

He was not used to being forgotten.

"Oh, I see," said Janey wearily. "I believe you must have spoken to Mrs. Aerial Harriman. She actually owns the store."

"I beg your pardon," said JW. "You are absolutely correct. We are dealing with the owner. Her daughter-in-law I presume?"

"No, yes, I am, sort of, well, her granddaughter-in-law, except, well, oh, sort of." Janey took a deep breath.

The Smiths looked especially confused now.

"I'll get her for you," said Janey.

Janey stepped from behind the counter and called to Misha. "Misha, would you watch the register for me again?"

"Sure," said Misha, coming back. "Happy to."

Janey went after Aerial.

"JW, look at that! A cowboy!" said Deidre, eyeing the part of the cowboy visible from where she stood.

She carried a large satchel type purse similar to Laurel's, but made of expensive leather and with a designer emblem on the front.

Rather than drape it across her body, she had tied the long handle in a knot and carried it as a purse.

"How much is it?"

"Only $11,000," said Misha, her tone indicating she expected a shocked response to such a cost. "It's our newest display. I designed it."

"But my dear is it large enough? We want to make sure we get the biggest and the best," said JW.

"Yes. Right, JW. Good point."

Misha rolled her eyes skyward but the Smiths were not looking at her.

"Oh, welcome! I'm so sorry I wasn't up here to greet you," said Aerial, breathlessly running up to the lobby.

Monica and Arthur followed at a slight distance.

"I simply must see to this, Arthur. We can continue our discussion with Miss Moon later."

Aerial reached the Smiths after her breathless trot and Janey relieved Misha, who went back to the unfinished display.

Monica and Arthur continued talking softly, their gestures indicating nothing had been solved.

"Mr. Smith! Mrs. Smith!" Aerial gushed a little. "I'm so glad you could drop by!"

"We did not just drop by, Mrs. Harriman. We have come more than 500 miles to see your famous displays. We are interested in a permanent display for our ranch. Our good friends on a neighboring ranch had the foresight to purchase one four years ago before the prices for the best went to five figures."

"Well," said Aerial hesitantly.

There was a display left that was less than five figures.

It was the long narrow display of carolers, an eclectic accumulation of mannequins acquired at various going-out-of-business sales and attired in colorful winter clothing.

To one side stood the song leader, holding a baton and facing a sheet music stand.

Other finishing touches indicated this was a group of singers performing carols in the holiday tradition.

Totally stationary, inanimate, and without sound effects, it went unnoticed by almost everyone in its position next to the blank spot on the back wall.

It was only $4,000.

Aerial was undecided if she should mention it. She wanted the Smiths to spend as much money as possible but she needed to sell them something. Anything.

"We only want the best that you have," said JW.

"Oh." Aerial felt happier. No need to mention the cheaper display. "Now you did want a Christmas display? Our Halloween displays are still available. They're being stored in our warehouse section over on the right side of the store and can still be viewed."

"Oh no. No Halloween stuff for us. We want it to be Christmas every day of the year at our ranch. And we want only the best. We have a huge enclosed courtyard just the right spot for the biggest and best display you've got."

"Oh wonderful! Come over here and let me show you…"

Aerial's voice trailed off as she took the Smiths to look at the displays.

Janey noticed that a number of customers had begun leaving without making any purchases and no one new was coming in.

The weather was getting worse.

If the Smiths had not been there, she would have tried once more to convince Aerial to close early as the police officer had suggested.

Arthur and Monica were seated on a bench near the front door as if they were unable to decide whether or not they wanted to leave.

They were talking softly but most of their conversation was audible to Janey although they didn't realize it.

"She can't stop me," said Arthur.

"What have we really accomplished? Should I get to work on this listing? Are there going to be lawyers involved?"

"My dear, do not distress yourself. Go ahead and leave and get some coffee."

"Not coffee. I've already got a headache."

Janey stepped from behind the register. "Arthur, can I speak to you for a moment?"

"Where are the restrooms?" asked Monica.

"On the left wall near the back corner of the store. Go past the shorter aisle that parallels the Santa Display, then turn left and go between that display and the Cowboy Display. You will see them then, right near the Cowboy Display," said Janey.

Monica went off.

"She could go around the Santa Display and be right

there," said Arthur.

"We direct all customers that way and usually go that way ourselves," said Janey defensively. "It poses less risk to the Santa Display. But actually I need a little time to talk to you about Randy."

"What has Randy done now?" Arthur asked Janey.

"Oh, I don't want to burden you, but too much is happening and you are the only one I can talk to about him. I want to wait to tell my parents until, well, things are more resolved."

"I feel for you my dear. I'm quite prepared for whatever he does."

"I hope so."

"Well?"

"Randy is having an affair," Janey took a deep breath, sounding more dismayed than distressed.

"My heavens."

"Apparently quite a serious affair. I think I am in some danger of being traded in."

"Are you sure?"

"No doubt, I'm afraid."

"I suppose it was inevitable. The one sin he had yet gotten around to. Just like his mother. She left, you know, when our marriage was about as old as yours. Left me with a son to raise. A son I had hoped would be a blessing, a consolation."

"Fortunately we don't have any children to be hurt."

"You must try to work it out, Janey. Maybe if you did have a child it would save your marriage."

"It would be impossible unless he gets out of the

store."

"You mean?"

"One of the display artists," Janey nodded.

Arthur looked at Misha in horror.

"No, not her." Janey looked around but did not see the person she was talking about. "The other one must be in the back. Laurel Moore."

"How long it has it been going on?"

"For some time now, several months at least." She smiled as if she were amused. "And right under my nose. I only found out about it last week. Aerial let it slip, quite subconsciously. She never realized-"

"Aerial KNOWS?"

"Yes, I think she approves. True love and all that. Laurel is her favorite here also."

"That woman, that evil woman."

"Oh, I don't know, Arthur. Maybe I'm wrong and they are all right. All we do is argue and I've been thinking if Randy really wants out-"

"You must not think that way, Janey. Marriage is sacred. You must preserve it all costs. No matter how unhappy you are."

They heard the high notes of Aerial's voice then. She and the Smiths came towards them.

Janey hastily went back behind the cash register and Arthur walked over towards the front bench.

At that moment two people entered the store and, had they made any gesture towards one another, it would have been assumed they were together.

The woman looked to be in her late 20s. She was an

incredibly beautiful blonde but in a soft very non-blonde way.

Her hair color was obviously not false, naturally honey yellow in color. Her skin was Scandinavian white, creamy with striking brown eyes.

She was not a tall woman, barely 5 feet tall. But she had an exquisite shape, large breasts, curvy hips, a waste not too tiny, but just right for her figure.

She wore professional looking clothes that still enabled her to appear feminine, black slightly rounded toe pumps, heels not too high, but high enough to look sexy.

The man on the other hand, was the epitome of 1980's fashion. His suit was obviously tailor made and the latest style costing as much as the average person made in a week. He had dark red hair and a ruddy complexion.

He was not really handsome so much as he was imposing. Over 6 feet tall he was easily taller than anybody else around, even JW.

But where JW was slim in stature, this man was bulky.

Both people carried briefcases and umbrellas.

Both immediately deposited the latter items into the pile, in almost grateful manners.

The blonde carried a briefcase that was slightly a little large and heavy for her.

She carried it in the manner that indicated she would like to set it down at the first possible opportunity.

But she did not.

Instead she walked past the counter and appeared to be immediately entranced by the Santa Display.

Seeing a woman crouching behind the animals, she silently stared a moment and shrugged.

Then, slowly and somewhat self-consciously, she began walking all around the store, shifting the briefcase from one hand to the other as she took in all of the decorations, disappearing towards the back.

As soon as the man, carrying an entirely appropriate and perfectly professional briefcase, turned from dropping his umbrella and faced the displays, the woman hiding behind the manger animals lit up.

It was obvious this was who she had been waiting for.

The man saw her too.

He was about to go to her when JW called out.

"Mark Brown! You son of a gun! What are you doing here? What a coincidence? Peggy here with you?"

He strode directly between where Mark Brown stood in the middle of the front lobby and where the woman had been about to emerge.

Alarmed, she ducked down an aisle filled with toys.

Mark Brown was torn only a moment before going towards JW and Deidre.

Aerial stepped back, suddenly upstaged.

But she rallied and walked over to join them.

"JW, Deidre, what a pleasant surprise," said Mark. "No, Peg is not here. I am picking up a surprise for her."

"Oh, Mrs. Harriman, surely you must recognize Representative Mark Brown. Our congressman."

"Of course," said Aerial, her face transparently revealing she didn't know him from Adam. "Representative uh-"

"Welcome, Representative Brown," said Janey, coming from behind the counter and rushing to Aerial's rescue. "All the way from Austin? How are things at the state capital?"

"At your service, Mrs. Harriman." He addressed Aerial genially, then turned somewhat stiffly to Janey. "I'm afraid though that I serve in Washington in the national Congress."

"Of course, from Washington," said Aerial, fanning her face with her hand, even though it was not at all warm in the store. "Ha, ha, how about that? Janey, look, a customer ready."

Aerial pointed towards the counter where a woman had placed a small artificial tree.

Feeling dismissed, Janey went back to the register.

"Yes, well," Mark glanced at Eileen who was staring at him unhappily from behind the display. "The weather in D.C. is much drier. I almost didn't make it here. If I hadn't had four wheel drive I wouldn't have made it yet. Oh, and Mrs. Harriman, I think I have fished out one of your employees. I found her stranded beside a car in rising water. I think she is still outside trying to get the mud off her shoes. Fortunately, I have vinyl flooring in my jeep. Her car drowned out before she could escape Sand Waves. Oh, here she is."

Chapter 6

A very wet and muddy Laurel came through the front door. She was dragging a large sharp cornered case with both hands, her umbrella unopened and clutched against her side with one arm.

"Laurel, my dear, I did not know you left," said Aerial. She took off her own coat and put it around Laurel's shoulders and led her towards Janey.

"I specifically told you not to leave," said Janey angrily. The customer departed directly between the two workers with an amused look on her face. Monica, returning from the restroom, also smirked as she heard the conversation drifting down the aisle she was coming up.

"I was just trying to get home. I have a cat that depends on me. She needs to be fed, and I didn't want to get stuck here." Laurel started to cry. "I had an appointment to sell makeup tonight also. I had my cosmetics case in the car and when I was afraid the parking lot might flood and it might get wet and I went to get it. It was turning dark so I just kept going. I'm going to miss my appointment. This other woman in the apartment complex sells makeup. My customer will probably go to her now. I am dependent on the extra income I make working part-time as a cosmetics consultant. My situation is so tight I could hardly stand to lose a sale, no matter how small."

Randy came forward and it seemed he was going to take Aerial's place next to Laurel but then he stopped short, staring at Janey who was staring back.

"Let's get you out of those wet clothes. We probably have a costume that will fit you. Come on, dear. Leave your briefcase in the manager's office. Maybe I need some more makeup. I'll look at what you have."

"Thank you," said Laurel, sniffling, dragging her large cosmetic case with her. It was an expensive waterproof finish that looked like leather.

Aerial and Laurel headed towards the costume rack that stood adjacent to a dressing room.

It was the same type of portable temporary cubical structure as the manager's office but with much higher walls.

A floor length mirror was attached to the outer side of the small door as well as there was a similar one on the inside.

On the aisle, front right, was a promotional arrangement of small to moderate size pieces of luggage, space rented in the store by the luggage maker.

Laurel set her cosmetic case there, intending to retrieve it later and put it in her mini-locker if it fit.

Weighing slightly more than most women her height, Laurel was unable to find a practical female costume that would fit her. But she would be able to wear jeans that went to a pirate costume made for a man by rolling up the cuffs.

The white silk shirt would be little big on her but not too much. She left the other trappings of the costume, a vest, hat and plastic sword hanging on the rack.

"At least we're selling these theatrical costumes, particularly the men's costumes. I placed a large order before Halloween. There's almost none left!" Aerial chattered happily through the dressing room door to Laurel as she changed.

"At least it's comfortable." Laurel came out in the costume and surveyed herself in the full length mirror.

"You look adorable," said Aerial.

"If she couldn't get out, we can't leave the area. Can we?" said Arthur, as he came over to the rest of the group at the same time as Laurel and Aerial returned.

"And now it is dark," said Deidre. And all the others realized it as well.

"I might can get back out," said Mark. "But I have only room for one other passenger. And I'm not sure we could make it back. I think we can still get around inside Sand Waves. But the outer exit is flooded."

Sand Waves had only one exit out of the colony in order to minimize the number of cars that could come in.

This had the effect of creating a bottleneck whenever a significant number of residents needed to get out at the same time.

Those routinely making the long tedious commute to Houston automatically incorporated enough time in their morning routines to accommodate this traffic jam.

And those same corporate employees invariably did not get home till late at night. As it was Friday, many people would already have come home earlier than normal even without the flooding.

Those who had not made it yet were going to have to spend the night in a hotel somewhere outside of Sand Waves.

"I don't know why the designers of this Command Designed Colony did not allow at least one small hotel inside the boundary," said JW.

"It would be so much more convenient when we come to shop," said Deidre.

"It looks like, with this emergency, Deidre and I have nowhere to go," said JW. "We heard on the way here, the part of Houston where our hotel is located is totally flooded in."

"Is it all right if we bring our luggage inside the store?" asked Deidre. "We have a low sitting automobile and if the water rises very much more, everything we have will get wet."

"Of course," said Randy.

"We can move the car to a higher place," said JW.

"Anyone else need to do that?" asked Randy.

Everyone else was already parked as high as possible.

JW and Deidre grabbed umbrellas and prepared to brave the rain to get their baggage, cursing the designers of Sand Waves as they went out into the elements.

"And we all know what even the finest hotel in the finest part of town is inevitably used for part of the time," said Arthur.

"It is idiocy not to have a hotel, I think," said Janey.

"The powers that be here didn't want transients staying here," said Randy. "It is practically impossible to even get an apartment."

"That's right," said Monica Moon. "The only apartment complex is a very small set of units hidden in the back of the colony, used primarily by persons temporarily displaced by the uneven buying and selling of their houses. Most agencies keep one or two permanently rented and on standby just for that reason. For the public, rents at these apartment complexes are 50 percent higher than comparable apartments just down the highway and there are no long term leases ever signed. This discourages riffraff."

"It is a way to discriminate against minorities," said Misha.

Mark looked at her sharply.

"Oh, I do not think race has anything at all to do with that," said the congressman.

"We do not need permanent apartment dwellers in Sand Waves. It is bad enough that they allowed those two condominium complexes," said Monica.

"I lived in one of those apartments," said Misha. "Then they found out I was not white and I was evicted. That's why I live in Houston now."

"You were evicted, Misha?" asked Aerial, with concern and empathy that surprised most of the others.

"I doubt that was it. Probably you didn't pay the rent. But based on your position here and how little money you must make, I don't know how you got in in the first place," said Monica.

"How do you know I am not Asian royalty? You bi-"

"Misha, remember Miss Moon is our customer- ah, guest," said Aerial, quickly cutting Misha off.

"Excuse me." The woman hiding came from behind the display where she had been watching. This was a good opportunity, she thought, to establish a legitimate presence in the store without attaching any suspicion. And let everyone know a black woman was present. "Sand Waves is 98 percent white," she said, speaking politely, controlling her temper, as they stared at her in surprise. Some with hostility. "It may be 1982, but Sand Waves is nearly an all white enclave. I am one of the two percent." She spoke softly in the direction of the man she secretly loved. "The statistics are correct aren't they?"

The congressman flushed a bit and did not reply.

He was well aware she did live in Sand Waves, in a condominium complex where she was the only black person residing, purchased with cash by her lover and put in her name.

Mark knew this because he was the man who loved her behind the scenes.

"That appears to be the situation, ma'am." Mark addressed her as if she was a stranger.

Although it hurt a little bit that she could not acknowledge knowing him, it was still a thrill to be spoken to by him in public. It made her feel more like a person.

Avoiding eye contact with Mark, she addressed Janey. "Did I hear someone say the road outside the area is cut off? But we can still get home if we live inside Sand Waves?"

"I would suggest that you leave immediately," said Janey, not without kindness. "Things could get worse."

"There are blacks living in Sand Waves," said Monica Moon. "There is the famous retired actor Monfried Santost, one of the first African Americans to win an Academy Award back in the 30s. There is the famous baseball player Clip Pointpar, famous for breaking racial boundaries in sports in the 1950s. There is Amelia Mattworks, the famous jazz singer of the 1920s."

"I hear she is now nearing 100 years old," said

Aerial.

"You sound like an advertising commercial," said Misha to Monica.

"I believe all those people live in mansions in the back part of Sand Waves that is accessible only beyond gates patrolled by security guards 24 hours a day. Isn't that right?" said the congressman.

"Yes, that's right," said Monica, annoyed at him for revealing that information. The gated sections were not a publicized part of the colony. Their inhabitants did not want their existence known.

"I knew all these people live in Sand Waves," said the black woman. While their location was obscured, the presence of celebrities had been publicized in the marketing of the colony. She wondered if the marketers thought home buyers were so naïve that they believed superstars lived just down the street from the tract houses purchased by moderate or even high income corporate workers.

Well, maybe some people were that stupid, she thought. *But not me.*

"Most of the blacks here either live in million dollar mansions beyond the patrolled gate or right near it in the highest class neighborhood mansions that sell in the hundreds of thousands," she said to Monica, pretending she believed this was news to the real estate agent.

"I am sure blacks are well represented in all Sand Waves communities," said Monica. "Are we acquainted? Ms.-"

"No, we are not."

"What is your name?" Monica persisted.

"My name is Eileen-"

"Actually, African-Americans aren't well represented here," said the congressman, interrupting. "That is one reason why I am here this week to confer with the Colony Federation and black and Hispanic area representatives about the demographics."

Eileen felt a flush of gratitude that he supported her statements.

"I was just planning to leave," said Eileen, in response to Janey. Dealing with the different ways society treated people stressed Eileen and she never pursued the subject long.

"Didn't you hear what they said on the radio? No one should leave," said Mark.

Eileen looked gratefully at him. She then hastily looked away, hoping her look had not betrayed her love for him to the others.

But they were indifferent to her emotion.

"Well, Congressman, something needs to be done about the flooding. Not just in Sand Waves. Your district must include more territory than here. The flooding in this part of Texas is getting worse and worse," said Janey. "The entire southwest part of Houston flooded the last time it rained like this. That's where my parents live. We didn't have this problem in the north. No five hour traffic jams during rush hour either. Wet, slush, mud, and 80 degrees in November. So damn muggy, I have sinus headaches all the time."

"Go back up north if it was so much better," said Laurel, but she spoke so softly from behind the unfinished display that Janey did not hear. Laurel gave up on the box cutter and ripped the tape by hand. Misha picked up the box cutter and picked up a different box.

The two junior employees glanced at each other.

Laurel pushed several boxes over to the side. "These boxes don't get unpacked, Misha," she said, wondering why Misha had suddenly taken a notion to actually work at this particular point in time.

JW and Deidre came back in, each struggling with four pieces of luggage and both now soaking wet.

"Well, I wouldn't want to live anywhere but Texas. But this is a dreadful place if you ask me," said Deidre.

"I personally don't see why anybody would want to live here," said JW. "We native Texans laugh at the idea of cutting down all the trees to build a house then replanting two bushes in a tiny yard when there are hundreds of thousands of acres of land available, not just down the highway, but all over the state. Apparently Yankees think a tiny lot with the two required trees is as spacious as a-"

"We find Yankees a derogatory term," said Monica. "And many people from the more sophisticated parts of the country are appalled at the lack of restrictions. They don't want to buy a house where any entity could purchase the land next door and build any type of establishment. With no zoning in Houston, and Galveston platted hundreds of years ago, nothing can be done to stop it. The mishmash of businesses and residences throughout Houston appalls most of my clients. They feel at home in Sand Waves."

Where strict colony federations, legal because they were voted power by the majority of original hand picked residents, can control the neighborhoods and keep property values high, she thought silently. *And my commissions maximized.*

"Do you consider Yankee a derogatory term?" Randy asked Janey, the idea occurring to him for the first time despite their having married five years ago.

"I- well, I am more from the Midwest. Although we moved around when I was a kid and did live in the North for a while," she said, vaguely. Janey did not want to admit in front of Monica's strong assertion about the insulting properties of the word, that the song *Yankee Doodle Dandy* always came to her mind, along with the movie of the same name starring Jimmy Cagney, when she heard the term.

And it was one of her favorite movies, frequently on the *Late Late Show* on TV. She liked the song, too.

"I'm more concerned about the constant flooding that threatens my home than what names I might be called," she said.

"That topic is also on the agenda," said the congressman. "Unfettered development is part of the discussion."

"It is a vicious lie that development promotes flooding," said Monica.

"All the paving gives the water no place to go," said Laurel.

"This flooding can't last too long. I can make everyone comfortable here," said Aerial.

"We have a lot of room in the back and in the side warehouse," said Janey.

Eileen was looking at Mark. Complaints about

socioeconomics had left her completely now. She was excited at the prospect of being trapped with him, even if they had to ignore knowledge of one another. Yes, segregation had been fought and the battle thought won.

That it had quietly re-emerged in this Command Designed Colony of 25,000 might be a cause for concern, but right now she was in the presence of the man she loved and very rarely saw.

And despite his calm and politically professional demeanor, the cut of his eyes to her at random showed her that he felt it also.

"Well," said Monica. "I'm not sure I don't want to try to leave anyway."

"At least here we're safe and dry," said Arthur.

"I see your employee has changed clothing," said Deidre to Aerial. "Is there something we could dry off with? And maybe change clothes ourselves? We don't want to break into our luggage here in the lobby."

"We're packed so tight, we might never get the suitcases closed again," said JW.

"Oh, I'm so sorry. Come with me. We have theatre quality costumes here, all kinds and all sizes. Let me take you to that section and anything you want to change into, you can borrow. We have lots of cowboy-type costumes."

"And hotels will be totally full everywhere around here with flood refugees," said Randy.

"I wanted to leave earlier. The policeman warned us to go. But no! We had to stay open. We had to stay," said Misha.

"Maybe we can still get out of Sand Waves. If we go

south to Galveston instead of north towards Houston?" Monica wondered.

"I hope you have a costume for a tall man like JW," said Deidre to Aerial as they went towards the dressing room.

"Misha," said Janey. "Get your radio out. Flip it on."

"No, I will not!" screamed Misha. "You would not let me listen to it when I wanted to."

"I have a radio," said Mark.

He pulled it out from his briefcase and turned it on.

Massive amounts of rain have fallen in the last two hours in Southwest Houston areas.

A flash flood warning is in effect for all Southwest Houston area communities including Clear Lake, Webster, Seabrook, Dickinson, Friendswood, Pearland, League City, Bacliff, San Leon, Beach City, Texas City, Sand Waves and the Galveston Island.

Everyone in the vicinity is advised to take shelter. If your structure is not in danger of flooding please remain where you are.

All streets and freeways are closed. If you are in a structure in danger of flooding, leave as soon as possible. Or get to the highest level of that structure as soon as possible.

This is an emergency--

Randy flipped the congressman's radio off.

The announcement was going into a repetition mode.

"So folks, I'm afraid no one is going outside of Sand Waves anytime soon."

73

Chapter 7

"Those other places are west of us," said Monica. "I don't see why they think Sand Waves would flood out if it hasn't already. The flooding goes from east to west normally."

"The rain is just coming down harder there right now in those areas. More rain is on the way," Mark reported.

"We are south of Houston. Everywhere south of Houston floods," Janey said.

"We cannot go northwest to Houston right? That is cut off?" asked Eileen.

"What if we go due west?" suggested Laurel.

"The highway to the west is already flooded out," said Mark.

"What if we go due east?" asked Eileen.

"Nothing there but a wildlife preserve. No highways. No roads," said Randy. "No lights, too dark to see anything."

"Due north?" Laurel persisted.

"Well, we might could reach Baytown but it is unlikely," said Randy. "We would still have to go northwest, that's the way the roads run. Due north there is nothing but chemical plants. They would be closed down in this emergency. We could not get through them."

Although it still might be possible to make it to their home, Randy and Janey knew it was their responsibility to stay.

"Our house should be all right," said Randy. "It is in the highest part of Sand Waves. The least expensive parts are the highest."

Aerial returned with JW and Deidre.

The West Texas couple looked mildly worried but felt confident.

They had their luggage inside, their car parked as high as possible and it was fully insured.

Plus they had both found perfectly fitting cowboy/cowgirl costumes that were actually almost identical to what they had been wearing when they arrived and wore every day of their lives.

Only their tight fitting blue jeans were slightly inferior brands and their western shirts were now different colors than they had previously worn.

And JW complained that the hat that came with the costume was black instead of the white color he favored.

"I thought there would be a lot to choose from," Aerial had apologized.

They had discovered only one male Western costume on the racks, which fortuitously fit JW. "I guess we must have sold all the others."

When the talk turned away from any possibility of leaving to the practicalities of staying, Misha became openly upset.

She started crying.

"People are going to drown!" she wailed. "And there's nothing I can do."

The others all stared at her for a moment, dumbfounded by her emotion but their attentions were quickly distracted.

"There's water coming in the front door," Janey yelled. "We have to keep it from the displays."

"I'll get all of the push brooms out of the warehouse." Laurel ran down the aisle towards the back right section of the store.

"No! They're not in the warehouse! It's so crowded in there with the off season displays that didn't sell, the brooms are in the unused office space now."

Randy started in that direction.

Laurel did an about face and also went towards the back section on the left side of the store.

The electric lights flickered off.

Then flickered back on again.

There was a little pop near the front doors.

Randy turned around and came back, going to the doors.

"The auto mechanism is shorted out," he said.

"Where is your breaker box?" asked Mark.

"It's right by the restroom, actually hanging on the side wall between the restroom and entrance to the office space where the brooms are. Follow Laurel if you want to check it," said Aerial. "It's so high up in the wall, most people need a step ladder to reach it. Randy is the only one of us tall enough to reach the switches without one."

"It is not the breakers," Randy asserted. "The electricity must be flashing outside. The doors can be operated manually. We can push them open and closed."

"I just wanted to know where it is located," said the congressman.

"They slide on a track?" JW asked Randy, thinking, *he could be an inch taller than me.* He adjusted his new hat.

"Yes, they are heavy but we can manage them," said

Randy.

"I think we should make an announcement," said Aerial. "Janey, use the PA system and say, oh, what should she say, Congressman?"

"I think you need to alert people to the fact that the road leading out of Sand Waves is impassable. Do you know how many people are left in the store?" asked Mark.

"No. I, well, there's all of us here and the Smiths-"

Janey picked up the PA microphone, turned it on and touched the sensitive section.

It popped.

"Ladies and gentlemen, customers here at Luxuries and Innovations, can I have your attention please?"

She paused.

"Will all customers please come to the front lobby? We regret this inconvenience if you have not finished your shopping but there is a weather emergency."

Aerial rushed towards Janey and waved her arms frantically.

Janey cut the microphone off.

"What?"

"We don't want to alarm them. We don't want a negative connotation to their visit to the store to stay with them."

"No, Aerial," Janey sighed. She turned the microphone back on. "Ladies and gentlemen, there's no cause for alarm. However, it would be helpful if everyone would come to the front lobby of the store so that we can better explain the weather situation. Thank you."

Everyone in the lobby started looking around.

No customers emerged.

Laurel returned with four brooms.

As Randy and Laurel were working to sweep up the water, JW and Deidre began moving their luggage onto the unfinished display platform.

Randy handed a broom to Misha.

Janey took the other one and they began pushing the water back out the front door.

"Shut the door and lock it," said Janey.

"Randy, how many people do you think are still in the store?" asked Aerial.

"I counted four. This lady here," he looked at Eileen expectantly, "Ms.-"

"Eileen," she said promptly.

"-was one of them. One was wrestling with a Christmas tree. He ought to be up here soon. I think there's someone in the ladies restroom," said Randy.

"I'll go take a walk through and see if I can find anybody." Misha had not finished speaking before she started down an aisle.

"Turn the music off. I think people just aren't paying any attention. When the music stops, they tune out what I'm saying. They think I'm a commercial," said Janey.

"That's about right," said Laurel, as she put the brooms away.

The water had subsided like a lost errant wave.

Just then the man struggling with the large artificial Christmas tree box came up, dragging it behind him.

This took everyone's attention for a few moments.

"Sir, where do you live?" asked Randy, as he went to

help the customer.

"I'm just in the next neighborhood er- colony over," said the man. "I am in a borrowed four wheel drive pickup. I think I can make it if I can pay for it in a hurry."

"Just take the tree and come back and pay for it later," said Aerial. "I have some sheeting you can put over it. Randy, go to the warehouse section and pull the tarp off of one of the out of season displays there and bring it to this man."

"That's okay, ma'am," said the man, pulling the tree towards the front door. "I don't care if the box gets wet, it won't hurt the tree if it gets wet. I don't need the instructions. I can put together an artificial Christmas tree without them. I'll come back and pay for it as soon as this is over. I appreciate it so much, you trusting me this way. I may not have the chance to use the truck again for a while."

"You're so very welcome," said Aerial.

Randy and the man forced the front doors back open and carried the big box out into the rain. Randy came back a moment later, soaking wet.

He pulled the front doors shut and locked them.

"This will help keep the water out," he said. "That man barely got away without the truck drowning out. The parking lot is flooded, the streets surrounding it impassable. No one else is leaving."

The water had stopped coming in the front as soon as Randy secured the doors.

They could see it in the still dim cloudy light from street lamps, flowing along like a little stream right up next to the front walls.

"What is our actual geographical situation here?" asked Mark. "I've been here many times but never paid attention. Now it is raining so hard I cannot even see out the windows."

"The store sits on a raised section of land and the parking lot slopes downward from the building for a short ways. But then it climbs back up to reach the street level which is much higher than the lowest section of the parking lot, but lower than the building itself. If fortune holds, the streets and parking lot may completely flood but the building should remain dry."

"Please God, that be the case." Arthur spoke softly.

"Oh, yes!" echoed Aerial.

"I'm going to make sure the back door is secured," said Randy. "The back end of the building is a little higher. So if water is not coming in here in the front, we should be okay there."

"Aerial, you should not have let that man take off with that tree. Wasn't that a $200 tree? You don't know that he's ever going to come back and pay for it," said Arthur.

Janey silently agreed, going back to the counter.

"He had an honest look about him," said Aerial. "And what does it matter? If the flooding is all that bad, if water gets into the store, so much merchandise will be ruined, it will not make any difference if the man never pays for the tree. I just hope he gets home and is able to have a nice Christmas with his family."

"Well, Christmas is several weeks away," said Arthur. "I do not anticipate this will ruin Christmas for anyone. Christmas is not dependent on weather, location or any earthly condition. Christmas will come no matter what the circumstances."

"We still have three people unaccounted for," said Randy. Janey reached for the microphone again.

"Here is one of them," said Randy. "Just wait, Janey."

He was followed by the deliveryman who had previously brought in the new ornaments.

"You left!" said Laurel, anxiously. "How did you get back in?"

"The back overhead door was completely unlocked," said Randy. "The alarm was turned off. Anybody could come and go as they please back there."

"I almost got out of Sand Waves with my delivery van, but I had to turn back at the exit onto the highway," said the deliveryman. "Our company policy, in a situation like this, is for me to attempt to return to the last place that I had checked in by phone. So I came back here. It was just easier coming in through the back door. The front parking lot was already too flooded for me to even drive the van around there."

"I couldn't find anyone else," announced Misha, as she came back into the lobby, a little breathless from having run the store's perimeter.

At this moment the beautiful blonde woman came forward from the path that led to the restrooms.

She was still lugging her oversized briefcase.

"What's going on?" asked the blonde.

"You can't hear the loud speaker in the restroom," Janey explained to the others who were beginning to express confusion as to why this woman didn't understand the situation.

"And who are you?" asked Randy, shivering a little as his wet clothes were starting to get really cold, as the air-conditioning was still running.

"My name is J. Daphne Martin," said the beautiful blonde. "I am with Finest Southland Life Insurance Company. I had come by hoping to talk with Mrs. Harriman about the insurance."

"Is there a problem with the insurance, Aerial?" Randy looked alarmed.

"Randy, you have got to get out of those wet clothes," said Aerial, taking him by the arm. "There's no problem with the insurance on the store. Miss Martin sells life insurance. You'll note the word 'life' in her company name. You need to go back to the costume rack so you can find a costume that will fit you that you can change into."

"But-" Randy wanted to protest but he suddenly began to shiver seriously and realized she was right. He had to get out of the wet clothes.

"Janey, do you think you could assist your husband?" said Aerial as she and Randy passed by the counter. "I feel I should stay here with our guests."

The delivery man discreetly moved towards the front door as if he felt like he was intruding and not deserving of the term 'guest'.

"Misha." Janey sighed with exasperation. "Take over for a moment please."

"Happy to," said Misha.

"I don't think there's any need for anybody to be at the register right now," said Laurel.

"Don't mind me, I'm nuts," Janey yelled backward as she went down the aisle. "Force of habit."

"What are we going to do, JW?" Deidre addressed her husband but he was at a loss for reply. "I don't think we can leave our luggage here."

"Don't worry," said Aerial. "We have some accommodations available, uh, in the back. My late husband had offices in the back corner where there are some desks you can stack your luggage on. As long as we stay dry, we're safe here. Let's pray that the electricity doesn't go out. We've been through some bad floods and never lost power at all, most of the wires in Sand Waves are underground. Only the wires coming into the colony linking us to Houston are aerial, like my name."

She laughed weakly at her pun.

Nobody else smiled.

"Yes, she's right. We've been through some storms and floods and never lost power, or only lost power for a very short time. But sometimes on perfectly sunny days the electricity just goes out for no good reason at all," said Laurel.

"Let's say a prayer aloud," said Arthur. "If you will join in a circle with me, we will say a prayer for the safety of our families, our homes, this location and ourselves."

Everyone turned and looked at Arthur for a moment. He remained nonplussed and spread his arms open.

"Anyone? Join me?"

Laurel then immediately went to his side.

Monica stepped forward reluctantly as though she thought it was expected of her.

JW and Deidre willingly joined arms, with Deidre next to Monica.

Mark stepped beside JW and Eileen raced to his side, linking her arm with him.

They stole a glance at one another.

The delivery man shuffled forward standing next to Eileen who was now totally oblivious of everyone, except Mark.

Aerial took Mack's other hand.

The insurance agent completed the circle, standing between the deliveryman and Arthur.

Only Misha fell back, sulking.

"You are welcome to pray with us even if you are not of the Christian faith," said Arthur to Misha.

Misha stood up abruptly. "No. I don't like anyone to touch me ever. I will go and see if Janey and Randy need help in the back."

Misha rapidly went down an aisle as Arthur began intoning a prayer and all those in the circle bowed their heads.

Chapter 8

Randy returned in dry clothes as the prayer finished.

Janey and Misha came behind him.

"Don't laugh, this was all that was available that would fit me," said Randy in a low voice. "Mr. Smith took the one costume left with jeans."

JW and Deidre were busy hauling their luggage towards the back offices under Aerial's direction.

Laurel laughed despite the circumstances. The pants and shirt were part of a costume sold by the store as Count Dracula. Randy was wearing the white formal dress shirt and satin tuxedo pants with a tone on tone stripe down the side. Sans the cape, mask, tie, and top hat, he merely looked overdressed.

"Now you are overdressed rather than underdressed," said Janey.

Randy ignored them both.

"I have been working on a plan," he said louder to the others. Little attention was paid to his change of clothes by anyone else since the new clothes did not look like a costume. "It does look like we may be here for several hours and we insist all of you should be made as comfortable as possible."

"I don't see how we can possibly be comfortable here," said Monica Moon. "Are we all going to sit in Santa's sleigh?"

"I am sure there are some chairs somewhere," said Laurel. "There is the unused office space in the back."

Aerial had already thought of that. Upon return, she and the Smiths rolled three office chairs into view.

"Actually, well, there are rooms upstairs where we can all possibly spend a comfortable night," said Aerial, somewhat reluctantly. "That would keep us safer in case the waters rise and flood the downstairs."

"Upstairs? This place has no upstairs," said Janey, bewildered. "There is no attic space over the warehouse section and the attic space above the retail section has been closed off since Aerial and Marcus bought the building."

"No, Janey, you are wrong," said Aerial. "The attic was remodeled into an upstairs apartment last January when the store was closed for vacations. I had it done discreetly and have kept the door leading up there securely locked, at least I think it is locked. Anyway, a display is rolled in front of it every morning and moved back every night when I return after the store is closed and you all go home."

"When you return?" asked Janey incredulously. "What do you mean when you return at night?"

"You live here, don't you Aerial? I noticed you are here so much more than ever before," said Laurel.

"I sold my house in Sand Waves ten months ago and I have been living over the store ever since," Aerial confessed. "There's nothing wrong with that. It is tradition, if you know history, for store owners to live over their stores-"

"Not in Sand Waves!" Monica Moon declared.

Deidre and JW looked at each other and returned to the bench.

"Yes, I am afraid I must ask you to keep this confidential as it is against the restrictions here, but such a silly restriction and why would anyone care?" asked Aerial

"We do need to have the radio in a fairly central location," said Randy cautiously to the others, as if he felt he needed support.

"It is MY radio," said Misha.

"Remember, I also have a radio," said Mark, wondering why they did not appreciate his radio as much as Misha's. "But the batteries are low."

"We can settle that later, just don't let the battery die, my dear," said Aerial.

"We have batteries here in the store." Janey cast her eyes at the battery display which was stocked with every possible imaginable battery sold in retail stores in more than ample numbers.

"Oh, right, so we do, well that's that then. Arthur would you help Randy move the display that hides- I mean blocks- the door to the stairs? Randy considerately comes back every night to help me with it and has done so all this past year. I am so grateful."

"That is why you left home every night?" asked Janey.

"We'll talk about it later," said Randy as he pointed out the display to Arthur.

It was the long narrow Carolers' Display.

They pulled it to the right, filling in the blank area along the back wall to reveal an unfinished wood door that opened to crudely built block stairs in a narrow passageway.

"Let's all go upstairs and work on getting comfortable for the night. Fortunately there are several small rooms- and we can divide up reasonably well-"

JW and Deidre once again joined the group but

before Randy could continue, Misha jumped up and started towards an aisle.

"I have to use the bathroom," Misha announced and strode briskly down that aisle. But she instead of turning left to the restroom, she turned right and went almost full circle around the back of the store, and back up the right side to the third elaborate display for Christmas 1982, located between the costume racks/dressing room and the display of artificial trees in the very back right corner which came just short of hiding the warehouse door.

Every year nearby Galveston celebrated the current Dickens craze with a festive city-wide celebration known as Dickens on the Strand, named for the famed writer and a well-known city boulevard. Innovations for the Seasons capitalized on this by having a Dickens-like display in time for the festival each year and advertising it to participants at the festival, just a short ways away.

Delighted to have another Dickens experience, the tourists came to Sand Waves to see. The current period scene was titled *Victorian Christmas Wedding* but was commonly called the Sleigh Ride Display.

This year, due to not selling the Sleigh Ride Display for two previous years in a row, the display was freshened with the addition of new mannequins. Its main focus was happy newlyweds, the groom in a tuxedo and the bride in her wedding gown with her veil, seated in a sleigh, amidst a snowy background, *Jingle Bells* playing. The sleigh was pulled by a horse, which moved its head from gazing forward to looking back at the couple. This was the repetitive motion, the only one, but there was a sound effect other than just music. The horse neighed as he looked back.

The couple, gazing at each other in happiness, surrounded by Christmas presents, remained stationary.

New mannequins, two bystanders, male and female, both in formal Victorian fashions, a woman in blue satin with a bonnet with muff and a man in a top hat and cape, carrying a cane, were added this year to somewhat disguise that this display was going on three years old.

They were also stationary.

This kept the cost down as did the fact that the female had no hands behind the muff.

The store was able to purchase her at a going-out-of-business sale from a Houston boutique hit by a tornado, also acquiring at low cost a male mannequin, also with damage.

The new male had taken the place of the original groom.

The groom became the male bystander as the damage on the new male mannequin needed to be covered by the bridal gown.

Therefore this display only cost $14,000 retail, but with a similar profit margin as all the others.

Like all the others, it remained unsold.

Misha studied this display for a few moments and opened the back of the radio.

She picked the smallest Christmas present in the sleigh, a box about the size of a Barbie doll box, opened it and took the bills from the radio and put them inside.

She closed the box and retied a ribbon around it, then continued on.

Chapter 9

"Are there any restrooms upstairs in your living quarters?" Janey was asking Aerial as Misha left in the direction of the downstairs facilities. Janey was thinking, *how could such renovations be done without anyone noticing? Especially me.*

"Oh, no, I just come downstairs to the public restroom," said Aerial. "It's no trouble at all. I rarely have to go at night."

"The changes to the upstairs merely included adding outlets and some ventilation, and a small airconditioner that vents through the roof. I hooked onto the electrical connections in the warehouse, which are on a different circuit, so as not to strain the circuit that powers all these lights and displays. I just rerouted through one of the vents and fed the wires through there." Randy pointed at a corner, right far side of the store, where electrical wires were coming through a hole in the partition for the warehouse. They ran, exposed along a little ledge near the ceiling, through the vent hole and up into the attic.

"So that's why no one reported this. No one saw any sign of an airconditioner," said Monica. "We keep an eye out for any signs of the homeless trying to sneak into any unused buildings in Sand Waves. That is the tale tell sign of someone living where they shouldn't be that we look for. After all, you cannot survive without an airconditioning system in this part of the world."

"Do the homeless have airconditioners under the bridge, JW?" asked Deidre.

"They have the open air like us on our rangeland,"

said JW. "That is all anybody needs."

"Where did you find an airconditioner made like that?" asked Laurel.

"A boat airconditioner. Marcus and I had a sailboat before he died and the airconditioner vented up through the cabin roof. I thought it was very clever of me to think of that for my loft," said Aerial. "Even if viewed from the air, all the store airconditioners are up there. It is just smaller."

"This violates every code in the book," said Monica.

Everyone ignored her.

JW and Deidre went back to the bench.

"Yes. I miss that boat," said Janey. She was still staring at the rough opening for the missing vent when she saw a small head peeking down through it.

"I had to sell it, of course, I couldn't sail it alone even if I did not need money. I miss it too."

"Is that a cat?"

"Arthur, you should have come sailing with us some time," said Aerial. "You missed out on that. Oh, Cassius! He's gotten up in the vents again. He goes along that little ledge and slips through the hole in the wall and gets into the warehouse. Kitty! Kitty! Come down from there."

"You've got an animal in here, too?" exclaimed Monica Moon. "Unlicensed and unregistered, I presume!"

"Certainly not, my cat has all his shots and he is registered with the colony federation. I paid the $50 annual fee for pets. He is a legal cat."

"Not in a store, he's not. There's no animals permitted in stores in Sand Waves."

"That's another issue, I need to meet with the

federation members about," said the congressman. "Not allowing service animals in the stores out here is causing problems."

"A cat running around in this place could be a hazard with all these lights and wires," said Arthur.

"He never comes down in the store. I keep him exclusively upstairs with me. Only he gets through that vent sometimes and over into the warehouse area," said Aerial, with concern for her kitty.

"I'll put up with some kind of screen across it to stop that problem," said Randy. "After all this is over. When I get time."

"And I suppose you use a space heater for when you need heat despite the dangers of those things? Really," said Arthur. "You don't think a cat is dangerous around something like that?"

"Obviously you've never had a cat, Arthur. Cats are not stupid. He's not going to run into a space heater."

"You will do no such thing," said Monica to Randy. "You have no right to do any type of modifications to any building in Sand Waves."

"So we will have to come downstairs for bathroom facilities? Any plumbing up there at all? What about a kitchen? What do you do for food?" Janey asked Aerial.

"Oh, I have one of those new type of- what do you call them- microwave ovens. It will cook almost anything. And I have a hotplate. Plumbing was, well, not practical. Beyond us. Sorry, I'm not complaining, Randy. I'm afraid I use a wash bowl and pitcher for washing up when I am upstairs."

"No need to apologize, Aerial. I just wish plumbing was within my skill set. But it just is not. And, Ms. Moon, we will have to have a discussion of your precious deed restrictions and other rules and regulations versus my constitutional rights to work on my own property, some other time. I am part owner of this building, technically. Legally I may make modifications to it."

"My God! Aerial! You don't have a shower or bath? That is unsanitary," said Arthur.

"I- well- when no one is here I can wash up quite nicely in the downstairs restrooms. The sinks are large and there are three of them, I just hook up one of those little sprayers to the spigot and there is a drain in the middle of the floor-"

"Aerial, we don't need any more details. We can imagine-"

"And the store restrooms have those hand dryers that replaced paper towels. You know, they save energy by not cutting down trees so there's less paper. Anyway. They are terrible at drying hands but I can dry my hair very well with it, so long as I keep repeatedly punching the button. That is if I don't go to the hairdresser, which is really my last luxury. Sometimes I have to forgo that in order to have money for the washateria. But fortunately this week I had enough for both."

Aerial patted her hairstyle which was drooping only slightly despite the humidity.

She obviously frequented older beauticians trained to style in the teased coif made fashionable in the early 1960s by Jacqueline Kennedy before she became Jacqueline

Onassis and let her hair hang straight like most women in the early 1980s.

"Washateria?" asked Misha in confusion, as she returned from the bathroom.

"Laundromat," Janey translated.

"There is no way this is not going to have to be reported to the authorities," said Monica. "Your living like this violates all kinds of safety and health codes, much less the deed restrictions for the property."

"It's not much better than those homeless vagrants living out under the river bridge," said Arthur, suddenly hearing what Monica was saying.

"Well really. I might be one of those homeless if I didn't have this place. And if it weren't for those stupid restrictions, I could have a bathroom and kitchen put in upstairs and be in accordance with the safety and health codes," said Aerial.

"The homeless living out under the bridge are under court protection until there is an appeal," said the congressman. "We cannot force them out. Most of them are the newly unemployed who lived in areas like Sand Waves just a couple years ago. With rents at all time highs, construction unable to keep up with housing demand, and interest rates through the roof, only the wealthy can get into starter homes. Places like Sand Waves are going to have to allow low cost apartments sooner or later."

"Never!" said Monica.

"I tried to find someplace to go," said Aerial. "But any place I could afford had a long waiting list. There's waiting lists for places that aren't even built yet!"

"I had no idea this was going on!" Arthur exclaimed. "I would have done something."

"I should have seen it," said Janey, looking resentfully at Laurel who was squirming under her gaze.

"I didn't know anything about it," said Laurel.

"If it weren't for your oppressive laws and codes, more people might have shelter over their heads in this storm right now instead of cowering under the river bridge," said Misha.

"We need to concentrate on our own predicament and what is going on here in the store. Mr. and Mrs. Smith, could you also rejoin us? Okay. For us to come downstairs as far as restroom use, I think this will work," said Randy. "Although each bathroom has three toilets, if we allow only one person in at a time, that will help respect privacy. All agreed to this?"

Everyone unanimously agreed to that tenet without any discussion.

"I have to go to the ladies' facilities right now," announced Deidre, and she took off.

"I can represent both of us and relay the arrangements to my wife," said JW, as everyone indicated frustration at still another delay.

"Great. Thank you, Mr. Smith. Now I will fix a sign on the restroom doors indicating in use or not. We have some of those around here somewhere- where you move a tab back and forth to indicate the status," said Janey. "What else? What do we do now?"

"Let's just go on upstairs," Randy suggested. "I think it will work out like this. The Smiths can have a room to themselves, as they are the only married couple."

"We are also a married couple," said Janey.

"Yes, I mean among our custo- among our guests," said Randy. "Anyway, there are six more or less different areas upstairs. A tiny living room, a dinette, a bedroom, and three storage areas we had to make for all the stuff that came out of Aerial's house. With your permission, Aerial, I have worked it out this way. The Smiths can have the bedroom. Ms. Moon and Ms. Martin can have the general storage area which is almost empty. Congressman, if you and my father can use the dinette, the delivery man- I am sorry! Your name, sir?"

"Mack Moore. That's Mack, just like the truck, not the clown. And Moore with two o's and e on the end."

Unlike the Smiths, the deliveryman had never moved out of earshot, but still remained inconspicuous.

He had remained as close to Eileen's side after the prayer circle broke up as he possibly could.

Eileen had welcomed his chitchat at first, thinking it was a good thing for the congressman to see someone else interested in her.

Another white man at that.

But eventually the big deliveryman began to creep her out a little.

She tried moving away from him towards Mark and that had worked.

He had backed off.

"Okay, you and I, Mr. Moore, we will be in the little living room. Aerial, Laurel, and Janey will be in the section where Aerial's excess furniture is stored. And Miss? Ms.?"

"Just call me Eileen."

"You, and Misha here, can be in the room where Aerial's extra clothing is stored. It will be crowded. But if we all cooperate and are considerate of one another, we will at least be able to spend a reasonably comfortable night. There are Christmas quilts and pillows enough for everyone. On the shelves on the second aisle."

"If someone could help me get those," said Aerial, anxious to make sure the more expensive ones were not chosen.

"I will," said the deliveryman.

"Mr. Moore, so nice to meet you!" Aerial extended her hand as she walked towards the deliveryman. "And with the same name as Laurel."

"No relation, of course." The deliveryman was fairly tall and looked to weigh about 275 pounds. He towered over Laurel even more than JW loomed over Deidre. "This is the first time I've had the pleasure to meet any of you."

"Ha ha, yes those common names. Harriman is bad enough. Having the last name Moore must be a nightmare," said Aerial.

"My married name was actually Moore," said Monica Moon. "I reverted to my maiden name after my divorce."

"Try Smith," said JW to Aerial.

"Or Brown," said Mark.

"Monica! You've been married?"

The visible shock that Arthur showed at this statement caused all of them to stop and look at him with some surprise, especially the members of the party who suspected the seriousness of his relationship with her.

"Oh, er, Arthur, I meant to tell you, dear. It was a long time ago. I was very young. I, er, rarely even think about it. It was just for a short time."

"Well," said Arthur, recovering quickly but feeling a little embarrassed. "Course, I was previously married myself. Ha ha, that's where my son Randy here came from."

The strangers among them quickly lost interest.

Everyone grabbed their bedding as Aerial and Mack passed out the pillows and coverlets.

Arthur moved away from Monica, stood beside Randy and put his hand on Randy's shoulder.

He had to reach slightly as Randy was 5 inches taller than his father.

"Well, can we go ahead and proceed?" asked Randy, uncomfortable, but he did not remove Arthur's hand from his shoulder, rather letting it slide away naturally as the two men shifted positions to move out of Misha's way.

She pushed her way forward and took center stage.

"So," said Misha, having taken all this time to digest the arrangements. "You put the black girl and the Vietnamese together."

Eileen looked with alarm at Misha but with also some amusement and understanding.

She is so young, Eileen thought.

Randy looked confused.

He had known Misha long enough that her youthful appearance no longer registered with him.

When she failed to act like an adult, as she frequently

did, it confounded him.

"I can assure you, I did not think of that at all, I was looking at room size and the sizes of people. Laurel and Aerial need a little more space, and Janey is related, sort of, to Aerial."

"Oh, thank you, Randy!" said Laurel, with real hurt.

"I'm not that overweight," said Aerial indignantly. "Just no longer have a really good figure." Aerial's analysis of herself was accurate. She was out of shape, not seriously overweight. She had a hard time finding clothes that disguised this fact. "I still weigh less than 140 pounds and I am almost 5 feet 5. I am middle aged you know. What do you expect?"

"I'm sorry Randy. I understand you are only thinking of me," said Laurel, allowing a little patronization into her voice.

"Are you saying you would resent being with a black person?" Eileen asked Laurel, who was actually thinking with alarm that she weighed as much as Aerial, despite being only 29 and Aerial being 51.

At least I am a little taller, she thought.

"Maybe you resent being with a Vietnamese," said Misha to Eileen.

"Oh my God," said Randy. "Please people-"

Just then a scream sounded down the aisle.

It was a scream not devoid of fear, but containing a little triumph too. JW jumped, ready to rush to his wife's rescue as she came into view, but there was no need.

Before the others could react, Deidre came back up the aisle dragging a man by the arm. A man, coming reluctantly, but without any real resistance.

She had his arm twisted behind him.

He had an amused look on his face.

"Look what I found coming out of the men's facility as I was going to the women's!" Deidre yelled. "Good thing I know Tay Quond Dow."

"Madam, please let go of my arm. I am coming willingly," said the man, as they reached the others, all of whom were speechless at the sight of his clothing.

"Who are you?" Aerial managed to say.

"Let him go, Deidre. This is most undignified," said JW.

Deidre complied with her husband's command.

"Thank you," said the released hostage, shaking himself a little.

"We must ask your name, sir," said Arthur more forcefully.

Janey gave a little gasp and then caught Randy's eye.

No one watching them could doubt that an invisible message passed between the husband and wife.

But no one was watching them.

Everyone else was looking at the newcomer.

The man indicated his red and white suit, stroked his long white beard and touched his pointed hat.

"I would think that it is obvious I am Santa Claus," he said.

Chapter 10

"That's one of our costumes we sell," said Janey, after a moment. "I recognize it."

"Who are you, sir? Please remove the hat and beard. What are you doing here?" asked Arthur, remembering that the store sometimes had actors play Santa.

But it was too early in the season.

The men, Mark, Arthur, JW, the deliveryman, and Randy had formed a confrontational semicircle in front of the costumed stranger.

Deidre had slipped around them and joined the women, all having moved close together in a defensive posture, save for Janey who remained in place and folded her arms.

"Now, gentlemen," said Santa. "I have good reason to be here. I am a devotee of Christmas and a longtime fan of the store. I admit the storm has driven me from my home under the bridge. Yes, I said under the bridge. But I mean no harm. My own few rags were completely soaked and this costume fit me so well I just couldn't resist."

"Are you saying you're one of those homeless creatures that live under the river bridge?" asked Monica.

"Well now-"

"We cannot turn him out," said Janey. "He'll drown out there."

"Poor man," said Aerial. "I know what it is like not to have any place to go. But we need to find some better clothes for you."

"Aerial!" Randy spoke sharply. "Let me handle Santa Claus. Dad, can you help Aerial show the others upstairs

103

while I take Santa to the costume section and get him better attired. Janey, stay down here for a moment. I need to talk to you about- about food. Yes, food. Food that we have in the store and how we are going to divide it up. Mostly candy, folks, I'm afraid. There is a little coffee, some crackers maybe. But we won't starve. Okay, could you take a better inventory, Janey?"

"Um, all right, Randy." Janey was more than pleased at Randy's continued forcefulness. Randy could be commanding but it usually did not last long before he remembered himself and withdrew. Arthur, too, was looking at his son with some amazement.

"Are you sure you will be all right?" Laurel asked Randy. "You don't know who this stranger might be."

"I think he must be some kind of criminal," said Misha.

"Randy, find out exactly who this man is before you let him come upstairs with us." Arthur had no problems giving orders but as he looked at his son, he was surprised to see Randy was not flinching at his command.

He dropped his attempt to intervene.

"We can let the ladies get settled first," said JW. Deidre clutched his arm in a manner that indicated she didn't want to go anywhere without him.

"We'll be fine. Please do as you're asked," said Randy, somewhat abruptly.

Somehow Randy taking charge made all of them, those who knew him, and those who did not, see the seriousness of the situation.

Everyone complied with his requests.

None of the others were interested in dealing with Santa anyway.

Everyone was getting tired and the thought of a semiprivate place to rest had become very inviting.

They all started up the narrow stairs one at a time as Randy took the stowaway with him to the costume section.

Janey followed Randy at a distance.

"Where have you been all this time? Several of us had searched the store numerous times to make sure no one was hiding."

"Santa blends in very well in almost any Christmas display," said the man, as he pulled a Harlequin costume from the rack.

Janey automatically surveyed the displays to make sure there had been no harm done to them.

Nothing looked out of place.

"Not that one." Randy took the Harlequin costume away from Santa and hung it back up. "How about a Chicago gangster? Those clothes are near to normal street wear. I was just too tall for the pants. So had to go with Dracula when my clothing got wet. By the way, where are your real clothes?"

"Hanging on the costume rack," said the man, as he held the gangster's suit against himself and looked in the full length floor mirror attached to the outside of the dressing room door.

The door had a mirror on the inside as well.

The shirt was loose fitting. The coat was roomy with many pockets.

It would be better than the Santa Claus or Harlequin

costumes.

"This outfit will do nicely. Fits me, I can tell."

Janey looked at the floor beneath the racks.

Sure enough a puddle of water had accumulated under the costumes. But otherwise nothing seemed out of place.

As Santa changed in the dressing room, Randy said to Janey, "I will put our newest guest in with me and move the delivery man in with my father and Mark. There should be no objection to that. The reverend might make a new convert. The congressman is a man of the people, after all."

"By the way," said Janey. "Does Aerial store her personal garbage in the warehouse? I just opened the door for a moment to there to see if those lights were working. You know they are on a different circuit. They are still working. But I got a whiff of an odor that wasn't good."

"Yes, she has to put it somewhere. She is supposed to use plastic bags instead of those paper bags from the grocery stores. She is stretched to the limit money wise. And even the purchase of garbage bags is a bit much for her sometimes."

"I wish I had known you were helping her."

"I almost told you many times, but she forbid me. Swore me to secrecy. She is proud. She won't take any financial help, just my handyman skills, little that they are. This is hard on her."

Janey took his arm. "Let's go on upstairs and explain the change in the arrangements to the other men. I'm sure Santa Claus can find his way up the stairs himself."

Chapter 11

The congressman could not sleep.

He crept silently out of the dinette, when he was sure both the delivery man and Arthur were slumbering, and passed the sleeping Randy and the stranger.

He stopped before the door where Misha and Eileen were quartered.

Fortunately the door was nearer the stairs than the sleeping men.

He scratched at the door as he imagined the cat would do.

He was rewarded with an answering tap.

They had both had the same idea.

Lights had been left on upstairs but there was no light on the stairs.

Mark went first, feeling his way down cautiously and as quietly as possible.

Safely downstairs, Mark waited by the staircase door, but far enough away to quickly hide in the Carolers' Display in case the wrong person came out.

The Christmas lights were not turned off in the retail establishment, but rather dimmed.

The fluorescent lights overhead were dark.

So the store glowed with hundreds of colored lights against the dark outside, where the steady downpouring of rain indicated the flooding persisted.

The Christmas music was silent.

The store had a weak echo.

To avoid detection, silence was needed.

Eileen was well aware of this.

She made no sound at all as she slipped from the staircase, stood a moment, then saw Mark as he stepped out in front of her.

Only a muted whimper escaped from her as they came together tightly, holding on to each other as if letting go would mean losing the other forever.

They were so involved in their embrace, that they did not see the third person slip by, also having come silently through the staircase door.

They did not see the streaked blonde hair swinging lightly on the shoulders of that third person as she slipped directly sideways and blended in with the Carolers' Display.

Her mind registered them, but only vaguely as she was focused elsewhere.

"Oh, Mark! It has been so long!" Eileen breathed softly as, still clutching one another, she and Mark slowly walked down an aisle.

"Too long," he murmured.

"Where can we go? We cannot stay right here. Someone is liable to see us. And if we cannot go to the restrooms-"

"There's a warehouse area over there. Let's go there."

"Okay." Eileen took her heels off so they would not click on the hard floor. "My, this floor is cold."

"I have a better idea. There are some offices in the back that have carpet. Let's go there instead." Mark took her by the elbow and led her forward.

"No, I'm afraid we will get caught there," she said softly, as she moved with him. "I hate living like this."

"I know, I know, but let's just make the most of this

moment right now," Mark said, as they started towards the warehouse.

Monica Moon came out from behind the Carolers' Display and opened the staircase door.

Behind it were JW and Deidre.

They came out somberly and stood in front of her.

All had successfully slipped past several sleepers, who, if they noticed, had concluded the insomniacs among them were all going to the restroom.

"All right," said Monica furiously. "I'm here. What do you want? This is the third time I've run into you two this month in a city of three million."

"Like you Monica," said Deidre. "We frequent the 'in' places."

"I don't know why we are having had this meeting now under these circumstances."

"Because we are here now and there's nothing else to do under these circumstances. We need to get this over with. We have been needing to talk to you and you refuse to see us at your office," said JW.

"I don't know what you think this will get you. Following me hasn't accomplished anything. Meeting down here in secret like this isn't going to either. We might as well go back to bed and wait out the storm."

"This is no ordinary storm. It's a massive flood. We could be here for days," said JW.

"We need a little more time, Monica," said Deidre.

"Don't count us out yet," said JW.

"I told you before, if you can come up with the rest of your percent money then you'll still be in the hotel deal.

You knew the terms when you signed on. You were going to come up with a certain percent of the operating capital. If you could not meet your part of the bargain you forfeited your initial investment."

"But I can't take that kind of a loss right now," said JW. "We have had some unexpected claims against West Texas."

"All our capital is tied up there right now. It is only temporary," said Deidre.

"You know the cost went way over the estimation you first gave us," said JW.

"That was not a binding estimation. You people should have plenty of money. Shopping here for $25,000 Christmas displays."

"Shopping and buying are two different things. I wanted to see the place this hotel scheme is going to put out of business. I did a little research and found out a few things about the store. It's one of the few places in this colony that is even close to being family oriented that's not connected to sports. They provide entertainment all year long with their animated displays. It has big potential," said JW.

"I am not concerned about that. That type of entertainment brings in no income," said Monica.

"Santa Claus will be here soon for the children to take pictures. There has to be money in that," said Deidre.

"Look, every holiday they have costumed actors came and pose for pictures with children in coordination with the photography studio. They have the Easter Bunny, Uncle Sam on the Fourth, a witch or something similar for Halloween. They are losing money on all that."

"But during the holiday season people come from all the world to see the displays," said JW.

"All free. And people come to Sand Waves during the holidays anyway. Relatives of all the corporate employees relocated here come to see their families," said Monica.

"Rather than put this place out of business and build a hotel here, why not find an alternate location and let this establishment continue? If we weren't so strapped, we might even be interested in investing in it ourselves. Or we could arrange for a legitimate mortgage to purchase this place and find someone more competent than that silly woman to run it. Just give us another month."

"There is no other location in Sand Waves that will work," said Monica. "This place is losing money. I intend to marry Arthur Harriman. He stands to profit considerably. I will be getting my real estate commission and ultimately the proceeds from the sale of the place as well. A smooth transaction depends upon Arthur convincing his son and his stepmother, galling to call her that as she's only a year older than him, to cooperate. Legally Arthur can force it to happen. However, it would be nice not to have all the unpleasantness they could cause. It's going to happen within the next two weeks and at that point in time you're going to have to come up with your share or lose all of the money you have put into the project already."

"We had some unexpected losses in the stock market," said JW, hoping to strike a note of empathy. A recent dip had hurt almost everyone. "We are cash strapped at the moment. It won't last."

"Only fools play the stock market. The real money is

in real estate. What about the ranch?　Does it have any mortgage value?"

"Just give us three months, Monica," said JW.

"Please, Monica," echoed Deidre. "Or just let us out of the deal."

"So your ranch is mortgaged to the hilt," Monica concluded. "You can drop out of the deal. You just don't get your money back. My hands are tied. What can I do? I'm not the only other party involved. You know that. We can't give you such a concession without giving all our other investors such an out. Why the project would fail completely."

"I'm not concerned about other investors. I'm only concerned with my share. And if I don't get more time to get my money out-" JW took a step forward.

"I seem to hear menace in your tone. Remember I am your only chance to get your money back. And if I do get you out of this project, it will cost you, maybe all that you have put in so far."

"Considering that we're all going to be cooped up here until who knows how long, you know it's just possible your paramour might come to find out your motive in cultivating a relationship with him," said Deidre.

"You wouldn't dare interfere in my personal business," said Monica, through clenched teeth.

"And a word to the wise to his son might alter the situation as well," said JW.

"Randy Harriman is a disgraced fool. He's nothing more than a stock boy around here. He has no influence over his father."

"He seemed to have taken charge tonight," said Deidre.

"A regression to the past. I've no doubt that his spinelessness will return when the sun comes back out. He is of no consequence. He has no influence with his father, I tell you. If you two, either of you say anything at all to Arthur or Randy Harriman about the hotel, about my financial arrangements with you, or anything to anybody else about me, I will kill you both."

There was silence for a moment.

"You haven't got the guts to kill anyone," said JW, but his voice shook a little.

"I wish we had never met you," said Deidre, somewhat inadequately. "Let's go back upstairs, JW. We're wasting our time talking to this woman. We need to consult our attorney. We're going back to West Texas when this flooding situation is over and make our lawyer get us out of this mess."

Deidre turned away from Monica and marched up the steps. JW followed close on her heels.

Monica ran her fingers through her long blonde hair streaked with brown.

She spent $50 a week on color treatments for her hair which, despite the fact that she was only 38 years old, was already beginning to turn a wintry gray.

She thought grimly how hard she had to work for her money when all the Smiths had to do was keep their inherited ranch on an even keel financially.

She wasn't sure which one of them had inherited the ranch.

Certainly they both acted like they were entitled royalty.

I'll show them what entitlement really is, she thought.

And she was about to follow the ranching couple, when she heard a noise.

She had forgotten about what she had glimpsed when she first came down.

Now it registered.

She quickly stepped up on the Cowboy Display and stood totally still. In the dim light, she hoped she would easily be taken for another mannequin.

She had to stifle a gasp when she saw Eileen and Mark, arm in arm, come from the direction of the warehouse, stop in the aisle and embrace tenderly and indulge in a long kiss.

This is the golden treasure at the end of the rainbow apparently deposited in this doomed little store just for me, thought Monica Moon, and she felt just as triumphant as the victorious cowboy standing next to her.

Chapter 12

"It was wonderful," Eileen murmured to Mark, and laughed the gentle laugh of a happy lover.

"It was a little stuffy in there," he commented with amusement.

"I know it was. It was more than stuffy. I remember that smell coming from some of the ditches in Georgia."

"Well, you know I have a poor sense of smell. Must be the tarps covering those displays," said Mark. "I think these are some type of plastic."

"Most tarps are made of a water repellent coated canvas," Monica announced, as she stepped down from the display.

Mark and Eileen stared at her in astonishment.

Before they could respond to her statement, before they could even move, Monica pulled a small 110 camera from her purse and snapped their picture.

The flash cube gave off a slightly burnt odor as it faded out.

"That won't be a terribly amorous photo. And it may be a little dark but any photo of the two of you holding each other tightly will do," said Monica, her voice trembling with elation.

Eileen gasped and pulled away from Mark.

Mark took her by the shoulders. "Darling, go on upstairs. Go on to your assigned space. Let me handle Ms. Moon. I will deal with the situation."

"But-"

"Go on, don't worry, Eileen. Ms. Moon is a woman of the world. There won't be any problems."

Eileen looked frantically at him but he seemed so calm and composed.

She did not really have any alternative.

She opened the staircase door and went inside.

Mark turned to face Monica.

"Well, Congressman, so you and Ms.- whomever- I'll find out her name- are not the strangers you pretended to be earlier."

"Mind your own business, Monica." said Mark.

"I am minding my business. I live in your district. An adulterous affair with a black woman. That is really going to go over well in your reelection campaign in this conservative district in Texas. You are already in trouble for supporting federal gun restrictions. This will provoke a 100 percent turnout in Sand Waves alone. Just to vote against you."

"Okay, Monica. What's the price for your silence this time?"

"Ordinarily cash would do. But as it happens, I need a special bill overriding the CF's prohibition against hotels in Sand Waves."

"What? Are you crazy? The colony federation could better approve my relationship with Eileen."

"Yes, but they are only 12 votes. And the real power doesn't even live here. They'll get over having to accept a hotel, if you do it soon, long before the campaign has to start. You have just been reelected. That will also help in counteracting the idea that Sand Waves is an all white enclave that wants to keep some people out."

"But it is an all white enclave, and I know for a fact it

didn't start out that way. What has happened? What's going on out here that's keeping all the minorities out except for the rich and famous?"

"It is so small and legally ambiguous, the fact that is it is all white doesn't show up in any legal way."

"I know to live in Sand Waves, a high paying job is automatic, therefore secondary," said Mark. "But there are many upper middle class and middle class blacks in the area but none of them live here."

"You didn't know that when you established your little concubine in the condominiums?"

"Eileen has told me she rarely see anyone black, rarely sees anyone Hispanic, unless they were servants to the ultra-rich or are ultra-rich themselves."

"It takes more than just good deed restrictions to maximize property values. Since I know you're not going to be telling anybody, let me tell you how it's done. We real estate agents do more now than just patrolling the neighborhoods and reporting and untidy yards or disallowed vehicles violations. We have a system."

As Monica explained, both she and Mark failed to notice that Eileen had slipped back through the staircase door, silently moving over to the side.

It was her turn to blend in with the Carolers' Display.

Monica's slightly high pitched voice dropped a little as it adopted a didactic tone.

"It's very simple. We have ethnic real estate agents that are paid very well to steer minorities away from Sand Waves."

"You don't think you're creating a dangerous

situation out here? You don't think the criminal element is going to see what's going on?" asked Mark. "For word soon will get around that people can find a white haven in Sand Waves. What kind of people do you think that will attract here?"

"All we have to do is point to the famous minorities living here," said Monica. "And the ones that are really rich but not quite as famous. They take care of the problem."

"I think you're playing with fire!"

"On the contrary, Congressman. I think you're the one playing with fire. Now you are going to get that bill for me about the hotel or I'm going to have your little romantic escapades on the front page of every newspaper in Texas."

Chapter 13

Eileen had heard enough.

Any chance of being alone with Mark was gone.

Still unseen by either Mark or Monica, she quietly slipped back up the stairs, remembering...

The first time she had driven through Sand Waves just to see what the area was like, Eileen had noticed it.

Other people driving near her were all white.

That was spooky enough.

She felt the spookiness but did not understand it at first.

Maybe she had happened on a white funeral procession or something.

But the real telling moment was her observations upon driving by an elementary school where the children were all outside playing.

She actually stopped the car and stared at those children for a good five minutes trying to figure out what was wrong, trying to see why the scene was so unreal, why it looked like something out of the movies.

Then she understood.

It was 1978, but-

The children were all white.

Mark had purchased the condo for her and put it in her name.

Rumors were allowed that she was the mistress of an important personage and was to be left alone.

She was left alone.

Now four years later, not much had changed.

The dip in the boom, which did send shockwaves across the Houston area, still was no match for the recession up north.

Companies were still coming to Houston, just at a slower pace.

Demand for ultra-luxury goods was down a little.

The nasty word 'unemployment' was beginning to be heard.

But Eileen knew that as long as her lover favored her, she had no financial worries.

She was secure and alone in Sand Waves.

Misha was already asleep on large pillows that had been placed on the floor for her and Eileen to make beds.

Soft Christmas lights had been left glowing throughout the upstairs so that all the trapped guests could find their way around in the strange surroundings.

Eileen wasn't sure, but looking at the face of the Asian girl, she could almost swear that Misha had cried herself to sleep.

Eileen sank down beside her and prepared to do the same.

Suddenly she froze as she heard movement under the blanket next to her.

And it did not come from Misha, who was out cold, snoring away.

As Eileen held her breath, totally still from terror, a warm fuzzy bundle plopped down on her neck and put its nose to hers.

Eileen relaxed, tears still coming, but she couldn't help but laugh a little bit at her fear of Aerial's cat.

She grabbed the cat gently with both hands and pushed the kitty off her neck, petting it at the same time.

The kitty meowed softly.

Eileen wasn't sure if it wasn't a protest that a stranger was holding him, or was a welcoming meow, grateful for a little attention.

"One thing, Kitty. You need a bath. You smell terrible." Eileen laughed a little as she whispered to the cat.

The cat did not reply but nestled itself under the covers and began bathing itself in the hundreds of years old feline tradition, purring at the same time in response to Eileen's gentle stroking.

"You're going to have to stay under the covers tonight with me," said Eileen, pushing the cat a little further down. "I don't think a kitty bath is going to help. You need soap and water. Go curl up down there at my feet so I don't have to smell you."

As if he understood, the cat made his way under the covers, nestled against Eileen's feet.

Eileen had been hoping the kitty would be her foot warmer all night long.

But when she awoke a couple hours later the cat was gone and it was still only 2:30 AM by her watch.

Her roommate was still snoring away.

She stared at the soft colored lights.

They put out no warmth.

Without the comfort of the animal, the tears Eileen had postponed earlier came now, and she sobbed uncontrollably into her pillow.

Chapter 14

There was no letup in the rain and daylight was not much different than darkness when Janey crept down the stairs the next morning.

She was silently thanking the Lord that the electricity had still not failed.

The dim Christmas lights still guided her way throughout the store.

She went to the phones.

God was merciful but phones were still dead.

She looked at the large sack of trash that had accumulated in just a day and a half.

The garbage of all the people trapped in the store, plus Aerial's personal trash had been brought down last night to make precious room for everyone upstairs.

Janey grabbed the trash bag and start pulling it down the aisle towards the warehouse.

Might as well get it out of the way completely, she thought. *There's no way they're going to stay cooped up upstairs. Once they all wake up they'll be down here at least part of the time just to get some space.*

Janey could hear Aerial's cat meowing as she opened the door to the warehouse section.

Randy has got to fix it so that cat cannot get in here, thought Janey. *We can't have the cat on the displays. He is liable to damage them somehow.*

Cloudy rainy daylight came through from the skylight causing the warehouse to have an eerie glow.

Heavens, it smells terrible in here! What kind of garbage can Aerial have? And how has she lived here all this time and we never smelled any garbage before? Janey thought, as she watched the cat climbing on the tarp that covered the Witch's Display.

Suddenly, the cat just seemed to go crazy, clawing and scratching the tarp, wildly meowing loudly as it did so.

Oh no! There's a dead rat in there, Janey thought. *That explains the smell. I'm going to demand a refund from those exterminators. It's only been two months since they've been here. How on earth am I going to get rid of a dead rat in the middle of this flooding? Guess I can at least put it in the trash bag. Maybe that will help.*

And she went to the Witch's Display and unzipped the tarp.

Randy was still sound asleep. It had been an exhausting day yesterday and he was one of the last to relax enough to literally fall asleep.

All the men- Arthur, the deliveryman, and the congressman- except JW- were in close proximity to one another.

Everyone had to pass Randy and his roommate to get to the staircase. Randy was still awake when Mark had come back up, but he pretended sleep.

His pretended sleep did not work when the deliveryman had come out.

The larger man accidentally kicked him, causing him to jump.

"Sorry, fella. I just couldn't sleep," he whispered.

Randy indicated that he understood. The call of nature. He looked at the sleeping figure beside him. *How can he sleep through all this?* Randy wondered.

"I wasn't going downstairs for the bathroom," Mack Moore had said, patting his ample belly. "I'm just hungry."

"Some candy over on that table." Randy had directed him.

He would better fit into that Santa suit, thought Randy, with some cruel amusement, although he was too sleepy to let the thought linger.

"Thanks, guy." Mack had gone back to his section and Randy could hear the deliveryman chewing the hard candy, as he felt sleepy again.

The next thing he remembered was Janey shaking him and whispering.

"Randy, get up. You got to come downstairs right now."

"Janey, what are you doing up so early? It is going to be a long day regardless-"

"Listen, wake up! And wake up Santa Claus!"

Randy grinned and stretched. He glanced at the man sleeping next to him. "You mean Al Capone here. He sleeps like a log."

"Just do it," she said with urgency. "Bring him downstairs, quietly. Don't let anyone know."

"What is it?" said the man, waking up during the middle of this conversation.

"Your masquerade is about to end," said Janey. "Get up and come with me. Both of you. Right now!"

Chapter 15

Janey had rezipped the tarp over the Witch's Display and lit some scented candles nearby.

The flames were drowned out by the fluorescent lights overhead.

As soon as they saw this scene, the men in costumes knew what was wrong.

They both recognized the smell. It was unmistakable to them.

Incense could not mask it.

"Plate," said Randy. "I'm out of it. This is your call."

"You have some gloves anywhere in this place, maybe with some of the costumes?" Plate stepped up on the platform of the Witch's Display.

"I have some right here. I grabbed some on the way up to get you two," said Janey, pulling them from her smock pocket and handing them up to him. "Unfortunately, I didn't have any on when I first unzipped it. I thought, maybe a rat-"

"Okay, it's okay," Plate took the gloves and began unzipping the tarp. From where they stood, nothing seemed wrong except the odor. The Witch's Display looked untouched in the bright light save for the fact that the witch had been stopped in the middle of her motion, slightly bent over, clutching the huge spoon in the middle of the cauldron. She needed electricity to straighten up.

"It's in the cauldron," said Janey, covering her mouth and nose with her hand. "You have to climb up there and look down in it to see."

"Just don't touch that switch." Plate knew the

warning was unneeded but he couldn't help issuing the command. The Harrimans took no offense.

"You got a good look, Mrs. Harriman?" Plate cautiously approached the cauldron, positioning himself next to the witch with great care. There was one spot where he could get a view of the victim's face without disturbing any detail on the display.

"Yes. I don't know him," said Janey.

"Randy, would you?" Plate moved out of the way.

Randy covered his mouth and stepped on the platform and took Plate's place. He shook his head.

"He answers the description of the one of the robbers. We had tracked them to Sand Waves. That's why I was here." Plate stepped back down onto the floor.

"We figured that," said Randy, following him.

"I appreciate you two keeping my secret," said Plate. "I knew you recognized me from my previous visit, Mrs. Harriman, despite my Hollywood sunglasses. And of course, I know Randy from when-"

"From my failed career as a policeman."

"From when he was on the force."

"So what do we do now?" asked Janey.

"My only real robbery suspect here is the deliveryman. But I have no idea if he was the other robber. We never got a description of him. It doesn't seem likely. They don't fit together well. But you never know."

"I'm not sure how we can keep this quiet. Apparently someone already knows," said Randy.

"Let's not keep it quiet. But let's tell everyone it must be an accidental death. Some kid. And this was not much more than a kid. Some hazing prank or something," speculated Plate.

"That goes on around here?" asked Janey.

"Yes," said Plate. "It is kept quiet. But it does. Let's keep my identity from the others right now, if we can."

"Do you want me to zip the tarp back up?" asked Janey.

"I'll do that," said Randy.

"Yes, go ahead," said Plate. "Mrs. Harriman, could you go upstairs? Wake up anybody that is still asleep, and get everybody assembled in the lobby."

"Yes. of course."

Janey was happy to leave the warehouse.

She heard the tarp being zipped as she crossed back into the main part of the store.

Forgotten, the cat shot through the door between her legs.

"Kitty," she said. "I've got to get ahold of you."

She scooped up the cat and carried him tightly under her arm as she made her way upstairs to carry out Plate's request.

"What's going to happen now, Kitty?" she asked, absentmindedly petting him to stop him squirming in her arms.

"Meow," answered Cassius.

Chapter 16

Laurel had found chairs in the back office area. Aerial had allowed her dining room chairs and a barstool to be brought down so that everyone had a seat in the front lobby.

The chairs were arranged in a semicircle facing the counter. Janey perched on the barstool behind the counter and Randy stood next to her.

Laurel took the seat that was closest to them.

Next to her, the delivery man, who shared her surname, plopped down wearily.

Then the Smiths, Misha, Eileen, the congressman, Arthur, Monica Moon, and the insurance agent.

The latter's chair was pushed a little out of line as if she did not quite want to be identified as one of the group.

It was early in the morning.

Several of them were still half asleep.

None of the seated people were at their sharpest yet.

"Where is Santa Claus?" asked Misha, with a snicker.

"What is going on here? Randy? Janey? Why are we all assembled like this?" Aerial spoke for them all.

"Please just be patient for a moment. Everyone relax. We have an announcement."

Plate waited until they were a little settled in before he stepped from behind the display.

He was still wearing the Chicago mobster clothing but somehow it no longer looked frivolous on him.

The seriousness of his manner, so unlike his character portrayals of yesterday, belied the costume.

"Ladies and gentlemen, unfortunately my real clothes are still damp, but I do have my identification. And both Mr.

and Mrs. Harriman here can vouch for my identity. I am Lieutenant Sinclair Plate of the Sand Waves Police Department."

"What are you doing here like this?" Mark began to question him.

The others murmured and looked at each other.

"Hear me out, please. Congressman, I have good reason to be here. Please, everyone listen to what I'm saying."

Plate waited until the murmuring had stopped and he had the attention of his audience once more.

"I won't tell you there's no cause for alarm with the situation. We are trapped here by the flooding. That, in itself is serious enough. But I appeal to your good common sense and better judgment to please keep your wits about you when you hear what I am about to say. While the flooding is posing no danger to us as long as we remain here in the building, to try to leave is to risk the possibility of drowning, all the cars are flooded in the parking lot. None of them are going to run."

"So you're saying we're safe here," Monica interrupted him. "Are you afraid somebody's going to try to leave anyway? We're not stupid."

"Please don't interrupt, Madam," said Plate. "I don't mean to be rude. But I need to get this information to you and I'm trying to do that with the least amount of anxiety and stress as possible."

This pronouncement had the effect of creating more anxiety and stress.

Arthur stood up. "Something going on that we don't

know about in addition to the flooding?"

"Dad, please sit down."

"I just want to help."

"Sit down, Reverend Harriman," said Plate. "Your skills may be needed when the time comes. At the moment it's necessary for me to be in charge of the situation."

"What situation?" asked Aerial. "Randy has been doing a fine job-"

"There's been a complication," said Randy forcibly. "Lieutenant Plate is now in charge of our emergency situation here. All aspects of it."

"I suppose you are going to explain why you came here posing as a derelict," said Mark.

"Odd as it may seem, my little undercover caper may have nothing to do with the situation at hand. With no communications available, there's no way for me to know."

Plate glanced at his pager.

It had gone off numerous times but there was no working phone to answer any summons.

"The complication Mr. Harriman has spoken of is that a body has been found in the warehouse."

Audible gasps came from his listeners.

Plate attempted to continue with a minimum of pausing, necessary to allow the gasps to play their course, but not allow more dialogue to begin.

"It looks like it was an accident. Someone, for some unknown reason climbed up onto one of the displays and was accidentally killed," said Plate.

"I've been looking at all the displays all this time," said Eileen. "Which one are you talking about?"

"We'd have noticed a dead body," said Laurel. "Some stranger must have snuck in while we were asleep and left it."

"You say it was an accident?" asked Mack.

"The body is in a display in the warehouse which was covered by a tarp," said Randy. "Umm, no one has, umm, actually been back there for a while. It's possible this was some type of hazing incident. The victim looks to be quite young, possibly a teenager. Maybe he is one of the homeless from under the bridge and he took shelter in the warehouse. And by accident the electricity was turned on."

"That couldn't be," said Aerial. "The switches are deliberately too far away for anyone to be too near the animation parts and turn on a switch at the same time."

"She's right. They have to move to a safer spot," said Laurel.

"There's been so much of that hazing going on lately all over the city, I hear about how bad it is from the other delivery drivers that have kids in college. More than one person could have been involved."

"Yes, that's right," said Laurel, supporting Mack's words. "News like that was in the *Chronicle* last week."

"Where exactly was the body found?" asked Arthur. "I hope we can rule out suicide?"

"There is no question of suicide, Dad."

"It looks like an accident where the display killed him," said Plate emphatically.

"An accident, surely," said Mack. "We have them all the time at work, not just on the roads. People are careless."

"Yes. Where? How could anybody possibly get hurt

on one of the displays?" asked Aerial, wringing her hands. "Even if a switch was flipped by accident or by someone doing some kind of hazing, the motions are not that powerful."

"Ma'am, you'd be surprised at what the smallest machine part can do to a person if it hits just at the wrong spot," said Mack.

"What do you say, Lieutenant?" asked Mark.

Plate looked down at the floor as if he could not quite explain.

As he searched for language, Janey spoke up.

"Aerial, the body was in the witch's cauldron. It appears he was a teenage boy and he was killed by the animatronics movement when the witch stirs the pot with her spoon. Maybe that movement was more powerful than we thought."

"Oh my God," said Aerial.

Arthur bowed his head as if in prayer.

"Who was this boy?" asked Daphne Martin. "My clientèle includes several families with teenage boys. Can we know who this person was?"

"I am afraid he has no identification on him that we could find," said Plate.

"When can we see him? See if anybody knows him?" asked Laurel.

"Shall we form a line? Go in one at a time? Lieutenant?" Daphne persisted.

"This is not the movies or TV," said Mark. "What do we actually do, Lieutenant?"

"I honestly don't know what protocol is in a situation

like this. Right now, I'm not inclined to let anyone see the victim, but I will go ahead and describe him and then if any one of you is inclined to think that you might know him- well, let me just describe him-

"He's less than six feet tall. Hard to tell. Possibly weighed a hundred and 30 pounds, has a small goatee, curly black hair, loose curls. But in a-" Plate searched for the right words, "-relaxed Afro perhaps?"

"You mean he is black?" Eileen asked.

"Yes, ma'am. He is African-American. We can be sure of that. Looks like he possibly died sometime very early yesterday or possibly late the previous night. Forensics is not my field."

"No, he wouldn't be one of my clients," said Daphne with some relief.

"You don't have any black clients?" asked Eileen with a little hostility provoked by the fact that the dead boy was black and the overall situation in general was causing her to feel more conscious about her race than she was used to.

"Yes I do," said Daphne, not at all defensively. "But I can count the teenage boys I have insured on my ten fingers. None of my African-American clients are teenage boys. I do have a couple of black families with girls-"

"Do you think that this could be someone you know?" Plate interrupted, looking at Eileen. "Miss-"

"No," Eileen said slowly. "I am from Georgia. I don't know many people here. No teenage boys." She looked at Mark, thinking, *because of you I don't dare know very many people here at all. I don't dare socialize, go to church, or do anything except wait for an opportunity to meet with you. I have to keep to myself, stay away from anybody because I might not be able to trust them if they found out about us.*

Eileen could have related in detail the plot of every soap opera on daytime TV.

She saw every new movie that came out every month.

She attended every new play at the Alley in Houston, alone.

She spent hours and hours every week at the numerous Houston area shopping malls, spending the generous allowance Mark gave her on clothes and jewelry that she had no place to wear.

She was well read on every topic of interest to every publisher in America and knew contemporary fiction like the back of her hand.

She spent hours every day writing long handwritten letters to her numerous family members back in Georgia who believed she was busy with a high paying secretarial job in Houston, and loved her for taking the time to write them.

They did not know she watched for the mail every day, hoping for a letter or two in return, and when there was a reply, that was the highlight of her existence.

Except for time with Mark.

She was suddenly aware of all this and equally aware that, while willingly she had made these sacrifices that brought such loneliness, this was the first time she had ever felt deprived.

Chapter 17

The police officer was in the process of asking the others if any of them felt they might know the victim. Everyone agreed there was very little possibility that anyone knew him as they did not know any black teenage boys.

Plate knew Randy was an exception, due to his past profession, but Randy had seen the body, and stated that he did know him.

The congressman might come into contact with black teenage boys on the campaign trail but it was unlikely he committed them to memory.

Daphne Martin further admitted most of her clientèle was white as most of them lived in Sand Waves. Her few African-American customers were people she was acquainted with that lived in Houston or Galveston.

Aerial, Laurel, Mack the deliveryman, all said they knew no African-Americans at all. Mack said his delivery route did not take him into parts of the greater Houston area with very many blacks. He did not get to know people on his route anyway. They were constantly moving to new locations, always changing. He did not live in Sand Waves but in a rural area north of Houston which was all white.

Misha claimed she only socialized with other Vietnamese immigrants and Vietnamese Americans and the only non-Vietnamese she knew were the people she worked with at the store.

Monica Moon said that one of her coworkers in her real estate office was African-American and that all black clients were referred to him. She did not know any teenagers. No teenagers of any kind. Period. When showing homes to prospective buyers, she requested they leave children of all ages with sitters or view homes during school hours. Children got in the way.

The reverend had no time for any socializing outside of the membership of his congregation which numbered over 3000 people, none of whom were any type of minority that he could recall.

In addition to holding many parties on their ranch, the Smiths boasted they led the social world of their small town in West Texas, population 287, a mix of 40 percent Hispanic and 60 percent white. They could recall maybe three or four African-American residents in the whole town, all over 60.

"We always invite them," Deidre assured everyone. "They are just so old, they don't come."

Eileen stifled a skeptic laugh.

Balancing this information with the protocol usually followed concerning a suspicious death, Plate felt justified in refusing to let any of them into the warehouse area at all, for any reason, much less to see the body. Everyone seemed to accept the idea of a transient seeking shelter or a hazing experience of some kind, gang related or even athletic team terrors. That the death might be murder, a thought that Plate was sure would cause panic, leading possibly to someone attempting to go out into the flood, did not seem to occur to anyone. Only he and the younger Harrimans, as far as he knew, had any idea murder was involved.

Plate wanted time to think the situation out. If the idea that this was murder got out among this group, it might not only frighten the trapped innocent, if the murderer was among them, that person might be tempted to flee as well.

He had been watching all their faces closely as he had asked each of them if there was any possibility they had known the boy. Aerial and Laurel had shown the distress associated stereotypically with sensitive women, tears and nervous agitation, upon hearing details of the young man's death, even more than Eileen, whose main emotion seem to be bitterness. Daphne and the Smiths had seemed indifferent.

Monica expressed disdain as had the delivery man, who openly said, "sounds like the kid brought on his own demise." This had caused multiple protests from Aerial and Laurel, as well as a rebuke from the preacher. In addition to condemning Mack's comment, the preacher had expressed appropriate prayerful solicitations. The congressman had expressed appropriate sentiment for a politician.

He could form no judgment as to how Randy and Janey were really reacting. They were behaving as responsible property owners and hosts to the group of people stranded in the establishment they managed. Trying to keep everyone else at equilibrium, they appeared to be ignoring their own feelings, whatever they might be.

They were the only two people that Plate did not really consider to be suspects. Arthur and Aerial may be related to Randy but Plate did not feel they were close enough to him to give them much more credibility than the others.

Plate knew Randy Harriman well enough that he was not at all worried that Randy would let any confidence slip.

He did not know Randy's wife as they had only been married a short time when Randy's behavior caused him to be dismissed from the force. Plate had actually spent more time talking to Janey at the checkout counter the previous day than he ever had while he and Randy were still colleagues. But wives of policemen usually were part of the enclosed circle of blue that routinely received special consideration and were expected to be trustworthy in return.

Still, it bothered him that he did not know what type of person Janey Harriman really was. He was counting on Randy to make sure his wife understood the necessity for keeping quiet.

He now recalled that Janey had been very prominently involved socially in police community activities and committees.

All that had been lost to her when Randy was fired.

She had lost her status when her husband lost his job.

Chapter 18

As Plate loitered around the door going into the warehouse, in what he hoped was a casual way for he was actually guarding the door to make sure no one got in, he thought back about the time that Randy Harriman had been on the Sand Waves police force.

Randy had been an exemplary officer.

Like himself, Randy had gone to the police academy after serving his two years in the army.

Like himself, Randy had not ever made it to Vietnam, drawing stateside duty in anticipation of the peace talks in Paris coming to a successful conclusion under Richard Nixon.

That Randy had landed a plum assignment on the police force in Sand Waves, which did not normally hire rookies, was probably due to the fact that his father was a prominent minister of a large wealthy congregation. But no one held that against Randy.

Nepotism ran rampant in Sand Waves in every possible way.

In fact, Plate had been the exception, in that his hiring was not connected to any prominent person or important relative in a high position but rather due to his record of achievements and his education.

Randy was a middle class cop in an upper class neighborhood.

The vast majority of Sand Waves' residents lived in homes, costing from $65,000 to less than $500,000, segregated by price ranges in neighborhoods defined geographically by a maze of similarly named streets, enclosed in boxes constructed of thoroughfares that held a smattering of nonresidential buildings. The lowest classes in Sand Waves would be upper middle class in the greater Houston area.

It wasn't that Plate considered himself upper class.

He just knew how to deal with the upper classes.

Randy had never learned.

Coinciding with the initial establishment of Sand Waves in the mid 1970s, when it had begun building its neighborhoods on the sand dunes between Galveston and Houston, (29.6825 north latitude and 94.7919 west longitude), there was an unofficial rebellion against the general socioeconomic conditions that had prevailed since the late 1960s.

The powers that created it envisioned Sand Waves as standing as a tower of strength against the prevailing tide.

While the majority of residents in the middle and upper middle colonies were transferred corporate employees from the recession stricken North, Northeast, and Midwest, there were a significant number of well-educated locals interspersed within.

By the time Randy was hired, Sand Waves was not a place of flagrant bigotry or white supremacy inclinations, but simply a place for upwardly mobile, well educated white people, who worked frequently with minorities, drank with them, lunched with them, made multiple business deals with them, but upon arriving home each evening, wanted to see white faces all around.

With its own separate school district, its own separate

places of worship (of every imaginable religion, all located within walking distance of each other), its own shopping areas, even its own hospital system (despite the great Houston Medical Center being just a short drive away), its own dramatic theatre, and movie theatre, and just about one or two of any other entity needed for modern existence (all strategically located so as to not mar residential structures), a family could move into Sand Waves and live there for the duration of their lives without ever leaving, if they could afford to.

Most could not.

Most had to work in Houston.

Few jobs were available in the Command Designed Colony and they were quickly filled, usually by relatives of the rich and/or famous.

Just a short time into his police career, Randy had run afoul of the powerful real estate agents in Sand Waves.

The real estate agents, perpetual monitors of this enclave, gave themselves credit for creating and maintaining the high property values in Sand Waves.

They saw themselves as the real police there, patrolling constantly with an eye out for those residents derelict in their attention to landscaping and property maintenance.

Up until the recent economic decline, reaching the area very late in the business cycle, from the time the colony began, anyone could count on buying a house in Sand Waves and being able to sell it for at least a ten percent profit in at most 18 months to two years. This guarantee of such a rate of return meant that anyone not planning to live there for a long period of time could purchase a house, hold onto it a couple of years, and sell it for a good profit, buying a similar house elsewhere at a lower rate and pocket the difference.

For the longest time, construction could not keep up with demand.

For those wanting to live there, the ideal plan was to buy in the highest colony in which a family could get a loan for the highest priced house their income qualified them. Then after a few years put the house up for sale and buy up into the next highest price colony.

This mentality kept everyone working hard to keep property values as high as possible, kept money flowing through the banks, much into the pockets of the real estate agents.

And it kept most middle class, and many upper class families, in enough constant never ending debt that they were easily controllable.

For their hard work in achieving this self-sustaining financial boom, the real estate agents felt they deserved special treatment from everyone including the police.

Randy had not been able to handle this.

He gave them speeding tickets despite the large real estate company logo signs plastered on their car doors.

He arrested their children for drug violations even upon being informed that the parents of the suspects were housing specialists.

The situation was agitated further when he refused to placate them by issuing citations to ordinary citizens for imperfectly kept lawns. Or for more than two cars parked in a driveway overnight. Or for painting houses without obtaining colony federation permission. Or for doing unauthorized repairs on their homes using unapproved workers. Or for violating colony federation rules by doing any home improvement themselves.

"Wasting police time," Randy told the real estate agents who filed these complaints.

They were not amused.

Finally they did what they did best. They banded together and used their powers of selection.

They had been honing those powers for years in much bigger ways than scratching one annoying cop.

They had fought the minority problem and, in their minds, they had won.

Minorities may have felt they had the right to live anywhere in any neighborhood in the City of Houston but this was not the City of Houston. It was an unincorporated section of the Gulf Coast.

Real estate agents subtly dissuaded minority middle class clients from moving in. This was made even easier than most would have thought possible by the inclusion of a significant percentage of real estate agents in Sand Waves who were black or Hispanic or other ethnicities.

These agents were interviewed and carefully selected by the predominant real estate agencies in the colony. They were given a psychological test ostensibly to determine how well they could work with their peers in teamwork. But actually the hidden aspects of the test scored them on their eagerness to make money versus their consciousness of racial inequality.

The agents scoring high in the former category were hired. Ethnic customers would be sent to them and gently steered away from Sand Waves. Of course, the ethnic agents got more than their share of automatic sales in Sand Waves from huge corporations devastated by the prolonged depression in the North and Midwest, moving their headquarters to booming Houston along with thousands of employees who were looking for neighborhoods just like those in Sand Waves.

The vast majority of these transferred corporate employees were white to begin with. If the companies had minority employees they needed to relocate, there was a different, less homogeneous master planned community just down Highway 59 and two others on US 45 that welcomed most anyone with a high paying job.

Along with Sand Waves, these neighborhoods reminded the transplants coming to Texas of the strict and precise types of building codes of their neighborhoods at home in their land-poor cities father north.

In Houston, they had to endure businesses right next to residences as Houston was the largest city in the United States where geographical zoning was prohibited.

In Sand Waves, transferees saw the average small lot with the required minimum of two trees as spacious. And while some established and prominent neighborhoods in the big cities were not overwhelmingly welcoming to the wave of middle class immigrants from the North, Sand Waves had been designed with them in mind. If they were white.

When subtle messages to middle class ethnic home shoppers failed, as they occasionally did, it didn't take long for those who bought homes, able to afford the slightly higher priced house than average middle class track home, to realize they really weren't welcome.

Soon they understood they would be able to sell their house for a nice profit, as home values were constantly increasing in Sand Waves.

They would be able to find just as nice of a neighborhood, a bigger house and decent size yard, for the same price, fully integrated, or even completely their own ethnicity.

But somewhere else. Not in Sand Waves.

To keep Sand Waves as pure as possible did not require active participation by the vast majority of residents.

But it sometimes required cooperation and always required apathy. Randy Harriman could never be apathetic about anything.

His emotions were easily aroused and any cause he adopted, he pursued with passion.

This made him an anathema to the powers that be in Sand Waves.

To get rid of Randy Harriman, or at least neutralize him, the real estate agents had begun a letter writing, official complaint filing campaign.

They bombarded the local newspaper with stories that showed him in a negative light.

They filed complaints with his neighborhood Colony Federation Board.

They set him up to fail socially and professionally.

Their only real obstacle to this campaign had been the social status of his father.

But they coped with Reverend Harriman's prominence by quietly supporting him and his church with their attendance, like Monica did, and finances.

This made their campaign against Randy look all the more legitimate.

There were constant warning notices from the CF every time a blade of grass grew over his curb, complaints about a dog he didn't even own but frequented his yard when the owner let it out at night, warning letters about anyone that parked in front of his house, even if they were unknown to him.

He had to prove in a colony federation hearing that he had paid the dues every year, prove that with canceled checks from each and every year he had lived there and so on.

After prolonged continuous harassment, Randy gave up.

He came to work drunk one Monday morning and the chief had no choice but to fire him.

Plate was completely sympathetic to Randy.

He had been treated terribly unfairly.

No one should have had to take the type of harassment, completely unwarranted harassment, which the establishment in Sand Waves meted out to him.

The problem was if a person could not take the civil harassment, which was really paper bullying, if such treatment caused that person so much stress they were impaired on the job, that person had no business being a police officer.

Police officers needed to be able to take far worse

treatment than chronic paper complaints and trumped up charges from bureaucrats that would never be taken seriously by the legal system outside of the Paper Powers existing in Sand Waves.

Plate had always suspected Randy came to work drunk in order to get fired deliberately so as not to have to work as a police officer again.

Randy had been good at policing.

He just didn't like the job.

So he ended it for good.

No question of ever returning to it.

But he also wrecked his social standing, which he had only been vaguely aware of, but his wife had reveled in.

Plate had not heretofore considered Janey's reaction to Randy's debacle and any damage it might have done to their marriage.

Being single, Plate did not have such thoughts uppermost in his mind automatically.

He was worried about it now.

Without the gun handy, the owner of the .357 felt very vulnerable.

No one had disturbed it in its hiding place downstairs but now that the body had been found, everything would be looked at in a more scrutinizing light.

And everyone was corralled upstairs.

Now, fearing the hiding place instead of being perfect, was too obvious, at the first opportunity the original substitution was reversed.

But personal searches might be undertaken by the cop at any time.

A new hiding place in the attic apartment had to be found.

It took a little thinking and a chance of getting caught in the wrong room but in just a short time the .357 was secure in another perfect hiding place upstairs.

Chapter 19

The semicircle of chairs around the checkout counter sat mostly empty.

The Smiths were sitting in two at one end and speaking quietly with each other.

Arthur and Monica were sitting on the chairs at the opposite end doing the same.

Aerial sat by herself on the bench, gazing across the lobby at the large portrait of her late husband which hung on the wall above the manager's office.

Janey had wandered to different places in the store to check the displays and merchandise.

Randy had relieved Plate for a time, keeping an eye out on the door to warehouse.

"What I'll do," he told Plate," is just sit here in front of the door and make like I'm doing store paperwork."

"I'm going to meander around and see what the others might be up to," said Plate. "I won't be long."

"Take your time. By the way I think Laurel went upstairs to nap so that's where she is."

"Okay."

The designation of accidental death was a brilliant move, Plate thought as he walked the aisles of the store. Everyone had relaxed after the initial shock.

He noticed the congressman talking to Eileen in the middle of an aisle.

That accounted for the whereabouts of everyone except the delivery man and Misha, but both restrooms had the occupied sign posted so they had to be in there.

He presumed.

Planning to shortly make his way back around to be sure about Misha and Mack, he found himself slipping back in the direction of the warehouse door.

But he stopped short of speaking again to Randy when he heard voices.

Randy was speaking in low tense terms and a female voice answering him was not Janey.

"It's time for us, Randy, time for us to be together. Monica Moon and Arthur Harriman are going to force Aerial to sell. I overheard them. There is no reason to stay."

Randy looked at Laurel, wondering what she saw in him, wondering why it was her that loved him and not Janey.

Why it was her that valued him and not his father.

"I'm lost, Laurel. I can't decide anything right now."

"Why do you lead me on and then hurt me?"

"I don't mean to hurt you, Laurel. This is not a pleasant situation for me. Janey is certain we are having an affair."

"We are having an affair. An affair of the heart."

Randy took Laurel in his arms then but held her back from kissing him.

"You're accused of the crime, might as well be guilty," she said. "Oh, Randy, I would go anywhere with you. Do anything to be with you. I don't care if we don't have any money."

"You might care in the long run. I am damaged goods, disgraced in the eyes of Sand Waves society."

"So, then, what have you got to lose? Let's both go away, far away from here and start over with a new life, new names even."

"Why should we do that? We would not be committing a crime. If I leave Janey for any reason, I would still want to be here."

"Then it's the store you love, not Janey. You want to work here. Well, if you want to work here, I want to work here too. Your problem is you're so eager to accept society's verdict that you're worthless. And Arthur and Janey's verdict that you can't be happy here. Why can't you see? Has it never occurred to you that I might know what's right for me and you might know what's right for you? That we might know better after all. That we are right and they are wrong. That we will be happy, could be happy, have the chance to be happy, to have that extra something. And the Janeys and Arthurs of this world will never know because they never cause anything but misery."

"That extra something? Janey and I had that extra something once…"

"I hate Janey," Laurel said, becoming suddenly vicious. "She is tearing you apart. She cannot stand no longer being a policeman's wife in Sand Waves. Losing her social position. Having to work here to make ends meet."

"Laurel, you must not speak that way of Janey."

"You should be happy the store will be sold. You'll have some money and we could go away."

"Shhh, Laurel, you don't know what you're saying, somebody is listening."

Plate flinched upon hearing those words, but he had not given himself away.

At that moment the tap of Monica's heels, briskly

151

advancing, sounded.

"Mr. Harriman- Randy," she said, barely glancing at Laurel. "This is a good opportunity for us to talk."

"Laurel, could you excuse us?" Randy was relieved to send Laurel away.

"Yes, sir," said Laurel, stiffly formal. She lingered by the luggage promotion for a moment. Then she walked away opposite from the direction where Plate still stood watching Randy. Plate fancied he saw her stop behind a Christmas tree, and that now Randy had two eavesdroppers. But he paid scant attention to her. Randy had moved with Monica behind the Sleigh Ride Display and left the door to the warehouse vulnerable.

Plate watched it and listened to Randy at the same time.

"Randy. I may call you Randy?"

"Yes, Ms. Moon, you may."

"Randy, we do need to get better acquainted. Your father tells me you are the type of man who puts others first so I know you will put him first in considering what to do about the situation with the store."

"Ms. Moon-"

"Monica. Please. Monica."

"Monica. I am having to choose between my father and a woman who has been like a mother to me, though she may be technically my step-grandmother. It's not an easy situation to be in and right now I do not feel like I can make any well grounded decision. Let's please drop the subject for the duration of this emergency situation."

Monica shifted her weight back and forth on her feet.

"Randy, let me tell you something." The sweetness had gone out of her voice. "This property will be sold. Your father and I will be married. That is all there is to it. There is nothing you can do to stop it. Now I don't care if you have any kind of relationship in the future with your father. Quite frankly, my life would be easier if you did not. And I'm warning you if you try to make it trouble for me, I will crush you. You're already washed up in this colony. I'll make sure you're hung out to dry."

Randy stood astonished as Monica turned and walked away.

Plate watched to see if Laurel slipped away from her hiding place to go back to Randy.

But she also went the other way.

The two women were bound to meet on their way to the narrow stairs and Plate wondered which one would step back and allow the other to go up first.

Chapter 20

Plate felt the warehouse was insecure. It was his responsibility to see that the body was not disturbed.

He was processing Randy's conversations with the two women. He feared he could not now count on Randy maintaining the mental discipline and concentration needed to help him keep the scene secure.

He waited a few moments and approached Randy, not mentioning what he had overheard, but requesting some suggestions as to how they could keep anyone who had an overdose of curiosity about the body out of the warehouse.

"Have you anything we can brace the door with?"

"There might be some nails in the back office somewhere. I'm sure Aerial has a hammer upstairs."

Then a frightened scream caught both men by surprise. Instinctively they took off running in the direction they believed the sound came from.

Plate got there first.

All the way across the store, between the Santa Display and the left outer wall, Eileen sat on the floor holding the back of her head.

"What happened?" Plate knelt down beside her.

She was rubbing the back of her neck.

No one was visible anywhere nearby.

Plate could not see any sign of an injury but the woman seemed very unstable when he and Randy helped her to her feet.

"I had walked over to see out the windows. But nothing but rain was visible so I was going back towards the lobby when it felt like something fell from the ceiling and landed on me."

Randy cleared some presents from the Santa Display and helped Eileen sit on the platform.

Plate started looking around for anything out of the ordinary.

"Are you sure you weren't hit from behind?" he asked.

Several of the others had come on the scene by now.

Plate asked them to please stand back.

"Something could have hit me from behind," said Eileen.

A lantern was on the floor nearby. Its label indicated it was an outdoor lantern which took a large six volt battery, causing it to be quite heavy.

"Could this have hit you?" Randy picked up the lantern.

"Don't pick that up!" said Plate, aggravated, his attention distracted from the injured woman.

Mark stepped forward to help steady Eileen.

"I'm sorry," said Randy, dropping the lantern quickly. "This is one reason why I am not a cop anymore."

"It's okay," said Plate.

"What happened?" said the congressman to Eileen, who despite the pain at the back of her neck, thrilled at his touch.

"I don't know. I didn't see anything."

By this time everyone was standing around the Santa Display.

Plate realized the door to the warehouse was totally unguarded.

Laurel pushed forward in front of the others.

"Here, let me take her over to the bench. We can sit down," said Laurel, trembling a little as she helped Eileen.

This person is so much like me, Laurel thought, as she and the congressman helped Eileen across the lobby to the bench.

Eileen was having similar thoughts.

"I'm feeling okay now. It just frightened me."

"Is it possible that the lantern could have fallen off the shelf and hit her?" asked Plate, as he started back towards the direction of the warehouse door.

"I don't see how," said Randy, following.

"It was on the unfinished display," said Misha, tagging along. "It was up on top of all those boxes that we haven't opened yet. It could have fallen and hit her if she had been just in the right spot."

"Is it possible?" Plate asked Janey, also keeping up with them.

"I suppose," said Janey uncertainly.

"I suppose you don't think I know what I'm talking about," said Misha petulantly.

"It had to have been an accident," said Laurel, catching up to them, a little breathless.

"Yes, of course, had to be," Randy said automatically.

Plate did not respond.

However, the idea that Eileen had not been the victim of an attack gave him some comfort.

But very little comfort.

Comfort full of doubt.

"We will put it down as a freak accident for right

now," he said. "I don't know what else I can do."

His last glance at the bench where Eileen sat, showed she was being attended by Arthur, Mark, Aerial, and Mack. Monica was not in sight.

The Smiths and Daphne had also followed him.

Plate used the opportunity to put them all to work finding nails, a hammer, and a board long enough to secure the warehouse door.

"Stay here, while I check the warehouse to make sure nothing has been touched," he instructed Randy.

He took a brief tour of the warehouse. The odor had gotten worse even though the tarp remained zipped.

He had no choice but to unzip it and look in the cauldron.

The body appeared undisturbed.

He quickly refit the tarp and rezipped it.

Mentally he timed himself as he did it.

Anyone could have slipped in and done the same while he and Randy were distracted by Eileen's cry. And left no trace of a disturbance, just like he had just done.

Back out in the retail section of the store, he found Daphne waiting with a board, nails and hammer.

Assured by Randy that Eileen's mishap was nothing to be concerned about, everyone had gone back to their previous pursuits, except Eileen who had gone upstairs.

Plate secured the door.

He had already decided his barricade would have to do the work.

He could not watch the door and these people, not this number of them, all at the same time.

It was more important to watch the people.

The dead body was not going to go anywhere.

He thanked Daphne for her assistance somewhat brusquely and went off towards the Santa Display to take another look at where Eileen had her mishap.

"Was it an accident?" asked Laurel, coming up behind him.

"Oh, well, hard to tell," said Plate.

"Must have been," said Laurel, stubbornness in her tone. Fear as well. "What's going to happen next? What are you going to do? Search all of us?"

"I've no authority to do that," he said. "I've no probable cause."

"Then there is nothing to connect anyone here with the poor boy found in the cauldron?" Sadness replaced the fear in Laurel's voice. "It was an accident then. Misha was right. I wonder if that boy's death was an accident too. I hope so."

Without waiting for his answer, Laurel turned away and went towards the restrooms.

He saw her stop and stare blankly at the Cowboy Display for a moment before passing it and going through the ladies' door.

Plate had no doubt about the attack on Eileen being an accident.

He now totally disregarded what Misha had said.

Just like the death of the boy in the cauldron, he was certain it was not.

Chapter 21

J. Daphne Martin had work to do.

It had been a cinch to get Aerial to sign on the dotted line after they had all gone upstairs last night.

She had even written a check for the first month's premium and agreed to have the subsequent payments automatically deducted from her bank account.

People often balked at this idea, fearing forgetting the automatic deduction would lead to bouncing checks.

But the company was enamored with the idea of being able to get into people's bank accounts and swipe money out.

Few people understood that there was actually no limit to the number of times they could try, or amounts of money the company could extract.

So Daphne got an extra bonus for getting clients to agree to that little feature.

Plus it meant her renewal commissions would come in automatically and with stability.

Considering the gravity of the flooding situation, Daphne saw opportunity knocking.

One of those nice events that doesn't kill anyone who is not foolish enough to try to go out swimming around or canoeing in the floodwaters, yet an event that reminds everyone of their vulnerability and ultimate mortality, Daphne thought in happy summation.

Adding in the accidental death of the teenage boy, Daphne felt if she didn't get a policy written on virtually everybody in the store, except probably the congressman, who would have his own insurance agent already, she was a failure at her job, not to mention the money she would lose.

Fortunately she had plenty of applications with her.

And bank draft agreements and most other routine paperwork called for at various times.

It was nice to get the first month's premium in check or cash but just signing the bank draft agreement was enough to put the policy in force, providing the person was young enough and healthy enough not to need a physical and there were no high risk factors involved.

Aerial had already taken her physical, which consisted of a company employed medical technician coming around to take her blood pressure, earlier this week.

Anyone that age with any serious health problems had to actually get a physical by a doctor.

Aerial had no long term health problems and had not even been to a doctor except for a checkup in the last five years. Her age meant a nice high premium, a good commission for Daphne. She had purchased $25,000 of whole life insurance, a Supreme Policy, for $150.00 a month.

The only other person trapped here old enough to need a physical was Arthur. He looked healthy. If he didn't have any invisible issues medically, a blood pressure check from the medical technician would be all that was necessary.

However, the policy could not be effective until that happened.

So there would be a time delay.

Daphne put him last on the list.

That still left ten excellent prospects.

She decided to start with Randy as he was married and might be soon starting a family.

Janey would be next.

If they were a typical married couple, it would actually be one sale.

Rarely did she have to sell married people separately. They either agreed together to buy life insurance or, together, they turned her down.

Next she was going after the Smiths.

They were a long shot.

Chances were high they had a life insurance agent where they lived in West Texas. But they were obviously so rich, such a gold mine, if by some fortuitous turn of fate they had heretofore neglected that aspect of their finances, Daphne was ready.

And many people did.

Many people, otherwise devoted to detailed management of their financial affairs, put off that aggravating detail of dealing with their inevitable death.

When Daphne had first started selling insurance she had sold about ten policies when she first heard the phrase that, later on, she would hear many times over.

She had been in an earnest conversation with a nice man in his 40s, making wonderful eye contact, engaging him in every aspect of the benefits of purchasing life insurance, when during the course of the conversation he had said-

"This is the way I want things to be *if I ever die.*"

Daphne had laughed.

She had honestly thought the man was joking.

Her impulsive spontaneous laughter had almost cost her the sale. Fortunately she had stopped short. Her training, never to blurt out the first words that came to her head, coming in good stead this time.

She had not said what was in her mind.

What do you mean if?

It had taken her a few moments to stifle her mirth and go ahead with the sale. After that, now in her fourth year in the business, she realized the phrase was commonplace.

"If I ever die…"

"If", "ever", and "die" were words frequently used in the same sentence by people of all kinds from all walks of life, religious and secular, male and female, of any age, no matter how advanced in their field, or total failures at life.

Daphne had long ago suppressed the urge to correct the conjunctive word from "if" to "when". The phrase had taught her that her job was completely contradictory in nature. She had to make people feel good about purchasing a product that would only be used upon their death.

A death most people in contemporary society somehow thought there was at least a chance of not actually ever happening.

The stereotypical fatalistic attitude towards death supposedly held by a significant percentage of the public, according to the movies and television shows, was actually held by only a tiny section of the general population.

With those fatalistic people, and with the few devoutly religious people she encountered, when she had positively identified them, Daphne could share a laugh over the phrase used by the significant plurality.

Of course, she had to make sure any particular prospect was not one of those in the third attitude category towards death.

That of simply ignoring it.

Those were the hardest people to sell and a special interest bearing policy had recently been developed with them in mind. Daphne was selling it like hotcakes.

Still she heard even those people, who were in perennial detachment, say occasionally- "if I ever die".

Despite its intrinsic humor, the phrase reflected the blindfolded society she lived in, so it never failed to evoke both ironic and bittersweet feelings within her when she heard it and she would have to stifle a smile.

After the Smiths, Daphne planned to tackle the singles, usually among the harder sells.

The delivery man was a good prospect. Blue collar workers had less contact with professional life insurance agents than white collar workers, meaning less competition. Some life agents would not deal with them at all.

And people who drove all day long for a living knew, on any day at any time, the odds might turn against them and they might become a statistic, one of the daily traffic deaths in Houston.

Always at least one life was taken each day by a car wreck and sometimes the numbers ran into the double digits.

Daphne put him down as a probable.

Unfortunately most of the others were both single and female.

Women just did not buy as much life insurance nor

buy it as often as men.

Talking up the new day and age of equality sometimes helped, but frequently women simply didn't feel any responsibilities towards providing for those left behind.

Sometimes the addition of children helped. But most married women still felt it was the husband's responsibility to provide for the family and therefore only the husband needed any significant amount of life insurance.

And Daphne was pretty sure, just by looking these women over, childbirth may be in their futures but was certainly not in their pasts.

Monica was a better prospect than Laurel because she had more money and status.

Laurel was a better prospect than Misha, who was obviously still a teenager and probably not even going to talk to her at all.

Eileen was an enigma. Daphne had several single black women who were excellent clients, but many times such prospects told her straight out they were only going to buy insurance from black agents. Still, of all the people there, Daphne figured Eileen to be the loneliest.

That by itself made her an excellent prospect.

Then there was the police officer.

He was a high risk applicant. Her company's policy was that for such dangerous professions a routine investigation of the real level of hazard faced needed to be undertaken before the policy could be bound.

Daphne felt sure she could get him at least a minimal policy. After all, there was a difference between a traffic cop in Sand Waves and a policeman on the front lines in the

Houston barrios or wards.

Still, he was much in the same position as the preacher. No instant coverage available.

She spied a luggage display where she could easily stash the briefcase and it would not be noticed.

Daphne pulled out an application, a clipboard and pen.

She could discreetly carry these down by her side, whereas the huge briefcase would be too obvious, sending negative images as she made her approaches.

She wasn't going to be rigid.

While she had her mental list of people prioritized, she was going to be on the lookout for any good opportunity to slip into a conversation with any of the trapped perspective life insurance candidates.

A nice friendly intimate personal conversation that might lead to a good juicy sale.

She started stalking the aisles.

Chapter 22

"I took out life insurance many years ago," said
Monica. "My parents had bought me some when I was a
child and when I got married I converted it to a double
indemnity adult policy. I don't even remember the exact
amount but it's at least $100,000. I'm single with no
dependents and don't need any more than that."

"I understand completely," said Daphne. "I'm single
with no dependents myself. However, we do have these new
whole life with interest bearing annuity policies that are
actually bringing a high rate of return that's guaranteed to
never go below four percent no matter what happens to the
economy."

"What interest are they paying right now?"

"Ten percent." The two women were seated on the
bench as they talked business.

"I can get 16 percent on my CDs at the bank. Why
should I put my money in an insurance policy?"

"Well, there is a guaranteed factor of the interest rate
never going below four percent. And there's no limit on the
amount of money you can contribute to the policy in
addition to the premiums."

"Interest rates in this country are never going to be
below ten percent again," said Monica. "I'd be a fool to
take a guaranteed rate of four percent against the higher rate
I can get at the bank."

"Have you considered going over your policy taken
out years ago and making sure it is up to date?"

Monica stared at Daphne for a moment with sudden
new respect.

Daphne now appeared to her to be a female comrade in arms.

She was younger and perhaps made up a little too much, but here was another single career woman having to fight the daily battle against the men in a man's world.

"Actually," said Monica. "I haven't actually looked at the policy in years."

"You would have updated your beneficiary after your divorce?"

Now Monica was really stunned.

And impressed.

"My goodness, you know I don't know that chore was ever done. I don't remember. It was a hectic time 15 years ago."

Small automatic payments that came from her oldest checking account were so insignificant in light of her current income that Monica had stopped tracking those years ago. She just made sure she put enough money in it each month to cover them.

"What company was your policy with? Could it possibly have been with Finest Southland Life? I have some change of beneficiary designations with me."

"Well, I think it may have been with your company. I know South or South Something was in the company name. My husband and I had just come down to Houston from Ohio. Long before the current wave of Northerners came in. We were among the very few non-Southerners in the area where we lived. I remember thinking the company name was ironic. Maybe it was Finest Southland."

"We have been in business more than 81 years."

"Then there is a good possibility?" Monica sounded hopeful.

Daphne tried to believe this.

There were thousands of small insurance companies, specializing in the highly profitable life insurance field, which had the words South, Southern, Southwestern, Southland, Southern Hills, Southeast, or South Something Else in their names.

Then there were those with added adjectives- Great South, Great Southern, Great Southeastern, Great Southland, Finest South, Finest Southern Hills, Finest Southwestern, Finest Southland and so on.

Then there were those with added nouns- South Memorial, Southwest Memorial, Southland Memorial, Southern Hills Memorial, etc.

Then there were the names that added certain groups, although that meant nothing. They insured everybody. These included Southern Teachers, Southern Hills Farmers, Southeastern Bankers, Southland Teachers, Southwestern Fishermen, Southland Bankers...

The list was virtually endless.

"Odds are it's our company," said Daphne brightly. "We were one of the first companies to target Ya- I mean seek out people being transferred here from the North. If you or your husband worked for a company that bought its group health policy from us, then it's a good chance that an agent called on you to try to sell you individual life insurance. Our company usually makes most sales via visits in the home. While a few other companies do that, we specialize in it."

Like a few hundred thousand other companies, thought Daphne silently, as she smiled encouragingly at Monica. "Do you recall if someone came to your home?"

"Yes they did, I do remember that. Would my bank know the policy number? Surely they would have a record of the company name?"

Monica was now alarmed.

During the stress of her divorce, the thought of changing her beneficiary had simply never come to her.

Of course her exhusband had never mentioned it.

Undoubtedly he had changed his beneficiary when he remarried shortly after leaving her. Her male divorce lawyer had acted more like he was on her exhusband's side and had paid her needs and priorities scant attention.

"Maybe. Insurance companies operate under different names in different parts of the country due to the connotations associated with geographical names, so there's sometimes a holding company to which all the payments go to. It would be easier for me to just look you up on my computer."

Daphne licked her lips.

When she could get permission from customers to do computer searches, she could find out more about them and usually get a higher premium.

"I know getting information out of the bank is almost impossible." Monica spoke from experience.

"Here are some of the forms we use," said Daphne, handing her an application. "Maybe these look familiar? I know ours hasn't changed in 30 years. The company is quite proud of that. Every company uses a distinct form."

"I don't know." Monica fingered the application. "Could you let me see one of the beneficiary change forms?"

"I'll get one out of my briefcase."

As Daphne slipped over to the luggage stack to get the beneficiary change form, Monica scrutinized the application. There was one question she knew she could not answer in a way that would not cause complications if she attempted to take out new life insurance.

Her eyes found the problem question right away.

Have in the past five years you ever been diagnosed or treated for cancer of any kind?

Monica had been treated for cancer. The cancer had been declared resolved. She had kept her suffering a secret, fearing it would harm her career. Her mastectomy was cleverly disguised with specially designed brassieres, and perfectly tailored clothing.

She knew the possibility of recurrence was high. She spent most days pushing thoughts about cancer completely out of her mind.

She was self-disciplined enough to do that very effectively. But in this situation, the idea of recurrence had come back to haunt her.

Daphne arrived back with the beneficiary change form.

"I- I need badly to do this," said Monica, as she looked over the simple form. "Will it be legal?"

"As long as we get witnesses not related to the beneficiary, it will be legal if your policy is actually with our company. If not- well, I'm not sure. There may be a gray area there, or more likely- no, the change would not be effective if something happened. That's my opinion, but then I am not a lawyer."

"Well," said Monica. "I don't suppose it could hurt to go ahead and fill out the form."

"Of course not," said Daphne smoothly. "Then I can make an appointment to get together with you, maybe next week, and go over your old policy."

"Not being not sure where the policy is, what company it's with or anything- this is embarrassing. I'm a career woman and here I am not taking care of my own personal business."

"I quite understand. It's perfectly normal. Believe me, it happens all the time. You don't have to have the policy in hand. If you will permit me, I have a computer system that is connected with all the major life insurance companies in the United States. It will allow me to type in your name and vital statistics and, unless your name is extremely common, I can ascertain what coverage you have with which company."

"Well, my married name was Moore. The policy was taken out under the name Monica Moon Moore. And people with the surname Moon are almost as plentiful as those with Moore, I have found."

"Oh, yes? Well, Monica is not too terribly common. What is your middle name? It will be on the company record. You had to disclose it before they'd issue a policy."

Monica hesitated.

After swearing Daphne to secrecy, she wrote it down.

Daphne had heard a lot of names, but could not help

but feel humorless surprise.

"My mother hated me," said Monica cryptically. "Actually, she was an English teacher with a fondness for alliteration. She just thought I would get married and drop at least one of the names someday. And I should have known that a marriage to a man with the last name of Moore was ill fated by the gods."

"Oh, but that solves our problem. Your middle name is certainly a unique name. We will be able to find out what coverage you have and if you cannot locate the policy, we can get a duplicate. I have lost policy forms with me also. Did you want to wait or-?"

"No, I recall. I am sure it was Finest Southland." Monica's voice indicated the opposite, but the thought of her exhusband having any chance whatsoever to even remotely possibly profit from her death suddenly filled her with rage.

She suppressed it but it stirred her to action.

While she didn't seem to be in any danger, being trapped by floodwaters was a hazardous predicament by any definition.

"I want to sign a beneficiary change right now. I am sure that in court it would hold, as it will attest to my intentions, even if it is not your company."

"Okay." Daphne was thrilled.

Even if there were no money involved, just handling a transaction such as this made Monica her client and there was sure to be more profitable transactions in the future.

If good fortune saw to it that Monica's old policy really was with her company, so much the better. Daphne could have the number assigned to her for policy service.

While, unlike in the casualty business, there was no "inherited" commissions payable on life policies, Daphne would still become Monica's official agent in the eyes of the company.

If not, she would just requisition forms from the correct company and redo it later. Monica was expressing no loyalty to any other agent. Daphne felt certain Monica was hers and future business would follow.

"Who do you want to change your beneficiary to?"

"Well, I guess, I don't know. I don't know if I have any living relatives. I haven't kept in touch."

"A favorite charity? Beneficiary designations are a little tricky. The companies frown on beneficiaries not related, but charities usually have no trouble collecting if they're already firmly established like the Red Cross or the American Heart Association-"

"I am engaged to be married. Unofficially. To Arthur Harriman."

"Well, now, while a fiancé is not technically a relative, as far as insurance companies are concerned, that would be a sound beneficiary. Let's see, so who can we ask as witnesses? Has to be someone here other than Reverend Harriman, his son, daughter-in-law, or sister."

"She's not his sister. She's his stepmother. I prefer somebody that I have no connections with it all. Maybe the two employees?"

Daphne bit her lip. "I'll approach the one named Laurel. The other one doesn't look like she's grown to me. I know she has to be at least 16 to have a job here. And I heard her say to somebody she was 18. She looks more like she's about 14 or 15. Let's go with somebody besides her. How about the cop?"

"Fine, I don't know him from Adam."

Daphne went to find Laurel, who was working on the unfinished display, but could not immediately locate Plate.

Instead she also brought back Eileen, who had been lonely upstairs, so had come back down.

Monica and Eileen agreed they were complete strangers.

In response to Laurel's polite question, Eileen said she felt better although her neck was still sore.

Monica's personal business is a happy distraction for both these witnesses, thought Daphne.

Although Eileen seemed a little stiff and even hostile toward Monica, Daphne put that down to possible feelings of social alienation or just the effects of her mishap.

Monica pulled out some papers from her purse. "Did you need any identification?" she asked Daphne.

"No, nothing," Daphne replied, working on the form.

Monica put most of the papers back in her purse, but keeping two sheets out, she wrote something quickly, then folded them and set them down beside Eileen and Laurel.

Then she changed her beneficiary designation from her exhusband, Paul Moore, whom she only vaguely remembered as a romantic attachment that she frivolously legalized, then almost instantly regretted doing so, to Reverend Arthur Harriman, whom she planned to spend the rest of her life with. At least the foreseeable future of her life.

But as she watched the witnesses sign the paper she suddenly thought she had no more desire to see Arthur Harriman benefit from her death then Paul Moore or any other stranger in this world.

She resolved to live a long time, cancer or no cancer. Until recently she had never considered not remaining single for the rest of her life. She didn't want children and had planned, if she ever married, to be at least over 35, and to marry an older man who would already have children and not want babies. Her recent cancer surgery, while not affecting her fertility, was another good reason to avoid having children. No way would she want to bring a child in the world whose mother might not live to see it grow up.

"Thank you for being witnesses," said Monica to Laurel and Eileen. She handed them her sheets of paper. "Just my appreciation and a record of your actions in writing."

Eileen opened hers and read silently. *Thank you for witnessing my life insurance beneficiary change in November 1982, Cordially yours, Monica Moon.*

Laurel folded her note and put it in her pirate pants pocket.

"Keep those for future reference," said Monica, with a slight smile at Eileen. "Just in case there is ever a question."

"Good idea," said Daphne, finishing up the form.

Paperwork finished, the other women drifted away.

Monica was left alone.

Glancing around to make sure no one was watching, she lit a cigarette and drew a deep breath.

Chapter 23

Happily unaware that her new prospect was uninsurable, Daphne wrapped up the details of her upcoming appointment with Monica and suggested to Eileen that they talk.

Eileen declined, having decided to go back upstairs for a nap, the events of the day producing sudden fatigue.

Daphne turned to Laurel.

Flattered by the request to be a witness for Monica, she was in the right mood to talk to Daphne.

"I really couldn't afford any life insurance right now," said Laurel. "However, your timing is good. In this situation I thought a lot about life and death last night."

That's just what Daphne hoped to hear.

"We have a minimal policy premium of $5.00 a month," said Daphne, "if you allow automatic withdrawal from your bank account each month."

"How much would that buy me?"

"At your age, 27- I am presuming good health?" Daphne usually did not ask at this stage such a direct question about health but Laurel had something about her that seemed unhealthy in a vague sort of way.

Laurel nodded, however. "I am very healthy."

"About $1800 whole life. Just a funeral policy. I could get you a higher death benefit if you wanted term insurance but there's no cash value, no interest earned."

"I'm in good health now," said Laurel, looking over the application. "There could be a problem with my past."

"Oh?"

"This question here- 'Have you ever been treated for

drug, alcohol, or substance addiction of any kind in the past ten years?' "

"You have trouble answering that question?"

"Yes, I am a former, uh, I had an abuse problem."

"How long ago?"

"Less than ten years."

"You got medical treatment for this?" Daphne knew that private group treatment might not show up on the radar.

"Yes, I was hospitalized."

"Oh, I see, well you would probably be given a rated premium, if you are accepted, which would be higher than normal."

Daphne was fibbing.

Her company never accepted anybody that answered yes to that question.

She mentally ran through the list of auxiliary companies she occasionally dealt with, trying to recall if any one of them had sent out a notice lately that they were accepting former drug users.

Companies occasionally relaxed their standards and let a few high risks in to get premium volume up at a time of slow sales.

Air Pilots Memorial Life Insurance Company had sent a memo recently relaxing its restrictions on persons with ulcers and West Texas Ranchers was allowing in mild heart conditions, but she couldn't think of any company currently accepting former drug addicts.

"It was a terrible time for me." Laurel was now relating the experience to Daphne.

Daphne was used to this.

Frequently when a client admitted past personal problems that could affect an application such as drug use or previous criminal convictions, they felt the need to relate the situation in detail to Daphne, not knowing psychology class yielded the only C she had in an otherwise superb set of college grades averaging 3.8.

"I was almost finished with my degree. I even had a job lined up and had put a down payment on a condominium that had yet to be built here in Sand Waves. Two months before my graduation I was at a party. I don't know what they gave me, but just like they say in anti-drug literature, I was hooked at the first try. Soon I was doing heroin. I blew my finals. Lost my down payment. And that was money I had borrowed from my mother. And, well, you see where I have wound up."

"Oh, that's terrible," said Daphne. "Would you like to fill out an application?"

"My mother has been diagnosed with some type of new slowly developing dementia. I don't know what the future holds for her," Laurel continued. "I fear it may run in the family and I don't know what my long term status here at this store is."

Daphne's thoughts, heretofore happily dwelling on additions to her clientèle and new commissions, abruptly paused, and then caught up to the verbal conversation.

She had asked the routine question automatically but now realized the last thing she wanted now was for Laurel to apply for a policy.

"I'm thinking if I could get a policy, even a little one, that might look good in the future somehow, someway?"

Laurel sounded hopeful. "And my mother is in a nursing home now. In Ohio. If anything happened to me, paying for the funeral would be devastating for her. She needs all her welfare for her bills not covered by Medicaid. She's got nobody else to help her."

Laurel's eyes filled with tears.

I wonder if there's anything else, thought Daphne.

Laurel did not tell Daphne about her past suicide attempt, officially diagnosed as accidental when Laurel's doctor had been willing to conceal her suicide attempt in return for sexual favors.

Laurel felt sure anyone checking into her past medical history would only find evidence of the drug abuse treatment.

She wanted to tell Daphne badly but feared Daphne would reject her.

Already Laurel interpreted Daphne's silence as judgment and disapproval of what she had revealed.

"Do I have to have a physical to take out such a small policy?" she asked Daphne, allowing a little hostility to creep into her usually soft and sweet voice.

"No. No one under 50, normally, has to take the physical for less than $500,000. But if you report any serious condition, we write your general physician and get a report from him, no matter how small the policy."

"So it depends on what he says?" Laurel was a little placated by the unchanged tone of Daphne's voice.

"I tell you what," said Daphne, now fearing Laurel was going to insist on applying for insurance. Daphne was legally bound to submit any application that was signed, with or without payment, and the company frowned on too many unacceptable applicants. "Let me mail you an application. I think I might can do better for you with a different company. All I have with me is my main company's applications. Let me shop around for you a bit."

That was not true.

Daphne had every application she could possibly ever use in her briefcase.

"That sounds fine," said Laurel. "I don't have any car insurance either. Can you help me with that?"

"No, that is casualty insurance. It's a different license. I only do life and health."

Casualty insurance paid too little commission for a talented life agent to mess with. It did not require real sales skills, as demand was strong.

Daphne had never even applied for the license.

"Well, we don't have any health insurance here," said Laurel.

Daphne thought rapidly.

No insurance company was going to touch Laurel for health insurance, individually, and her status as an employee and past history meant that, Innovations, defined as a small a company with less than 50 employees, would be likely be denied group health insurance as well.

Daphne did not often write group insurance. It was a lucrative field but still very much a man's game and required a lot more work and follow up than the individual policies she preferred to sell.

But she occasionally sold individual health insurance policies when asked.

"I'm not up to date on my health requirement right now," Daphne lied. She hoped she was lying ambiguously enough that if she were ever called on the carpet she could wriggle out of it. "Health requirement" could mean anything.

"And our individual health premiums start at $29.99 a month."

Daphne had forgotten that this would be a lot of money to Laurel.

She thought of that truthful, dissuading barrier too late to avoid the lie.

Daphne hated lying but a certain amount of deceit was just necessary in her profession.

"I couldn't get you anything cheaper anywhere."

At least that statement was true.

That sum bought only paltry coverage at a high deductible.

Premiums were soaring in the health field and good individual insurance was out of most people's reach, even if they qualified, unless they had a high paying job.

And most high paying jobs provided free or low cost health insurance.

"Okay. Just starting with life insurance might be best. If those are the premiums, it's all I can afford right now anyway." Laurel looked in her pocket for an unused piece of paper to write down her mailing address. "I wish I had thought about life insurance earlier. I would like to leave my mother something. I'll be looking for that application in the mail."

Mack approached them while Laurel was still writing

her address down.

Laurel looked at him, handed the paper to Daphne and moved away.

"I'll get this right to you after all this mess is over with," Daphne called after Laurel.

"I couldn't help overhearing," said Mack.

Daphne looked up and down his large frame, wondering if his weight was out of the normal range on the company's rating scale. If so, he would be rated for a higher premium also. And, like the police officer and the minister, there could be no instant binding coverage.

"I just wanted to let you know I don't need any insurance," said Mack.

"Oh. Oh, well, okay there. I appreciate your letting me know that, thank you." Daphne turned around and walked away from him, mentally crossing both him and Laurel off her list.

The Smiths were a washout as well.

Like the congressman, they had a life insurance agent in their hometown. It was ethically forbidden for Daphne to solicit a sale from them once she was told that. They could come to her and insist on purchasing an additional policy if they wanted to. But she could not ask for their business.

That was a fine line ignored by many agents, but Daphne abided by it.

She did not intend to be a life insurance agent for too many more years.

She had not intended to ever become a life insurance agent. It had been the best job offered to her when she had gotten her college degree in 1977. The only job offered in the Houston area where her parents and all her family lived.

Despite there being low unemployment in Houston, compared to just about every other major city, most firms wanted new employees to be willing to relocate.

Daphne liked her hometown. She planned to stay in the Houston area all her life. She saw no sense in moving away, even for a short period of time, just to satisfy the unreasonable demands of some corporation.

She had planned to only work for the insurance company a short while and get some experience to put on a resume and get a better job. A "real" job. But selling insurance had turned out to be the better job.

She was making far more money, with a lot less effort, than any other female that she knew who had graduated with a similar degree as hers. Or any degree for that matter.

Having survived her company's brutal training period quota, she essentially worked for herself, under the guidance, but not control, of a general manager. And she had wonderful benefits comparable to the best corporations in Houston and most importantly, she made all her own appointments.

After a lifetime of adhering to school schedules, her time was now her own.

So she was not about to risk an ethics charge and take away any of the livelihood of any other agent. For in the long run, one or two customers here and there were not going to make any real difference to her.

She told herself that in the future she was going to leave the insurance business behind and pursue an exciting career in a different field when she was ready. She had so many interests, journalism, sociology, art and the new fascinating field of computers. She had taken classes in all those fields as electives in college while pursuing her business degree.

It vaguely nagged at her that she had no real plans for any career in these fields. That she would probably have to go back to school and get another degree to make such a radical change. She didn't really want to do that. But there was no hurry. She was only 27, still young, had plenty of savings in the bank, and could go back to school at any time to change the course of her future.

Daphne only secretly acknowledged to herself in her daydreams what her fantasy plan for the future was. She envisioned falling in love and getting married. Preferably to a man on the socioeconomic level to which she had become accustomed to as a result of living in, and servicing her mostly wealthy clients in the elite high income environment of Sand Waves.

This idea of a supporting husband was contrary to the ideal of the emancipated woman that she aspired to be. But that was not why it bothered her.

The thought of having to find a man who would love and accept her as she really was, plus make at least as much or more money than she did, frightened her.

Because she was unsure such a man really existed.

Chapter 24

Luncheon occurred in the same setting as the death had been announced.

With Aerial's permission, Randy brought a table down from her apartment. She had almost no food but did have a loaf of bread, some lunchmeat and a few condiments, in addition to the plentiful Christmas candy routinely stocked by the store. There was going to be enough for everyone to have at least two sandwiches.

Janey began preparing the sandwiches as Randy arranged the chairs around the table, positioned adjacent to the counter.

Plate was still hanging out mostly near the warehouse door.

The others had been roaming the aisles, or taking naps upstairs, or getting together for a game of cards at the counter.

There were numerous Christmas themed decks on the store shelves as well as a host of Christmas themed games. While sacrificing the inexpensive card decks for the group's entertainment, Aerial had not yet offered the more expensive games, hoping the group would not be there too much longer and she could avoid at least some financial loss even if it was minor.

No one had offered to purchase anything.

Misha had received permission to open a Christmas version of *Chutes and Ladders* and was trying to convince anyone to play with her. So far, Aerial and Arthur had been her only partners, standing in the manager's office, using the top of the time clock for a makeshift table. Each had begged off after two or three games.

She was seated at the foot of the manager's office, her back against the half wall that formed one side of it, waiting to snare another player.

Mark's radio, designated the official source of news, reported extensive flooding continuing, with thousands of people being held prisoners in their homes.

Phone service was still out in the Sand Waves area. Emergency and rescue personnel, when they could venture out into the rain safely, were concentrating on rescuing people stranded in the middle of the freeways, on the roads, in the ditches, and homeless camps under all the overpasses and bridges, and other areas where their lives were in danger.

It was going to be a significant while longer before they got to people who were trapped in relative safety. Those people were being advised to be patient, communicate with friends and family if possible, but not to expect any real attempt at rescue until the water started to subside and all those in harm's way were out of danger.

Shelters were full of people who had to evacuate low lying areas as their homes began to flood. Most apartment complexes were asking first floor residents to leave while second and third floor and above occupants were being advised to remain at home.

Hotels were emptying their first floor rooms in anticipation of the floodwaters rising even after the rain stopped. Second and third floors in every hotel in the greater Houston and Galveston areas were full.

Hospitals moved all patients above the first floors.

Leaving an area that was safe, dry and on relatively higher ground, no matter what the circumstances, was just plain foolish, admonished all government and safety officials.

Anyone safe, not threatened by rising water, medical emergency or any other immediate life threatening event was asked by county civil authorities to please remain in place until the emergency was over.

The rain was still coming down.

"Ladies and gentlemen," said Plate, using the opportunity of them all being within hearing distance at the same time during lunch.

He felt the PA system should be saved for any emergency that might arise. It was a little fragile and overuse might kill it.

Plus there was the inherent risk in crying wolf.

Everyone, except Misha, was seated in the semicircle around the table.

"So far we have been fortunate that we've had no power outage here. Undoubtedly that's due to most of the cables being buried deep in the ground here in Sand Waves. However, we cannot be sure this will continue. If we have to spend a second night here, we need to think about emergency lighting provisions. It was brought to my attention that last night, while lighting was adequate upstairs and downstairs, the staircase was completely dark. There is no way to safely have permanent light in there."

Plate had found an old black and yellow flashlight stored in the unused offices. It was more reliable and he kept it for himself.

Trying to be inconspicuous, he had left most of his

police gear in his patrol car, which was originally parked far away from the store in order not to attract attention and now was inaccessible due to the floodwaters. With him, he had only handcuffs and his gun.

"Mrs. Harriman has been generous enough to offer us any and all battery powered lighting instruments the store stocks," Plate continued. "As we have plenty of batteries, all we need to do is procure the lights we want to use, make sure they're working and keep them with us at all times."

"So after lunch," said Randy, "each of you can go find something easy to carry. Just check with me and let me know what you're taking so that I can correct the inventory. Please accept these as our gifts. Please, each of you take only one. I think the most convenient for most everybody will be the old fashion Christmas lanterns. They may be a little awkward but they do put out a good light and have a handle, making them easy to carry. They are located on aisle three."

"Even though it is daylight, if the lights go out, except for here in the immediate lobby area, this store is going to be dark," said Aerial. "We have some Christmas lights arranged in the bathroom but, on the staircase going up to my loft, there is no way to light it without stringing hazardous cords that would likely trip someone. And I don't have a whole lot of light upstairs since there are no windows."

"So everyone please select a light and keep it with you," said Plate, in summation.

Most everyone took Randy's advice and went for the Christmas lantern.

Only Misha found a *Star Wars* sword that lighted up like a flashlight.

Mack found a similar version of the same toy, only larger.

He and Misha ripped open the toys and had a pretend sword battle for a few moments.

Plate stood and watched them.

"You are letting me win," Misha accused Mack.

"No you're just too quick for me. I am a slow, fat old man," Mack laughed.

Plate thought Mack was exaggerating.

He had to be in his late 20s or early 30s.

It was his weight, some signs of a scraggly beard trying to grow, and hair beginning to thin, that made Mack look just a little bit older.

"I think the big guy is letting her win," said Laurel, coming up next to Plate.

She caught Mack's eye and they smiled at each other.

The battle went on.

"Do you live here in Sand Waves, Miss Moore?" asked Plate.

"I used to," said Laurel. "I had some hard times and lost my home here. But I'm hoping to get back here. I love Sand Waves."

"I would not live here," said the deliveryman, a little breathless from the battle which Misha had just won,

"Come on let's play again," she begged.

"No, I am tuckered out," said Mack, coming to join Laurel and Plate.

"What about you, Officer? You live here?" asked

Laurel.

"Yes and no," said Plate. "I'm one of those transient apartment dwellers in the one apartment complex. So I don't count. Where do you live, Mr. Moore?"

"Originally from Idaho. Now, I'm way over in West Houston," said Mack. "If I could get back home, I'd be high and dry. My area doesn't flood like this."

"How long have you been delivering merchandise in this area?"

"Well, now, let's see. I was assigned to this area, oh about eight months ago."

"You get to drive your vehicle home at night?"

"Oh, no sir! I drive to a central location distribution center from my house, pick up my delivery truck there and most of the merchandise will be there also. It's just that I'll have to make multiple trips. The truck is only so big. They think by giving us these small dinky trucks it saves gas. But it's just the opposite. We got to make more trips."

Laurel wandered away as Plate and Mack continued talking. Plate was trying to engage the deliveryman further but Mack seemed disinclined to want to continue the conversation. Plate wasn't sure if he could hold the deliveryman's reticence against him or not.

A lot of people, who were not murderers or robbers, did not really care to converse with the police under any circumstances.

He noticed when he finally stopped attempting to talk to the deliveryman, Laurel came back around and started chatting with Mack. They walked towards the display of Christmas trees together.

Everyone had wandered out of the lobby.

Plate walked in the direction of the restroom and found himself on the same aisle as Monica Moon. They nodded to each other, each planning to pass the other without any words, when they both heard a loud click.

Making eye contact with Monica, Plate put a finger to his lips.

She remained quiet.

He also motioned for her to stay still.

This she did not obey, following him closely as he crept in the direction of the sound which seemed to come from the register.

Plate held back his arm to stop Monica from passing him when they came to the edge of the aisle and saw what had made the noise.

Her back to them, Misha had opened the cash register and was removing the rest of the money.

Chapter 25

Monica rapped Plate on the shoulder, frantically pointing at the thieving girl.

Plate shook his head and motioned for Monica to be quiet and stay back.

Misha took the money from the cash register, opened up her locker inside the manager's office, took out her purse, and stuffed the money inside.

The small purse was already so full of money, she had a hard time keeping the bills from popping it back open.

Finally, she took a paper bag wrapped the purse inside of it, put a rubber band about it, put it back in her slot, and locked the mini-locker.

"Do something," Monica whispered furiously in Plate's ear.

"Shush," he told her.

Even in a whisper his voice held enough command that she shut up.

Misha, glancing around a little nervously, stepped down out of the manager's office and sat back down at the spot where she had left her game.

She pulled her transistor out and put in the earpiece.

Plate grabbed Monica Moon by the arm and led her towards the Cowboy Display until they were out of Misha's hearing range.

"Why did you not do something?" Monica hissed at Plate.

"Not right now. I have more important fish to fry," said Plate. "I'll report the petty theft to the Harrimans and see what they want to do with it. But I don't want to disrupt the harmony we've managed to achieve here in this situation just yet. Can I count on your discretion for the moment? If you are needed as a witness later on, I will contact you."

Monica looked into the eyes of the policeman.

"Okay, Officer, you have my word. I will not cause any disruption."

"Thank you," said Plate. "I think the Harrimans went back upstairs, I will go and speak with them about this right away."

Monica watched as Plate went through the staircase door, then she turned and went back towards the lobby.

Misha was still seated in the same place, engrossed in her music.

"Fancy a game?" she asked, when she saw Monica staring down at her.

Monica reached down and grabbed Misha by both arms and pulled her to her feet.

"DON'T touch me!" Misha yelled.

"You little thief," Monica hissed.

Misha's eyes went wide with fear.

"Don't tell on me, please," she begged.

"I hate you nasty foreigners coming to this country and taking jobs from Americans. And then steal from your employer on top of that."

"I- I can explain- I'll put it all back."

"Get that money back out of that locker right now," said Monica.

Misha obeyed her.

Monica unwrapped the purse, opened it and counted

the money.

When she finished counting, she folded it and extracted two bills.

She pushed them at Misha's breast.

"That is what you get to keep," Monica said. "I'll keep quiet this time. You had better keep your mouth shut too. If you say anything about me, I'll not only accuse you of being a thief, I'll kill you later."

"I- okay- okay- thank you," Misha bowed in Asian subservience. "So good to me. Thank you, Madam."

Monica pocketed the money and looked satisfied. "I'm glad we understand each other. If these nincompoops that run this place ever discover the money is missing, I'll back you up. I'll say I saw the delivery man take it."

"So grateful, so appreciative of such a wonderful patron," said Misha, inclining her head in deference once more. "Anything I can do to serve you, Madam?"

"Hmm, there may be some things you can do in the future," Monica said thoughtfully. "Maybe. Maybe not. Just remember what I told you. Remember too, that congressman's a friend of mine. I can have him look into your parents' immigration status. Even if they are legitimate, I can cause some trouble. So remember, you talk, I can bury you."

Monica turned and walked back towards the staircase door.

I needed some pocket change, she thought with satisfaction as she opened the door and went up the steps.

Misha stood watching Monica walk away with blatant hostility.

Then she opened back up the locker to put her purse back inside.

But before she did, she extracted a long metal object from further back in the locker, where she normally kept it behind her purse.

Putting the purse away, she now held a 12-inch dagger by its handle and stared at it, then looked back down the aisle towards the staircase door.

Chapter 26

The afternoon passed in acute boredom for all concerned.

There would be no formal supper.

Aerial scrounged through her refrigerator pulling out every bit of food she could find. She had nothing in sufficient quantity that could be divided. So everybody got something different.

And of course, there was plenty of candy.

News bulletins informed them that without a doubt they would be spending another night in the store. There was reasonable hope that rescue would come on Sunday.

Reasonable but not certain.

Catnaps were taken.

Card games were played.

Aerial found a couple of old board games among some unpacked boxes, along with some romance novels and they were passed around.

The snacks were consumed.

The storm had worsened.

While the sun didn't normally set until nearly 9 PM this time of year, by nearly 7 PM, due to the black clouds blanketing the sky, it was nearly as dark as midnight.

Plate requested that they all go upstairs for the evening, despite the early hour.

There was, he told them, always the possibility of rescue during the middle of the night.

Then there was also the possibility that, as the floodwaters rose, the downstairs might actually flood.

They needed to be prepared for either.

Everyone looked at their watches and complained it was too early.

"There's no more food, except lots of candy, for supper," said Randy. "Please get all the candy you want, take it upstairs, have a little and try to get to bed."

"We are so high here," Aerial protested. "It can't flood the downstairs very much. Usually all we get is rain water blown in the door by high winds."

"And this storm doesn't have much wind it seems," said the congressman. "Or it would've blown out of here already."

Plate held his ground.

He stopped just short of ordering them all to go upstairs. Actually he thought getting them upstairs would increase the security one hundred percent.

He still feared attempted exits into the flooding. Having them all upstairs meant they were that much further away from the exterior doors.

Eventually with some stalling that ate up about 30 minutes, they all reluctantly complied. Plate informed Randy that it would be a little while longer before he came up, indicating he would be in the restroom. He instructed Randy to go on to bed, not to bother saving any candy for him but to please find any coffee that might be left over and confiscate that.

Unfortunately, the store did not have a soft drink machine. So there was no other source of caffeine.

Plate had actually decided he was not going upstairs at all.

He went back to the front lobby and picked out the

most comfortable of the chairs, an office chair that rolled, and pushed it to the back of the store and positioned it in front of the staircase door.

He had the lantern, his useless pager and his .38 to keep him company.

Checking his uniform, he found it was still too wet to wear.

From behind some merchandise on a nearby shelf from where he had hid it, he pulled out the water stained copy of his latest science fiction novel, flipped it open to his folded down page, sat down in the chair and prepared to spend a long long night.

'… *leaving the bodies behind leaves us to become suspects in a murder investigation,"* said Karl Sabers.

"Don't let that concern yourself," said the all too *unpleasant voice of Ashley Claymore from the device in Karl's pocket.*

A few moments later a dark blue floating transport pulled up beside them. The side hatch of the vehicle opened and Claymore exited. Beside him were the two alien men that he was dining with earlier.

"Congratulations, you've done far better than I expected!" Claymore exclaimed at Karl.

Karl pointed his new sword at the old man. "You followed us!"

"I'm afraid the two of you are too valuable to leave unattended," Claymore stated with a smirk.

"I appreciate the compliment, although I do not know why you are including the slave girl, as I am clearly more valuable than anyone anywhere around here," said

the long hair tabby cat as he swiped his ear with his paw.

Claymore looked at the cat.

"While the slave girl is marginal, I do find Karl to be worth a lot, so don't discount him," Lightening further commented, wiping his face. "He's my source of cat food."

Claymore shook himself and turned away from the cat.

"You'll have to come with us," Claymore stated to Karl and Sophia, while glancing back at two aliens. "Caladi, Ellris, grab them...."

Plate shook himself. He was falling asleep.

He straightened up in the chair and tried to find where he had left off in the paperback.

He looked at his watch.

It was going on 8 PM.

"....Karl tossed his sword aside. He lifted his hands in the air. "I surrender."

"Good." Claymore then pulled a stunner pistol and fired a blue pulse at Karl..."

The paperback fell from Plate's hand as he dozed.

Chapter 27

The upstairs hiding place had served well, but the owner of the .357 revolver needed it now. A special pocket sewn into a special shirt kept it secure as its owner started downstairs.

Despite being wood, the stairs gave no warning creak as they were descended by shoeless feet. The person carrying the shoes had a light which was set on the lowest beam, carried under one arm with shoes under the other.

Slowly the staircase door cracked open.

The policeman's nodding head was bent over just the right way. The trick was to get the door completely open so as to get a clean strike without alerting him.

This was expertly accomplished.

The policeman slumped to his right as the chair rolled sideways. His assailant caught it before it hit the Carolers' Display.

In the dim colored lights, the attacker turned off the portable light and blended in with the mannequins posing as singers on the Carolers' Display.

Taking time to put shoes on, the attacker waited a few seconds, making sure nobody had heard.

Or was coming.

Then the dolly was removed from its hiding place among large tree boxes surrounded by the displayed decorated examples.

The policeman's slim form was transferred from the chair and slowly wheeled to the Sleigh Ride Display. The rolling chair would have accomplished part of this purpose but the dolly's manual lift made it easier to get up to the display platform. It was easy to remove the groomsman mannequin from the sleigh.

It turned out the mannequin had no legs, a fact hidden by the voluminous skirt of the wedding gown, and Christmas packages piled up all around.

The mobster's coat was removed from the stricken man, his police gun pocketed by his assailant.

The groom's coat was pulled on over the mobster's dress shirt.

The bride's skirt was pulled back and several packages moved to make room for the policeman's legs as he was seated next to the wooden bride.

In the chaos, money spilled out of one of the packages. In surprise, it was quickly snatched up.

The top hat was carefully placed on policeman's head, hiding the wound, and he was leaned against his new wooden partner in such a way to appear that he was romantically attending her.

The mobster's coat was hung back on the costume rack.

The half mannequin was stashed in the dressing room.

The briefcase, containing the bloodstained gloves, was retrieved from its hiding place within the stack of luggage.

The dolly was returned to its spot.

Quickly, for time was short, the guns were switched again.

The .38 was placed in the downstairs hiding place.

The owner kept the .357 in his pocket, intending for

that gun to be lost forever soon in the floodwaters. But it might be a good idea to keep the policeman's gun handy for later use.

Mission accomplished. There remained only keeping the appointment scheduled.

The manager's office was the designated meeting location.

The police officer's assailant headed in that direction.

Meanwhile, the person who had silently followed, taken over the hiding spot in the Carolers' Display, and had been watching from the limited vantage point behind the group of inanimate singers, debated whether it was safe to leave the cloaking refuge.

It was not.

More footsteps could be heard coming down the stairs.

The policeman's attacker reached the manager's office safely. Waiting there, it became necessary to crouch down in the small cubicle.

The noise on the staircase carried all the way to the front of the store.

"Eileen, where are you?" Mark had whispered urgently as he came down the stairs.

"Over here, darling. I was just inside the doorway."

"Where can we go?"

"This way," said Eileen. "I don't know why we didn't think of using the space before. We can even lock the door."

Arm-in-arm, they went off in the direction of the costume rack. Eileen pulled an evening gown.

"Would you like me to look more glamorous?"

"That's a great idea."

Eileen chose a form fitting satin pink strapless gown with matching full length gloves.

She forced her silky hair into a French twist.

"You'll look scrumptious, in that. Mmm," said Mark as he followed her into the dressing room, which, while small was still big enough for what they had planned.

Once inside, Eileen gave a little shriek. "Sakes alive! What is that! It's another body!"

Mark turned on his lantern. The legless mannequin was propped in the corner on the small seat in the dressing room.

"Oh, sakes alive!" Eileen exclaimed again, catching her breath.

"Probably planted here by Monica Moon to frighten us if we came here," he said grimly. "I'll just take care of this."

The lifeless, legless mannequin stared at him as he took it outside the dressing room.

After debating a moment where to go with it, he took it to the Sleeping Beauty Display, lifted it up on the platform and jammed it behind the princess' bed.

Then he went back to Eileen.

Deidre and JW contemplated the Santa Claus Display. Deidre held the old fashioned lantern while JW climbed up in the middle of the scene.

"Can you get them? Are they real?" Deidre asked urgently.

"Success, my sweet. I have them and they are real."

"Careful, remember what happened to the boy on the other display."

"Just don't flip any switches, my love," said JW, as he slowly climbed back down with the prize.

"Theft is breaking one of the Ten Commandments," said Arthur Harriman, standing in their way.

The Smiths, caught in the act, both looked like deer frozen in headlights as he shined his lantern at them.

"But if you share the cookies, I will not tell," said Arthur.

After a moment to recuperate from the shock of being caught with the cookies, the West Texas couple recovered their aplomb.

JW counted the cookies. "Certainly. There are 14 cookies here, so that means we can divide them with the rest of the group," he said.

"Of course, that is what we intended all along," said Deidre.

"Of course." Arthur smiled at them. "I think if you just give me one cookie per person, then you might be entitled to the rest. After all you found them and took the necessary actions to retrieve them."

"Thank you so much, Reverend," said JW, surprised. "That is most understanding of you."

"It's just a few cookies," said Arthur. "But what about those boxes of cookies on the display?"

"They are empty. When we picked one up, we could tell," said JW, picking up a box on top of the stack by the children mannequins, and tossing it to Arthur.

Arthur knew this box was empty the moment he

caught it. He put it back on the display.

"Looks like someone just took the cookies out and glued the box top back," said Deidre, carefully selecting the largest of the cookies to keep for her and JW.

On the way to the Santa display she had pinched a Christmas tree skirt from a large sloppy pile, located near the front on another aisle, to hide the cookies in.

Hoping Arthur did not notice she was using store merchandise to carry the cookies, she quickly turned away from the two men and started towards the staircase door.

"We'll be getting back to our space," said JW, following Deidre and then taking her by the shoulders.

JW steered her towards the back left corner of the store.

"What do you bet they have a supply of those cookies back in those offices somewhere?" he whispered.

"Brilliant, JW!" said Deidre and they headed that way.

Back by the Santa Display, Arthur stood with cookies in hand and looked around for something to put them in.

The box JW had handed him was too small but there were several larger empty cookies boxes on the display at the bottom of the stack, right in front of him.

He felt a little guilty for pulling one out of the carefully arranged display, after all he was disturbing a work of art. But it was just a stack of cookie boxes and he saw only one big enough for his needs.

Clutching the cookies with one hand, with his other hand he grabbed the desired box by the flap, pulled it carefully from the stack and shook it.

The stack remained intact, just with a vacant space where the box had apparently not been bearing any of the load.

In Arthur's hand, the box top popped open.

Several hundred dollars fell out.

Scooping up the money, while still safeguarding the cookies, Arthur went upstairs at once, intending to find the police officer.

The police officer's assailant was uncomfortable and close to panic, crouching in the manager's office. The .357 was pulled out of the pocket.

The louder noises had dissipated, resumed from different directions across the store, then died down again. Fortunately no one had come in the direction of the manager's office.

That was about to change.

More noise. Someone else was coming down an aisle.

It was too early, earlier than agreed upon, but hopefully, this was the right person. The right person at last. In the manager's office there was no place to really hide. Or to see. A person came out of the far left aisle, running towards the lobby. The .357 was ready to fire.

Eyes cautiously peeked over the short cubicle wall.

Just moments earlier, the assault on the police officer had been witnessed by this other person with cool detachment.

The hiding of the gun had been seen.

Emerging from the Caroler's Display, this person

suddenly felt much more confident. The lantern with the six volt battery was abandoned. It was a poor weapon compared to a gun. No opportunity had ever arisen to get ahold of the dagger. Taking it to finish the job after attacking with the lantern might have worked. But the gun would be so much simpler.

And now it was in hand.

Before proceeding to the manager's office, the police officer's .38 was removed from the hiding place it had so shortly occupied.

This person was calm and in no hurry. Care was taken to make sure the hiding place gave no sign of disturbance. The hiding place would not be empty long.

It would be needed again later.

There was a slight noise from the manager's office as the approach was made. The .38 was readied.

Time became an enigma. First there didn't seem to be enough time. Then there was plenty of time to accomplish everything.

The occupant of the manager's office sighed with relief and put the .357 back in the special shirt pocket. It was the right person, the new partner with papers needed for a clean escape. Carrying a case, with the papers inside, no doubt.

Quickly, without any greeting other than brief eye contact, they raced together to the front door and, having to set both cases down, they managed to get the door open, rain pelting them both as they faced the elements.

But only one went through the front door and a clap

of thunder sounded just at the right time to disguise the sound of the gunshot.

The one that remained on the inside was gratified to see the victim dive into the water in the deeper part of the parking lot to escape, trying to flee the bullet that had already hit its mark.

The shooter had a harder time getting the door shut working alone but finally was able to put the glass shield against the pelting rain back in place. And was able to get safely back in the manager's office with both cases.

Quickly a small lock was manipulated and the dagger was fished out of the locker and put into the case carrying the papers so desired that they had cost a life.

Then the other case was forced opened.

This was a bonus. Its contents, no matter what they were, would be incriminating.

The contents were placed strategically.

The case was abandoned along the way during the short sprint that followed.

A quick climb and the police officer's .38 was put back in the downstairs hiding place.

Another gun had become a ticket to the new execution method of lethal injection.

Fortunately, the thunder had drowned the sound from the shot.

But that might not happen again.

A more silent weapon was desirable.

Time was of the essence once more.

There was another appointment to keep.

And there she was, waiting by the staircase door.

Chapter 28

Monica Moon had slipped downstairs as quietly as possible. She was sure she had heard Misha come downstairs before her, so she had slightly delayed her descent. She didn't care if anyone was kept waiting.

She had actually experienced a little regretful consternation that her spontaneous blackmail of Misha might have been unwise and not worth the paltry $600 she had gained from it.

If Misha was downstairs, Monica wanted to know what she was up to. And where she might have hidden any more money.

Monica lit the cigarette she had carried downstairs along with her lighter. She was sick of being told not to smoke and inhaled the tobacco with relish.

To hell with them all, she thought. *I'll smoke whenever I want to.*

Monica was so focused on her cigarette, while at the same time intent on looking for Misha, that she failed to monitor what was going on behind her.

Too late she realized exactly who was downstairs with her.

It was not the person she thought she was supposed to meet. The person's face was still in the shadows, but she recognized the wrong skin color at the same time she saw the upraised arm.

"How dare you threaten me?" Monica exclaimed with bravado that she did not really have. "Where have you been? Why are you wet?"

The arm came down, and again too late, as she turned

away, crouching in defense, Monica got a peripheral glimpse of the long silver object held by her assailant's hand.

It was the intention of her killer to hide Monica's body similarly to the way the body had been hidden in the Witch's Display cauldron.

Out of sight in a display.

There was a space behind the bed that would be perfect for disguising a corpse, for a short time at least. The office chair was readily available for transport. It was easy to get Monica's body into the chair and tie it with holiday ribbon that would hold it long enough to get it to the front of the store, weighing it down with the case and dagger.

Pushing the office chair like a wheelchair, the body was soon delivered to its destination. But the body had to be pulled up to the platform by hand. This was tedious and difficult. And when that chore was accomplished, to the killer's chagrin, the space was cluttered with a legless mannequin, which if left under the body, would cause it to be visible.

The killer grasped the body once more and moved it off the mannequin onto the convenient, but highly visible, furniture. Trying to think frantically in what location the legless mannequin could be successfully hidden elsewhere, the killer felt the onset of panic. All order and method lapsed.

Time had run out.

The staircase door opened and closed loudly.

The case and dagger were still on the chair. The killer had to choose between returning the case to the arrangement of luggage and hiding the weapon or continuing to try to position the body so it would not be seen at once. The body was heavy, positioning it properly impractical and taking too long. After all the effort to get it to the right place, the killer abandoned Monica's body where it was, jumped off the display and grabbed the case, rapidly shoving it in the midst of the promotional luggage.

Above all, the dagger could not be returned to the killer's case. It had blood on it now.

Meanwhile, the staircase door twice more opened. Then once again.

Fearful of discovery, frantic footsteps circled all the way around the front, replacing the chair by the counter and the dagger where it had been found, then racing towards the back of the store.

But time held.

Those exiting the staircase door went towards the costume rack, leaving the door wide open.

The killer had a chance to slip behind them all and get back inside the staircase doorway.

Chapter 29

"I am sure I heard people going down. Several, not together, either," said Randy. "Plate has never come upstairs at all. Something has to be wrong."

"You're not going down there alone," said Janey, whispering so as not to wake anybody else.

"Stay behind me then."

Randy cautiously opened the staircase door but saw nothing out of the ordinary.

"I'm going to turn on the lights brighter," said Randy.

"Turn them on so we can see fully," said Janey. "Just don't activate displays."

"Okay."

"What is going on?" said Aerial, coming through the staircase door. Her voice was thick with sleep.

"I'm going to turn on the lights. Somebody is down here. I cannot find Plate. I want to make the lights come on, completely but without activating the displays. Give me a minute. That is a little tricky. I've got to hit just the right combination of switches."

"Somebody came back up the stairs after you two came down," said Aerial.

"Are you sure? How could have they gotten by us?"

"I'm sure. There was somebody that went right near me in the dark staircase. I didn't have my lantern. I forgot it. They didn't have any light on either," said Aerial.

"Must've been one of the women?"

"I don't know."

"As soon as I get the lights on we are going to find Plate and we're going to account for everybody. He specifically wanted everybody to stay upstairs."

"Well, maybe somebody had to go to the bathroom," said Janey, trying to reassure everyone, including herself.

"From what all noises I heard, there must be a long line," said Randy. "Here are the right switches, I think."

Sure enough the huge florescent lights in the ceiling flipped on, without activating the animation on the large displays.

Instinctively, protectively, Janey started to survey the displays to make sure there was no damage. She stared at the Sleeping Beauty Display with some consternation.

"Somebody's tampered with the Sleeping Beauty Display. It looks different, but I just can't see-"

Her words were interrupted by a sudden monumental flash of lightning so close, for several seconds everyone thought the building itself had been struck.

Thunder boomed, more lightning danced around. The lights went totally out and there were screams from every section of the store.

Then, as suddenly as the lights went out, they flared back on again, not only bringing back on the bright fluorescent lights, but initiating the loud Christmas music medley beginning with *Jingle Bells.* The animation on the three major displays quickly brought movement and all the mannequins appeared to come to life.

Janey's eyes had never left the Sleeping Beauty Display during the electrical short circuit and she was still staring at it when the power surged back on and the music played and the display started to move.

At last she saw what was wrong. Sleeping Beauty

was rising up. The Prince was leaning towards her, all normal. But there was someone between, caught in the middle of their mechanized, unstoppable embrace.

Janey screamed.

Randy stood entranced behind her. JW and Deidre came running from direction of the Santa Display. Mark and Eileen came running from the dressing room.

Arthur walked behind them, saw what was happening, realized at once it could not be stopped and what that meant. He ran to Randy's side.

Aerial screamed then. Daphne, Laurel, and Misha came out the staircase door, raced to the front and stood entranced with the others in the lobby at the exact moment that Sleeping Beauty and her Prince entangled in their embrace the trapped body of a woman with long straight streaked blonde hair and crushed it between them.

Only the woman's hair slowly becoming streaked with blood was visible as the fairytale characters clutched each other.

Then the animation continued. The Prince withdrew from his sweetheart and Sleeping Beauty reclined back down on her bed. The female human body between them draped dramatically forward, arms stretched over the head which now fell upside down over Sleeping Beauty's breasts.

As the fairytale characters withdrew and resumed their starting positions, the dead woman was unmistakably, easily identifiable to all watching as Monica Moon.

Chapter 30

The fairy godmothers started to fly.

The next stage in the animation had begun.

"Flip the switch, Randy! Flip the switch!" Aerial screamed.

Randy jumped out of his trance and sprang upon the display, frantically trying to remember exactly where the emergency switch on this one was located.

"Where is it? Where is it on this one?" he called out desperately. It was only moments before the enchanted lovers started moving towards each other again.

"Back behind the fairy godmothers!" Janey yelled trying to be heard above the music which was much louder than usual. "Over to the right behind the one wearing blue!"

A mannequin out of place, legless, was in the way. Flinging it behind him, Randy found the switch and flipped it just before Sleeping Beauty and the Prince started to move again.

The music and the animation stopped.

The lights remained glaringly bright. Every detail of Monica's body, draped across the inanimate body of Sleeping Beauty, now as lifeless as the mannequin, was visible to the small group of people standing before the display.

Monica's arms were outstretched, pulled by gravity towards the floor, as was her head, her distinctive features almost upside down with her hair falling from the crown of her head towards the carpet on the display. Her face was unmarred. Her eyes were closed. What blood seeped through her hair appeared to come from the back of her head, where some wound, not visible with the body in this position, had to be the source. Her gray satin finish suit was completely untouched, her tight blouse ripped slightly at the side seams, exposed by the jacket panels which had fallen open. Her skirt band was still tight around her waist. Her knees were bent over the knees of Sleeping Beauty. Her lower legs and feet were not visible as they draped on the other side of Sleeping Beauty's bed.

"Her jewelry is gone," said Aerial, and the normalcy in her speaking manner was like a splash of cold water on everyone else.

"We are all going to be murdered in cold blood!" cried Misha.

"What do we do?" Janey looked at Randy.

"Where is the police officer?" asked the congressman.

Realizing for the first time that he was not there, everyone began looking around, as if each one of them hoped to be the one to find him first, and somehow be rewarded for alleviating the situation.

"I don't think he came upstairs last night," Randy whispered low to Arthur.

"The hammer is upstairs under my bedding, go get it and get into the warehouse to see if he's in there," said Janey, nearby.

"If the door is still boarded up he couldn't possibly be in there, could he?" asked Arthur.

"Yes, there is an outside entrance," said Randy. "Go on. I'll join you as soon as I can."

"Heavens, son, we've been cooped up in here for so

long, I forgot about the outside."

Arthur left.

Randy repeated his information about the police officer to Mark, telling him also what Arthur was going to do and asking Mark to look around the retail section of the store.

Randy sent Janey upstairs to search for Plate up there.

"Miss, could you help me search?" Mark said to Eileen, with more stiffness than necessary. Eileen, still in the evening gown and hoping to avoid any explanation, gratefully nodded yes and the two of them went toward the dressing room from where they had emerged.

They could not quite wait until they were out of sight before clasping hands.

"What can we do?" JW spoke for himself and Deidre.

"Go up towards the lobby, and see if the damn telephone company has ever got the phones working again," said Randy.

Laurel walked over to Randy and put her hand on his arm. "I'm so sorry this is happening, Randy," she said.

He absentmindedly patted her bare shoulder, noting with mild disapproval she had pushed down her sleeves and collar, draping the pirate's shirt across her shoulders in the most provocative way possible. Before the flood and its consequences he would have enjoyed her flirtation but this was not the time.

"We'll get through this, Laurel. We will." He spoke in a dismissive tone and walked away from her.

Aerial and Misha both looked lost for very different

reasons.

Misha was remembering her confrontation with Monica Moon and wondering what happened to the money.

Aerial was wondering if her business could possibly survive after all of this murder and scandal.

"I am going to manipulate the lights so they remain on but all the special effects are disabled. At least I'm going to give it a try," said Randy. "It's all so interconnected, I am not sure I can do it completely."

Suddenly Misha ran over to Randy and grabbed him by the arm.

As much as she hated to touch anyone or be touched, the gesture captured his full attention.

"Somebody else isn't here," said Misha. "Where is the deliveryman?"

Chapter 31

He was dreaming. It was cold, but he was happy. Beside him he could feel the beautiful soft taffeta of the smooth white dress worn by his bride. It was raining but he didn't feel wet, only chilly. He snuggled closer to his bride in attempt to get warmer. She was not very comforting but still, this was a nice dream. He was in a sleigh, still in his wedding clothes, being pulled across the snow by a horse.

It was nighttime. No, then it was daytime. Then daylight flashed off and on. The horse turned and looked at him and neighed. Then it turned back. Then the lights went out. Then they came on again. But the horse was silent.

It had to be a dream.

But he had a really bad headache and he wasn't sure he wanted to wake up if it was going to make the headache worse.

"Officer, Officer." Daphne kept her voice low and she gently patted him on the cheek. "Officer! Wake up? Are you hurt? Are you okay?"

This was definitely a dream. No one could be that beautiful, no one could have such blonde hair. She couldn't be real. Too bad she was not the bride… His bride was just sitting there woodenly impassive, ignoring him.

"Are you hurt?" the unreal beauty was saying. "Do you know what happened? What happened to you?"

Plate opened his eyes and raised his head up slightly. He reached and felt the heavy hat and tipped it down over his eyes. Then he reached to the back of his head and felt the wound there.

He had enough experience to assess its seriousness without any panic. He felt a little more panic when he realized his holster was empty.

He pushed the wedding dress off his knees

"I don't think I'm seriously injured," he told the real woman looking at him with such concern. "I must have been hit hard enough to be knocked out for quite some time though. If you could just help me to make sure I can safely rise up, then I'll know pretty soon."

Daphne physically helped Plate as much as she could to steady himself as he climbed out of the sleigh, and over the boxed presents surrounding him. She got down off the display first, reaching up to him as he slowly bent over and allowed her to brace him as he stepped down on the floor.

He looked around to assess the extent of his dizziness, trying to take his mind off of the pain in his head. Without any self-consciousness or embarrassment, he allowed Daphne to continue to support him until he made sure he would be able to walk without falling.

He looked at his watch but he was too dizzy to be sure he was reading it right.

"What time is it? Do you know where Randy Harriman is?" he asked Daphne shakily. But he reflected, with a sinking feeling, that Randy probably had to surrender his firearm when he was dismissed from the force. And probably was denied a permit for a new one in civilian life, if he even bothered to apply.

"He is looking for you. We've all been looking for you. I think you've been overlooked in this display several times."

Plate laughed a little. "Must of been the top hat."

Daphne looked at her watch. "It is 1:17 AM."

"Then I have lost about five hours," said Plate.

"Do you know what happened?" Daphne asked him again.

Plate thought for a moment and said more to himself than to her, "I sent everybody upstairs and then brought a chair to sit in front of the staircase door to guard it for the night. I sat down and pulled out a book to read. That's the last thing I remember."

Daphne told him about Monica Moon.

Plate forgot his headache, momentarily at least. He looked extremely grim.

"Why don't you come up to the front lobby? You can sit down there. And we can let the others know that you are alive."

"That's a good idea," said Plate.

"And you aren't the only one missing, I mean-"

"Someone is gone?" Plate recalled his fear that someone, innocent or guilty, would try to leave despite the dangers of the flood.

"Yes, the deliveryman. That couple from West Texas found evidence he had, or somebody had, forced open the front door. And he is the only one unaccounted for, now that I have found- I mean you have been found."

Daphne and Plate reached the lobby where Aerial and Misha were sitting near the counter.

"Oh, thank goodness!" said Aerial, rising to meet them. "We had practically given you up for dead."

"Where is Randy? Do you know, Mrs. Harriman?"

"Oh, he is searching the warehouse area for you, and for the delivery man. Did you tell him, Miss Martin-?"

"Yes, I know the delivery man has disappeared," said Plate. "I'm not too surprised about that. But the death of Miss Moon is quite a shock."

"Why would you not be surprised that the delivery man has disappeared?" asked Daphne.

"Thank you for your kindness," Plate told her as he reached a chair and sat down. He gingerly felt more around the back of his head.

"Mrs. Harriman, have you any ice? This man needs a little medical attention. I would not know where to go look for it. If you can get something to use as a bandage, I do know basic first aid," said Daphne.

"Oh yes, of course."

"Mrs. Harriman, first, I need you to go and get your-go get Randy," Plate could not remember exactly what relationship Randy was to Aerial at that moment.

"Of course, I'll go get him right away," said Aerial. "Miss Martin, go upstairs to my refrigerator and get some ice out of my freezer, and there are some kitchen towels around there somewhere to wrap it in."

Aerial took off towards the warehouse. Daphne looked around for somebody else to send after the ice. She did not want to leave Plate right now.

"I may have a little information for you about Ms. Moon," she said to him, to stall leaving him alone.

"Really?" Plate tried to follow what she was saying

"Yes, as you know I'm a life insurance agent and I

was talking with her about her policies. She actually signed a change of beneficiary form in the presence of two witnesses here."

"Really?" he said again, dividing his attention between her words and his injury.

"Yes," said Daphne, worrying that the police officer was having a hard time focusing on what she was saying. "It's a bit complicated. I can tell you later. I'll go get the ice."

"No, go ahead and tell me. If I don't process it right this time, you can run it by me again later."

"Well basically, Ms. Moon had an old policy she had forgotten about and realized the beneficiary was her exhusband and so she changed her beneficiary to Reverend Harriman, her fiancé."

"Is that legal?" Plate asked.

"Yes. Although there is no legal relationship yet, fiancé is considered a valid beneficiary relationship by insurance companies. The only complication is that her policy might not be with our company and the change was done on our company form."

Daphne had a short moment of fear of getting summoned to court in a complicated lawsuit and almost wished she had just destroyed the beneficiary form as soon as she knew Monica was dead and kept her mouth shut. The witnesses would probably have forgotten all about it. If not, Daphne could always have said it went missing in the chaos of the situation.

It was too late for that.

"What made you ask her about something like that?"

Plate was a little steadier now.

"Oh, fishing for old forgotten policies. That's a common selling technique. One of my favorites. If they have a policy that is paid in full, like a 20 Year Life, or one they took out with bank draft payment that they've forgotten about- uh- that was Ms. Moon's situation. It'd been so long she could not remember exactly what company wrote the policy."

"Go on," the police officer directed. "Does that mean the change of beneficiary is questionable?"

"She was almost sure her policy was with my company. But if it wasn't, we are probably all going to wind up testifying in court when the conflicting beneficiaries start suing," said Daphne.

"I get to testify in court all the time," said Plate, with a slight smile.

"But you get paid for it."

"What else did the two of you talk about?"

"Nothing really, just small talk. Did you know her middle name?"

"No," Plate said, contemplatively. "I do need to get the full names of everyone here."

"Her full name was Monica Miami Moon."

"Monica Miami Moon? Poor woman." It was hard to tell if his sympathy was for her demise or her name. He did chuckle a little.

"Add in her married name and it would have been Monica Miami Moon Moore," said Daphne. "She made a joke that her mother was an English teacher who hated her, and her exhusband's last name should have been a warning from the gods that their marriage was doomed from the beginning."

"I would have taken that as a signal, too. Mothers! Anything else?" Plate was still smiling.

"Otherwise, that was about it. She seemed quite a lonely, unhappy person."

Plate's levity vanished quickly. "Okay. If that's all, go on and see if you can find Randy Harriman for me."

"Something else I wanted to tell you but I cannot remember it right now."

"It will come back to you. Just tell me then."

"Are you going to be okay here by yourself?" asked Daphne.

Plate felt for his gun forgetting for a moment it was missing. "I am beginning to wonder if I will," he said wryly. "I don't suppose insurance agents are armed these days?"

And as he spoke those words he wondered a little at the instant trust he was giving this young woman whom he had just met.

It went against his training but it felt so right.

"As a matter of fact," said Daphne, somewhat conspiratorially. "I have a concealed carry permit."

Plate looked at her in surprise.

Since the post-Civil War Reconstruction Texas Constitution effective in 1873, the Texas Legislature was empowered to control the movement of weapons in Texas.

Most current interpretations concluded it was legal to own a gun, even to have them in a vehicle, but not to carry them in public places.

Guns had to be transported unloaded and separate

from their ammunition. It was not impossible to get a concealed carry permit. But it was very difficult.

"How on earth did you get a concealed carry permit?"

"Well, let's just say I have an influential friend."

"Dare I hope you have the firearm with you? And that you would be willing to-"

"I'll get it right out of my briefcase. I stashed the briefcase right down that aisle that has a lot of luggage. Mainly because it's so heavy. I hate carrying it around all the time. And I did not want to go up and down the stairs to get things out of it. Papers, you know. Don't move. I'll be right back."

Chapter 32

Daphne was true to her word. In just seconds she was back with her large suitcase like briefcase. She knelt with it at Plate's feet. She twirled a combination lock and clicked it open. Inside, amidst a lot of papers, was a small open face black box.

Daphne flipped the lid back so Plate could see what was inside. She looked up at Plate almost like a puppy wanting approval. He looked down at the box in the briefcase and saw a shining black .32 caliber pistol.

He looked at it with unconcealed desire.

"Go ahead and take it," said Daphne. "I have been training with it. But I really don't feel very competent. It's for my protection when I go out into the Houston area late at night. Most of my business is in Sand Waves now but when I was first getting started in the business I went to a lot of really rough neighborhoods after dark."

Plate moved a little too quick to grab the pistol and almost fell off the chair. Daphne put her hand on his chest to steady him and he reached and clasped her elbow to get his bearings.

Their eyes met.

He took the gun then, examined it and noted with gratitude it was clean and in good condition and fully loaded. Standing carefully, pocketing it slowly, feeling enormous appreciation towards her, he also said a quick silent word of thanks to God to accompany the Hallelujah he felt like shouting out loud, but could not verbalize due to the attention it might attract.

For he was sure the culprit who had his gun did not

foresee this.

"Tell me more about how you got this permit." He felt guilty for asking but he had to. He was supposed to ask to examine the actual paperwork but he could not quite go that far.

She took the permit from the briefcase and handed it to him. "I have a lot of very influential clients who, in their concern for me, rigged, I mean fixed- well, saw to it I got this. One client is a constable, one is a judge- It's perfectly legal. Don't look at me like that. I don't sleep with them."

Plate flushed and it made his head hurt worse.

"They are just decent people," Daphne continued, "who were concerned for me when I first started out. I was going all over Houston most every evening alone to keep appointments with people I had never met before. And where I lived then, in Southwest Houston, there was a serial murderer rapist preying on women like me at the time. They caught him eventually, thank goodness, but not until after I moved to Sand Waves."

"I am grateful, Miss Martin," he said simply to Daphne, and handed the permit back without even looking at it. "Do you prefer Miss or Ms.?"

"I don't care," said Daphne, her heart pounding. *He is fishing to see if I am attached to anyone,* she thought with elation.

"I'd appreciate it if you go and get the ice now." He sat back down. "Don't forget to find Randy. And also find Janey Harriman."

Daphne rose without a word and half ran down the slick aisle in her heels towards the staircase door, concentrating hard so as not to slip, passing Aerial coming back with Randy.

Plate's head had cleared up a little bit by the time they reached him. But he didn't get up again.

"This is a hell of a mess," he told Randy. "What's the weather situation? Are we still trapped here?"

"Looks like probably at least until tomorrow morning." Randy relayed all the information he had about the weather reports and official requests for those not in imminent danger to remain in place.

"No phone service?"

"Estimates are phone service might be restored sometime tonight, could happen any time, according to reports on the radio," said Randy.

"It's just a question of when they can get to the wet cable and replace it," said the congressman, coming out from one of the aisles into the lobby. "Are you okay, Officer?"

"I will be. Randy is bringing me up to speed on what has been happening."

"Our lights went out briefly. We had a few power surges but we still got electricity because those wires are in the ground. Apparently we don't have any phone service because those wires are in the ground."

"I am confused," said Plate, his head spinning a little again.

"Let me explain before you decide this is some type of bureaucratic screw up that I'm responsible for," said the congressman. "I was involved in securing the utility connections for Sand Waves when it was first built and my dad used to work for the phone company. Old phone wires that connect to our new phone wires in the ground are actually coated with paper."

"Paper?"

"Yes, back from the World War II era, they used paper as insulation instead of the plastic coating used today. The copper wires were coated with paper and air pressure maintained on them to keep them dry. The flooding has caused the air pressure system to fail so the paper coating has gotten wet. That was Sand Waves' connection to the main phone grid. Thus the entire system has been knocked out."

"I see. That's what Sand Waves is connected to on the outside?"

"Right, and when paper coated cable gets wet it doesn't work."

"Why have we never known about this before?"

"Well, we've always known the risk with the paper coated cable. But it was so well buried that- well, it takes a flood like this, and this is already being called a hundred year flood, to actually penetrate all the barriers and get the cable wet. This is the first time it's happened since Sand Waves has existed."

"I see."

"To replace all the underground paper cable just because it might someday possibly ever get wet would be prohibitively expensive. The only way it will ever be done is if we totally abandon the phone system as we know it and go to some other type of sci-fi unknown technology.

"While it's not my fault we don't have phone service,

I think I can take some credit for the lights not going out. When Sand Waves was first conceived, I insisted on underground-"

Tuning the congressman out, Plate thought about the book he was reading right now. He wondered where it went in the confusion. The title began with the futuristic year it was set in, he couldn't remember the numbers, somewhere several thousand years from now, but the subtitle was *The Return of Cat*.

Cats had been extinct. Then through the magic of science one had reappeared, ready to serve its human in return for food. And one of the functions of this cat, which talked, was to periodically let the main character get a handle on the timeline of events.

The hero character was constantly bombarded with futuristic battles, attacks, ambushes and trickery as he attempted to save the immediate situation while not really completely comprehending what was actually going. Plus the hero was frequently getting assaulted or knocked out for some reason or another.

Plate was identifying with that character right now. He wished he had a talking cat like the one in the book to help him out. The cat rubbing against his legs at the moment looked somewhat like the cat on the cover of his science fiction book.

If only the real cat could talk.

"Meow," said Cassius.

He looked down at Aerial's cat and picked it up. A small section of the kitty's fur was sticky.

What can you tell me, Kitty? he thought, drawing it

close, then pushing it back as he detected two distinct smells on the cat. One was the result of the kitty having access to the warehouse area.

But the other was gun oil.

"Congressman, do you happen to be armed?" Plate asked, putting a halt to Mark's continued commentary on Sand Waves' utility construction.

"No indeed," said Mark. "I voted against the last attempt to allow the unlimited distribution of firearms. Everyone has said it was a courageous vote on my part. I had been leaning the other direction. But the attempted assassination of President Reagan last year clinched the issue for me. I knew at once how I was going to vote on the issue."

Now I know how I will vote next time, thought Plate. He turned to Randy. "You, Randy?"

Randy shook his head wordlessly. "Aerial won't allow a gun on the premises, even if I did have a permit, which I don't. We don't even carry toy guns in the store. Aerial doesn't approve of them as Christmas presents for children. The only toy gun in the place is the prop in the cowboy's holster in the Cowboy Display. The one in his hand is actually part of the statue itself and doesn't come off."

Daphne returned then with Janey and some ice in a bucket. Plate felt even more grateful to Daphne at this moment and it showed in his expression when he looked at her.

He was also appreciative of her discretion.

"What is the status of Miss Moon's body?" he asked

them. "Has anything been touched. Is there a way to rope off the display?"

"No, we haven't done anything. We've all been looking for you and the delivery man."

"I think it's safe to say he has gone. Just between us, he was my only possible suspect for being the other robber."

Plate waved Daphne's ice away for the moment.

"You mean you think the first murder victim was one of the Detached Robbers?"

"Help me construct a timeline," said Plate. "Maybe we can get a better handle on this that way."

"You're going to have to tell us what you know, also," said Daphne. "Why you were here earlier dressed as Santa Claus, claiming you were a homeless person. Otherwise we are not going to be able to make sense of anything."

Now Plate looked at Daphne with some reservation. While no one was one hundred percent above suspicion, he knew Randy Harriman as a fellow, albeit former, police officer. Janey was his wife. As far as he knew she had been a loyal police officer's wife and still retained that status in Plate's eyes.

The congressman was a well known public official, perhaps not above suspicion in his political dealings, but certainly not one of the Detached Robbers and unlikely to have committed murder.

But Daphne Martin was a total stranger, did not look the part of an insurance agent at all, and out of all of them, she carried a gun.

A .32 which she had willingly handed over to him.

That clinched it.

Whatever the consequences might be, he was going to have to trust these people and he felt like trusting Daphne Martin most of all.

Chapter 33

"I'm going to trust all four of you with some information that needs to not go beyond us."

Randy, Janey, Mark, and Daphne indicated their willingness to honor this trust. They had a timeline worked out in no time, once they had listened to Plate's narration.

He told them in detail.

"After killing the people in Houston, we got a tip that the Detached Robbers were on their way to Sand Waves because one of them had a contact here. We were tipped off that the contact would be meeting the robbers at one of the locations in Sand Waves that fit their MO. There was going to be one more robbery and then the Detached Robbers, now wanted for murder, were going to head to Mexico. They were going to be getting some help from somebody here in Sand Waves.

"Our informant, who had been helping the Detached Robbers launder the money but turned against them because he did not want to be liable for the murders, did not know which of the appropriate locations was the destination for the criminals. So a police officer was assigned to, well, blend in at each one of the possible locations. I was sent here.

"As you have already guessed, Mrs. Harriman, I did not leave after our initial conversation yesterday, but rather hid out back. After I got thoroughly soaked and realized I would drown if I didn't come inside, I came in through your unlocked overhead door, found a costume to blend in with the décor in the store in hopes of catching the robbers if they showed up. And catching their contact. I was going to surreptitiously signal Randy I was here. I didn't think he would mind. But I never got the chance before Mrs. Smith found me.

"The body in the witch's cauldron fitted the description of one of the robbers, the one the informant always dealt with. No one ever got a good description of the other robber. His clothing always disguised him in such a way that nobody could really say anything else about him, not even his race or, in truth, sex. We're not sure the partner was a man.

"The man calling himself Mack Moore was the only reasonable possibility, once we were trapped here in the store, of being the second robber. When the body in the cauldron was found, the obvious conclusion was that the second robber had, for whatever reason, killed his partner. This, being their rendezvous place with their accomplice, was where he came in spite of the murder. He brought the body in and hid it in the witch's cauldron. That Mack Moore was this man was a strong possibility, I realized at once. But the other possibility, of course, was that the body in the cauldron was not one of the Detached Robbers, had nothing to do with Mack Moore, who was an innocent man. A third possibility was the body in the cauldron was a robber, but his partner had brought him and dumped him and escaped before the storm got so bad. Therefore again, Mack Moore was a totally innocent man."

After completing the timeline, everyone studied it for several minutes in silence.

"Monica Moon must have been his contact," said

Janey.

"That's impossible," said the congressman. "I've known her for years. And she may have done some suspect maneuvers financially or real estate wise. She was not an armed robber."

"They had the same last name," Daphne recalled. "Was that really his last name? Did anyone see his driver's license?"

"I checked all identification against what I was told as soon as I realized the gravity of the situation. Only Misha had no identification. She claims she left it at home," said Plate. "I had no reason to question the ID Mack Moore showed me. But Moore is such a common name."

"Maybe he was her exhusband and he killed her when she told him she had changed the beneficiary on her life insurance. She didn't recognize him after all these years and he wanted revenge," said Daphne.

Plate was unsure if Daphne was enjoying a little joke to herself at his expense. He cut his eyes towards her. She caught them and smiled.

"As I said, it's not uncommon for more than one person, even in a small size group, to have the last name of Moore." Plate tried to look at Daphne with disapproval, but failed.

"Yes, that's Laurel's last name," said Randy.

Janey flinched. Hearing the name Laurel added to her stress.

"How do we know Mack Moore is guilty of anything?" asked Janey defiantly. "Maybe he was set up to look guilty. Maybe the real robber forced him to go along

237

and killed him. Maybe he's dead too."

"But nobody else is gone," said Daphne, realizing exactly what that meant for the first time.

"So, he's gone. He was the criminal," concluded the congressman. "Monica must have stumbled onto it. Seen him do something that gave himself away."

"No, that's not the point, is it, Officer?" said Daphne.

"Right, right," said Plate, surprised that she was the first to catch on.

"What is the point?" asked the congressman.

Randy and Janey could not see it either.

"The problem is, if the delivery man and the man in the cauldron were the Detached Robbers coming here to meet a compatriot. Well," said Plate, "the delivery man is gone. The other man is dead. But what has happened to whoever they were meeting? The delivery man had a high sitting four wheel drive vehicle. From what you have told me in the timeline we have constructed, he had plenty of time to get out of Sand Waves. Why did he come back?"

"He should have wanted to get as far away as possible," said Randy. "Unless-"

He looked at Daphne who looked at Plate.

"Unless his confederate was still here when the road became impassable? Is that what you all are trying to say?" asked the congressman.

"Then that would mean one of the people trapped here overnight was the co-conspirator, the contact they were coming here to meet," Janey concluded, the level of fear in her voice rising with every word.

"And if that contact was not Monica Moon?" Janey

asked.

"And I would bet the Smith ranch on that. Monica would never have consorted with that level of criminal." The congressman was adamant.

"Then that contact is still here with us. And we don't have any idea who it is," said Plate.

Chapter 34

At this point, Plate instructed Randy to use the PA system to let the others know he had been located and to please assemble in the lobby.

Plate suspected rightly that, tired of searching for him, but not wanting to be seen as slacking, they were all just loitering in the back of the store.

Everyone appeared in the lobby in short time and all expressed relief that Plate was not seriously harmed.

"You roomed with Miss Moon last night?" Plate wanted to confirm this with Daphne.

"Yes," Daphne replied.

"Did she have anything with her? Any luggage?"

"Just her briefcase. She lived here in Sand Waves. She would've had no reason to have any luggage. Just like me she slept in the same clothes she was wearing when she arrived."

Plate's first thought had been to reassign quarters so that the room Monica had slept in would be left alone. But after studying the situation, he realized that was not going to be practical.

"Would you have any objection to my searching the room now?" he asked Daphne. "You can distinguish your section from hers for me."

Daphne had no objection. Aerial concurred.

Asking the others to please remain patient and wait for him to return, he and Daphne went up the narrow staircase.

"Aren't you going to interview everyone, one at a time?" asked Daphne, as they reached the room where

Monica Moon and she had spent the previous night. "That is what everyone will expect."

"What do you think I'm going to ask them? Did they do the murders? They are all going to say no. Were you here when the killing happened? Well, yes they all were. I know that already. For the second murder at least. Everyone takes TV mystery shows so literally."

"That's all most of us have to refer to. Oh, I forgot, Monica had an umbrella. I saw it downstairs. It matched her briefcase which matched her clothes! Must have cost a fortune."

Daphne was no cheap dresser but she drew the line at excessive expenditures on clothing. Petite as she was, Daphne could usually get fine clothing of all types at a discount. But Monica had possessed the most common of figures. About 130 pounds, she had been of average height and had been small breasted. Competition for professional women's clothing in her size was keen.

Monica would have had to pay through the nose for form fitting designer business suits like the one she died in. Adding matching accessories would have made the whole price tag astronomical.

"Did you have any idea when your roommate went downstairs last night?"

"No," said Daphne apologetically. "I am a very sound sleeper. And if she had gotten up and left the room, I would have just thought she was going downstairs to go to the bathroom."

"If anybody else heard anybody come downstairs, that's probably what they thought too," said Plate. "It's what I would have thought."

They returned downstairs with Monica Moon's briefcase. It was easy to find her distinct umbrella among the pile.

He put the briefcase and the umbrella in the manager's office as everyone watched.

"Until I can locate a safer place for these, they'll be okay here. I'm going to ask you to all go upstairs, except for Mr. and Mrs. Randy Harriman. I am going to reassign quarters however, and will ask all of you that have a change to please move your bedding and personal items, if you have anything with you, to the location I'm about to assign you. I apologize for any inconvenience."

It was easy to rearrange quarters for the members of the group. Space was not quite as limited. There were two fewer people.

Janey was assigned to move in with Randy in the clothing storage closet, the smallest space, shared the previous night by Eileen and Misha.

Misha took Janey's place with Aerial and Laurel.

Eileen took Monica's place with Daphne in the general storage closet.

There was no change for the Smiths, or Arthur and Mark.

Eileen and Misha verbally applauded the justice of these changes.

Randy and Janey each silently anticipated being forced into a small cramped spaced together with a joy that surprised them both. They were each sure the other had no such feeling.

Plate further announced he would take over the living room so that no one could get to the staircase without passing him.

If Mack mysteriously showed back up, Plate would cross that bridge when he came to it. He considered it only a remote possibility.

Chapter 35

"Everyone please go upstairs and accomplish these transfers. Even if you're not relocating, please go upstairs and stay in your own quarters until further notice," said Plate. "I need Randy and Janey Harriman here. Reverend Harriman, could you and Mrs. Aerial Harriman tend to Randy and Janey's stuff. Would that be okay with you all?"

The others proceeded towards the stairs. Randy and Janey and Arthur and Aerial looked in turn at each other for a few seconds.

"Fine with me," said Randy.

"Of course," said Janey.

"I'll be happy to," said Aerial, looking with some dread at Arthur.

"It will be our pleasure," Arthur said.

He allowed Aerial to precede him down the aisle towards the staircase, staying several steps back from her.

Plate repeated his question to the couple before him that he had first asked Daphne. What time had anyone came downstairs last night?

Randy and Janey agreed they had no idea.

"It's possible any of them could have come down as far as I know," said Randy.

"I was not on guard for anything like this," said Plate.

"For that matter neither were we," said Randy. "Janey and I can't even alibi one another for last night."

"That may be a good thing," said Plate. "An alibi from a spouse does not help anybody. Can you genuinely alibi anyone?"

"I can't," said Randy. "I couldn't even alibi you."

"Let's assume for a moment, I didn't do it," Plate said sardonically. "Everyone had to pass you and me to get to the staircase."

"No one passed me for that purpose before nine," said Randy. "But after that, I was exhausted. A semi could've run over me and I don't think I would've noticed."

"I fell asleep pretty hard, too. I don't think either of my roommates came downstairs," said Janey. "But surely you don't suspect Laurel or Aerial?"

"Okay," said Plate. "Let's start with your employees. What do you know about them?"

"Misha and Laurel?"

That moment Aerial came out from the aisles into the lobby.

"I know, Mr. Police Officer, you asked us to stay upstairs. But I just couldn't. I can't get Ms. Moon's er-predicament out of my mind. My display's violated. I can't begin to explain in a way you would understand, but violating my display like that, does not just violate the artwork, but the spirit of Christmas itself."

"What are you suggesting?" asked Plate. "I can't allow anything to be touched. The Sleeping Beauty Display, and the Sleigh Ride Display where Miss Martin found me, are crime scenes. For that matter, the area right in front of the staircase door is part of the crime scene. It's bad enough I cannot fence that off, but there's no way else to get around."

"We have extra tarps," said Aerial. "Can't we cover the poor woman's body somehow, without touching it, of course?"

"No," said Plate.

"I've got an idea," said Janey, after a moment. "We have those floor-to-ceiling curtains we used last year, when we had the actress come and pose as a fortuneteller. We made a tent around her with those curtains, so kids could go in one at a time and get a more spooky experience. They are very lightweight material but not transparent."

"Suppose we put those curtains around the Sleeping Beauty Display?" said Aerial.

"Where are they located? Do you have to go into the warehouse to get them?" asked Plate.

Plate had already resealed the door to the warehouse and didn't want anyone else going inside for any reason.

"No, they're over in the little unused office section in the back," said Randy. "Before Aerial had to move here, she was rarely here long enough to use the office. It was mostly used for storage. Marcus's office is back there too. It's been closed up and unused since his death. A lot of stuff has been put back there. We stored the old courtesy booth safe there. The warehouse has gotten so full since displays stopped selling and we had to start storing them all."

"These curtains would not touch the crime scene at all? How do they hang up?" asked Plate.

"They hang from hooks on the ceiling. We have hooks all over the ceilings so they can hang anywhere in the store we want them. They wouldn't have to be too near the display, so as to make sure not to touch it," said Aerial hopefully.

She pointed to the ceiling and everyone looked to

discern the hooks she was talking about.

"I see them. They're all over the place. This is about a 12 foot ceiling right? How do you get up there to them?"

"We have a lift," said Randy. "It's a small lift and it's back in the office area too, actually right in front of it and behind the Cowboy Display. It's meant to be kept in the warehouse but I never got around to putting it back there after I changed the décor from Halloween and Christmas."

"You have a lift?"

Plate stood up, still rather slowly. His head still hurt but he was gratified he was no longer dizzy. He realized now he had actually seen the lift a couple of times when he surveyed the store area but it had never registered, so obscure it was among all the holiday décor.

"So is that okay, Officer?"

Aerial smiled with something that resembled happiness.

"Yes, let's get that lift out here. You can hang your curtains. If you have enough, hang them around the display with the sleigh also. And I want to make use of that lift," said Plate.

At Plate's instructions, Randy drove the lift to the center front of the store and parked it in the lobby, facing the counter with the register.

A few moments later, Plate was as high as the lift would take him.

From the center of the store, he could see the entire retail area of Innovations. What was a confusing maze viewed from the floor, was a clear diagram surveyed from where he stood near the ceiling.

To his left, at the front right of the store, was the little cubicle with short walls called the manager's office. Going clockwise, next was the small unfinished display, and then the large Santa Display.

The restrooms were beyond Santa with the tall narrow Cowboy Display in front of them. The unused offices occupied the back left corner.

Centered in the back wall was the staircase door with the movable Carolers' Display next.

The back right corner was the overhead door location with the display of Christmas trees almost blocking its view even from up in the lift.

The warehouse door was almost completely obscured by the trees but a little corner of it was visible from the lift. Then the large Sleigh Ride Display took up a big space.

The huge Sleeping Beauty Display took up the front right corner of the store and between those two displays was the small cubicle with taller walls that served as a dressing room with the costume racks in front of it.

That was everything, except a bench by the front doors, and the counter with the register and, of course, the store aisles in the middle of the building.

The end of the aisles from left to right held baskets of candy, Christmas ornaments, the old fashioned lanterns, dolls, and the luggage promotion, respectively.

Merchandise on the interior of the aisles was too numerous in type and content to be anything more than a maze of seasonal items and boxes of every possible size.

As well as memorizing this layout, after descending, Plate drew a little map on a piece of white copy paper.

Randy and Janey hung the curtains. The lift was returned to its original location.

Aerial went back upstairs. *The confrontation ahead of me will be easier now,* she thought.

Plate asked Randy and Janey to go upstairs also and request the others to wait until he called for them.

Plate started thinking further about the layout of the store, studying his penciled map.

Aerial, Randy, and Arthur, legal owners of the property, could give him permission to search the premises at will.

He looked around. There were thousands of individual items in the store, both on shelves and displays. Many items had only one unit on the shelf with the rest in their original cardboard boxes stacked behind the example. Boxes that could easily be opened and used for hiding a gun.

Multiply the thousands of individual items times their boxed duplicates and Plate could easily believe searching the entire store would involve an operation that required looking at a volume of merchandise that numbered more than six figures.

One item at a time.

Such an endeavor would be impossible without several more people, even if he let those he trusted assist him. And legally, he could not do that.

And there was the gray area of searching the quarters, temporary as they may be, of the other trapped suspects. An unsympathetic judge might rule they had the right to an expectation of privacy in the areas where they spent the night. And render any evidence he found useless.

On the other hand, somebody had his gun.

Plate took mental stock of how everyone was dressed.

Janey and Misha had on fairly loose fitting smocks and tight pants. Laurel had on the pirate costume pieces that fit her awkwardly but surely a heavy .38 would be visible on her. Still, she could maybe manage it, if it were positioned just right.

Daphne wore the classic professional female suit prescribed by the Dress for Success feminist crowd. This included a blazer jacket, matching skirt and tight button up blouse. Monica had worn the same, just more expensive, and the gun had not been on her body.

Aerial was in fluttering chiffon that made him wonder if she had planned a cocktail party before the disasters had hit. Eileen was wearing dressy pants, a pullover cotton knit and carried a bulky sweater.

Mark and Arthur were wearing traditional men's business suits complete with jackets. Randy was still in the fairly loose fitting Dracula pants and shirt.

When last seen Mack Moore wore his delivery uniform, pants, and shirt with a company issued wind blazer that protected against the rain.

JW and Deidre were both wearing the tight blue jeans and tight fitting western shirts of their costumes which were not costumes on them. JW wore a jacket in addition. Plus a cowboy hat.

Of them all, only Deidre could not have concealed a gun within her clothing. Aerial would have no choice but her bosom, so she was unlikely also.

The others all had clothing that could hide.

And Plate feared that whoever had his police gun, was keeping it concealed on their person.

He looked down at his own costume.

He was still wearing the groom's tuxedo coat over the mobster's silk shirt and pinstriped pants.

"Oh my God," he said out loud, rubbing the wound on his head.

A few moments later he held his police uniform in the men's restroom, drying the sections that were still damp with the wall mounted electric energy saving hand dryer, repeatedly punching the button to keep it going.

Chapter 36

Misha went right to her bedding in the furniture storage room and went to sleep.

The Smiths likewise retreated to their bedroom. Randy and Janey closed the door to the clothing storage room, made a space and tried not to make any sound.

Arthur and Mark waited impatiently in the dinette. Neither felt like going back to sleep.

Eileen went to the general storage room, luxuriating in the much larger space.

Daphne disobeyed.

She waited until everyone else was settled and whispered conspiratorially to Eileen that she just had to go back to the bathroom.

She slipped quietly down the stairs and around to the Sleigh Ride Display.

She decided that was as close as she could safely get without Plate spotting her watching him.

If she could not always see him, at least if anything happened, she would probably hear it.

She was not going to leave this man alone down here.

He had been struck in the head. It was even possible that he had a concussion.

There was a murderer loose.

Anything could happen.

Back upstairs, Aerial checked on everyone out of nervous consideration, before proceeding with her plan.

Eileen covered for Daphne's absence and everyone else assured Aerial they were doing the best they could considering the situation, and did not need anything.

Then summoning her courage, Aerial asked Arthur if she could speak with him alone.

"I'll be happy to step out and give you some privacy," said Mark, over their protests that they were the ones who should be inconvenienced.

"Nonsense," said Mark. "I'll just wait in the little living area."

As he closed the door to the dinette behind him, Eileen opened her door.

"I'm alone in here," she said quietly.

"What about when the blonde girl gets back?"

Eileen did not reply, but never took her eyes from his face.

He slipped through the door into the general storage closet with her.

There were no chairs left in the dinette area. Arthur and Mark had been sitting on the table since the chairs had been taken downstairs.

Now Arthur and Aerial perched on either side, Aerial's feet dangling.

"Well?" asked Arthur expectantly.

"I have accomplished our mission," reported Aerial.

"The poor dead woman's body has been covered?"

"As much as possible under the circumstances," said Aerial somewhat stiffly. It was odd to work with Arthur towards a mutual goal.

"I appreciate your tending to the situation," said Arthur. "I felt the request for some dignity for the deceased would be better received if it came from you."

"I put it in a different way than you requested."

"Oh, how so?"

"I pointed out how the whole, um, scenario violated the artistic beauty of the display."

"That's the problem with you, Aerial. Everything is art. You have no respect for the sanctity of God."

Arthur slipped off the table edge and stood. Aerial did likewise.

Aerial sniffed. "I did also say it violates the spirit of Christmas."

"Spirit of Christmas? Where is any spirit of Christmas in this place?"

"You never understood what was behind the Christmas Palace. Your father and I built the store to promote Christmas."

The store had originally been called the Christmas Palace, for the plan had been that it would only be open during the Christmas season.

Conceived by his father and new stepmother during the years immediately following his mother's death, during which he was a seminary student, the original name of the store provoked even stronger emotions in Arthur.

"But you turned it in to a secular profit oriented blasphemy, expanded to full time, altering its merchandise as the holidays progressed throughout the year, making Christian holidays equal to pagan rituals like Halloween."

"Well, the idea had been so successful, and Marcus said with the disposable income of a significant percentage of the population of Sand Waves being so high...we were making so much money!"

"You didn't manage to keep any of that money."

254

"Marcus said it was a brilliant marketing concept. Marcus said we were making so much money we could afford to put it all back into more merchandise and even bigger, more expensive displays. We hired artists like Jancy and Laurel. Randy would come by on his police beat. He met Janey and they fell in love. And- it was so wonderful. Then Marcus had to die." Aerial begin to sob. "And now it's gone all wrong!"

Arthur resisted the urge to put his arms around her to comfort her.

"There is hope for Randy and Janey, I feel that strongly. But my father died," he said, emotion causing his voice to tremble. "And in what state was his soul when he died?"

"Arthur," Aerial's tears were halted by shock. "Arthur, Marcus was a Christian. You don't think he -"

"He had strange way to show it."

"Everyone cannot show it like a brand on their forehead."

"That's exactly the way it should be shown. He made this place what it is. And what kind of a place is this? Have you taken a good look at the displays? Have you surveyed the merchandise you carry in your store that purports to represent a holy day, the second most holy day in Christianity? Toys, costumes, colored lights, sparkling tinsel, fairytale characters? Where is Christ?"

"We have a baby Jesus," said Aerial defensively.

"A baby Jesus in a Santa Claus Display?"

"Well, well, there's nothing wrong with that. That display idea was Marcus's last design concept. He thought

Santa Claus and Jesus should be connected somehow. Remember the Santa Claus legend's origin is in one of the saints?"

"My father was not a Catholic. He didn't believe in saints."

"You didn't know your father at all. You so resented it when he married me, and you were just a young boy, that you shut him out of your life. It was very very hard on him. It would have broken his heart but he did have faith. He was sure you would understand one day. And you didn't have any problems taking all the money that he gave you to go to college and become a preacher."

"I assumed that was directed by the hand of God."

"And so it was. It wasn't directed by my hand. I objected to it. That was before the business was so successful. We needed the money then. It was a sacrifice to give it to you for tuition and books."

"I always knew you were against me."

"You know, Arthur, you're 50 years old, but in some ways you have never grown up. If you had, you would've resolved your differences with Marcus before he died."

"I only wish I could have spoken to him about Christ before he died."

"I'll admit, over the 25 years I was married to Marcus, most of those years he was not, by any means of the definition, religious. But he was faithful and optimistic always. And what you don't know, what was kept from you because you kept your distance from us, even after you became a success and got a church in Sand Waves right next to us, is that shortly before he died, Marcus had a- a- a conversion experience."

"A conversion experience?" asked Arthur. "Under what circumstances? With what result?"

"You said Marcus wasn't a Catholic. You were wrong. Marcus converted to Catholicism before he died."

"That's impossible! He didn't have a Catholic funeral. I did his funeral myself."

"No, I- that was my failing."

"He converted to Catholicism under your influence? You are Catholic?"

"I am not Catholic. I go occasionally to a small nondenominational church, not in Sand Waves but, uh, not too far from here. I did not go to the Catholic Church with him. But I didn't stand in his way."

"Who influenced him then?"

"Well, he had some friends, other older men. They went hunting. Some of them were Catholic. I didn't know them really. Their wives were not real friendly to me. They all had daughters my age. Well, anyway-. And how do you know God did not influence him?"

Arthur was silent.

"Where were his Catholic friends when he died?" he finally said.

"Well, I think, it was hunting season. Uh, some of them, I remember, were at the funeral. You see, when he died so unexpectedly, I was in shock. His conversion experience had been very private to him. It had been so recent. I did not arrange for a Catholic funeral. He had been afraid to tell you. I knew I was already seriously alienated from you. And to not let you do the funeral, that to let you find out he had become Catholic, would totally break any bonds you had with me.

"I explained the situation to the priest. He didn't like it. But he couldn't do anything about it. I did allow a private Mass the night before you preached the real funeral. It was attended only by me, Randy and Janey, and, yes, there were a couple of his hunting buddies there. I think. I have a hard time remembering those days and I had hardly ever met those men. They all went hunting at ungodly hours of the morning."

Arthur was stunned at her opinion of him.

"I am not a bigot, Aerial," he said. "I respect other denominations of the faith. I might have taken a while to adjust but-"

Arthur paused. Aerial was silent.

"He was my father and never said anything!"

"I don't know what effect Marcus' Catholicism would've had on our store," said Aerial. It was just beginning to take hold of him when he died. But suppose we had a statue of the Virgin Mary out there and that poor woman had gotten murdered- and- and-"

Aerial shuddered.

"That just illustrates my point," said Arthur, regaining his composure.

"It illustrates my point," said Aerial. "There is a place for the lighter touch of Christmas. People need a way to celebrate and have fun without it constantly being shoved in their face that the end result was the Crucifixion."

"The end result was the Resurrection," said Arthur. "And what does this store do when the most holy day of

Christianity comes? Easter bunnies. An actor dressed up like a giant rabbit. Colored eggs. Easter presents! Since when do we give Easter presents? Send Easter bunny cards?"

"I suppose you resent it that your father became Catholic instead of coming to your church."

"I just told you that I would not have felt so. My father had the right to have converted to any form of Christianity. That is irrelevant. No denomination of true Christians would sanction turning Easter into a secular holiday. I have nothing against the Catholics. That my father came to Christ before his death, in any way, relieves a great burden from my mind."

"So can you now see that the Christmas Palace- I mean Innovations is our, was our- mine and Marcus's way- is now my way of promoting Christ? You may not agree with it, Arthur. It may not be your way. But it is what we- I- have to offer in this, in this secular little money and status obsessed colony. Christianity is not the norm here, times have changed, you know.

"Marcus believed we need Christmas celebrations to remind us of Christ. And no matter how far removed the tinsel and trappings of commercialization seem, every little ornament, every Christmas card, every tree, nativity statue, is well- I believe in some way touched by Him and by participating just a little- even if they don't believe- even if they are atheists- by participating just a little- it- well- He is pleased-"

Arthur wanted to lecture her about flawed theology but her words, inaccurate that they might be, had warmed him a little. And, thinking about Jesus, as he knew Him, he could not help but suspect there might be a glimmer of truth there.

" 'Pleased' might not be the word, Aerial," he said stiffly, but not unkindly. "The word might be um- uh, perhaps, 'encouraged'."

Aerial wiped away her tears and looked at him in astonishment.

"I know I'm too young to be your stepmother," she said. "But I was your father's wife. Can't there be some type of reconciliation between us? So we can be a family. With Randy, and maybe Janey- if they don't split up. If only they don't!"

Arthur was contemplative for a long moment.

"As my father's widow, you are entitled to my respect," Arthur finally said.

"Thank you, Arthur."

"Would you also say, as part owner of the store, I am entitled to some say about it?"

Aerial had forgotten the danger to the store for a few moments. That she could have forgotten was such a shock to her that she was at a loss for words again.

"With the assistance of Miss Moon, I was planning to force a sale," he admitted.

"Miss Moon! Oh, Arthur, I'm so sorry I forgot, she was your friend, your- your-"

"Yes I know. She had caught my eye. Strange I think yesterday I might have said I was attracted to her. It was purely platonic, of course. She was far too young for me. She talked disdainfully about families and children. She seemed to think I wanted children. At my age!

"I had no intentions- still, perhaps I did let her think… I was actually trying to introduce her to a deeper religious faith experience. She came to my church, but I feared she did not really feel much. Anyways. Whatever caused any other feelings toward her on my part, it must have been temptation, my feelings towards her died with her apparently. I have been spending some time contemplating that. Poor woman. I'm sorry she's dead. But do not count me as one of her bereaved. I only hope I, in some way, brought her closer to God. I doubt it."

"You never know," said Aerial kindly.

"Thank you," said Arthur.

"It would have been all right for you to like a younger woman."

"Aerial, on some things, no matter what, we will never agree."

"Okay, I understand. But what about the store? It must be saved. Your father's life is in this store."

"I will allow my father loved this store. I hope he found his life was really in Christ. Maybe he would have made changes if he had lived."

"Then perhaps if we reconsider how we approach the Easter season marketing campaign? Of course, Randy is a partner and would have to be consulted. Not to mention, I always considered Janey as sort of an unnamed partner and I value her opinions also. If they don't- if she stays. If Randy doesn't leave her." Aerial dabbed her eyes.

"I'm going to pray about it," said Arthur. "That is all I can do. I have no influence over my son."

"Well then. Well then. There's nothing else to do right now while this police officer investigates these murders. I will pray about it all, too."

Unexpectedly, Arthur began to weep.

Aerial went to him and put her arms around him.

"I do not weep for sorrow for my father," he said.

"I do," said Aerial, sniffling with him. "I miss Marcus so much!"

After a moment, when his tears had subsided, Arthur continued. "I do not weep for sorrow, but for joy at the news you have told me."

He did not push Aerial away. Instead he told her, "you should stop weeping also. We will see him again."

She stepped back, opened her eyes wide and stopped crying also.

Chapter 37

The morning dawned with everyone hungry and feeling the effects of abbreviated sleep.

Outside the huge store windows there was a slight change in the lighting which indicated darkness was over and somewhere above all the rain clouds there was the sun.

Just not visible.

The curtains were in place over Sleeping Beauty and her Prince. For the rest of the prohibited areas, Christmas wrapping tape marked off the spaces, colorful red and green print, rather than the standard crime scene yellow.

The trapped group also awoke to the request that they remain upstairs until otherwise instructed by Lieutenant Plate.

Back in uniform, traditional black shirt and pants, white hat with yellow band and a pale blue gray tie distinctive to Sand Waves police, Plate soon decided, after he spoke to them individually, they would be allowed downstairs if they wanted.

The long monotonous waiting for rescue might spark a rebellion if space for the group, confined more than 24 hours by now, was not maximized as much as possible.

And he was only one man. Although he had a gun.

Most of them did not know that.

Without mentioning weapons at all, he had left his holster empty for all to see and placed Daphne's gun inside a hidden shirt pocket designed for that purpose.

Daphne's gun was fully loaded but he had no back up ammunition for a .32 caliber.

Someone else had a gun too, he feared. His .38

caliber.

He wanted whoever had taken his gun to think he was still unarmed.

He was trying to keep tensions at the lowest level possible.

He had set up the front counter area so he could interview each person as they were expecting.

He was not hoping for anything. But no harm could come of it. And what else was there to do?

The rain had not let up.

It looked like it was going to be one more night. From the radio Plate heard promises of the restoration of phone service at any time now. But the phones were still dead. He hadn't bothered to replace the battery in his pager although there were batteries plentifully available.

What did it matter if his pager worked when he couldn't return the calls?

Informed about the arrangements downstairs, everyone had been asked to come one at a time down to see Plate.

Once the interviews were over, Plate promised, everyone would have freedom of movement about the store, as long as they respected the curtains and tape.

Most of the interviews did not take long.

The most promising interview surprisingly had been with Randy, although it only confirmed what Plate overheard just after the first body had been discovered and before Monica had been murdered.

Now it took on a different significance.

Plate had insisted Randy come clean about Laurel. It

had been a circuitous conversation but with results in the end.

"Laurel has been here about three years. She was hired before Marcus died. She had been in college studying interior design and had worked at a grocery store or two. She's always been a pleasant employee. She's not real energetic but usually shows up for work on time. Everybody has always liked her. She doesn't contribute too much to design of the displays but she's real good at executing Janey's ideas. And every so often she has a good idea herself. I don't know what more to say."

"When you checked her references, everything panned out? No red flags, I suppose? Or you would not have hired her."

"About that, now, as I said, Marcus was still alive when she was hired. I wasn't involved."

"But you would have checked the references of the other girl. Right?"

"Ummm, well, if they were checked, it would've been me."

"What do you mean if they were checked?"

"Look, Plate, I've had my hands full these past few months with Aerial moving in here. We needed another display artist. As I said, Laurel is not too creative. Janey couldn't do it all. The displays haven't sold well. I needed somebody with some creative talent to help redesign them. Misha appeared and, with just a minimum of instruction, she produced excellent drawings and insightful suggestions on how we could improve the displays. Plus she can touch type the ten key adding machine so she should be able to run the new register Aerial ordered."

"You just hired her? Check her driver's license? She was the only one who didn't have one to show me."

"I'm sure I must have."

"Umm, hmm. And her paycheck? How does she handle that?"

"She cashes it every week here at the store. So does Laurel. So do I. Even Aerial. We all do. Most of our business is cash. We get some checks and credit cards but not unless the total is three figures normally."

"Okay, you know anything else about either one of these employees?"

Randy hesitated.

"Randy, listen, two people have been murdered. Don't hold out on me now. I overheard your conversation with Miss Moore when you were watching the warehouse door for me."

Randy paused. "Laurel has had some problems in the past."

"What type of problems?"

"She had a bout with drug addiction. Lost her home or something like that. Had to drop out of college."

"Without checking any references, how do you know all that?" Plate asked.

"She's told me. We're friends."

"Friends?"

"She needed a friend. She confided in me."

"She has no family?"

"No- I don't know. She told me her family was all dead. Maybe she was telling the truth."

"She chose you for a friend? Not Aerial or Janey?"

"She chose me. There is nothing more to it." Randy's voice was not convincing.

Plate folded his arms and stared at him.

"There's nothing more to it on my part," Randy insisted.

"But on her part?"

Randy did not answer but the way he hung his head told Plate all he needed to know.

"Have you discouraged this girl? It didn't sound like you were discouraging her when I was listening."

"Not exactly. She is very sensitive. And things have never been quite right with Janey since I left the force. Janey seems constantly discontented. You know she has a degree and a high level of talent. I think she feels she has to continue to work here. Before, it was her choice to work here while I was a cop. And much of the artistic success of the displays is due to her, especially since Marcus died. But she feels trapped now. And my working here also is a constant reminder that our social status has changed. I like working here but she really doesn't understand this. I think she feels both of us needing the store for income keeps both of us artificially low."

"Did Janey know about your special friendship with Laurel?"

"She thinks it's worse than it is."

"Great."

Plate mentally reevaluated Janey. And Randy too. He had not foreseen that this was going on and was more worried than ever he had placed too much trust in them.

267

"I have been afraid Janey might leave me."

"So you have been keeping Laurel in reserve? Just in case?"

"It doesn't sound nice when you put it like that. I haven't led her on. Just perhaps not discouraged her as much as I should have."

"Be prepared, this may all come out. I will have to ask Janey some questions."

"Let me talk to her first," Randy pleaded.

"That's not exactly protocol."

"Listen, neither Janey nor I murdered these people. Surely you know that. Okay, so maybe I don't know Misha or Laurel as well as I thought I did. I am remiss on verifying employee references. Faulty on my employee relations. That doesn't make me a criminal. Let me go talk to my wife. We could not be forced to testify against each other no matter what we've done." Randy tried to smile.

"You might volunteer to testify against each other." Plate arched his eyebrow.

"Come on, Plate. From what I knew of you, when I worked for the department, yes, you follow the rules, but you also have a lot of common sense."

"All right. Let's say I don't think you or Janey are killers." Plate was back to the problem that he had to trust somebody in this situation. He had already placed his bets on who to trust and it was too late to back out now. "Go on back upstairs. Talk to your wife. Send the other Mrs. Harriman down."

Chapter 38

Randy had gratefully acknowledged his former coworker's kindness. He went upstairs, instructed Aerial to come down, then took Janey by the arm and led her to the storage closet where they had spent the night.

"What is it?" she asked, when he shut the door behind her.

"It is time for us to talk," he said.

"Talk about what?"

"Talk about us. Talk about Laurel."

"I don't want to hear anything about Laurel."

"Janey, don't be naïve-"

"Naïve! You think I'm naïve?"

"No, you haven't had much experience in life. We married young."

"Oh, so that's it! You think I'm so naïve, lacking experience at life because I was a virgin when I married you? Just because I don't sleep around. And I suppose Laurel is sophisticated?"

"Laurel has had a hard life."

"A hard life? She's had a hard life?"

"She has had a lot of experience in life that you have never had. Never will. She's never had anyone to protect her- and she's had to become strong- mature beyond her age."

"Oh, you idiot!" said Janey, furious. "She is strong is she? Strong because she was a drug addict? If you think that is strong you have a warped sense of maturity. A warped sense of strength."

"Warped?"

"Warped. What a child you are, Randy! That's not experience! That's not maturity or strength! You think all those people you put in jail back when you were a cop were strong? All those who made trouble-"

"You cannot compare Laurel to them."

"Really? Look, she was a person whose life got difficult and so she took that first fix or retreated into a false relationship with a married man. And you say she is strong? She is mature? She's had experience?"

"I-"

"When all she is- is weak."

Randy was silent.

"All she is- is weak," Janey repeated. "Weak."

"No. That can't be. The strong person is the one who goes through a terrible time in life, becomes a drug addict or whatever, then goes through a recovery."

"No, you are wrong. The strong person is the one who goes through a terrible time in life and doesn't ever become an alcoholic or drug addict at all. You think people that attempt suicide, they're experienced? Are mature? The mature person is the one that doesn't attempt suicide at all."

"But it is trouble that makes you strong."

"No," said Janey. "It is God who makes you strong."

Randy had no answer to this.

"The strong person is the one, like Aerial, who never loses faith in God, who finds God in her trial. The one who never gives up on life in the first place. Who doesn't declare bankruptcy, sees it through and pays their bills. Who hangs on. Figures out a way to live without resorting to camping under the bridge."

"You've been talking to my father again. You are both wrong. It wasn't Laurel that was weak. It was me."

"Really? How do you figure that? Laurel couldn't handle college so she took drugs. She couldn't handle life so she tried to commit suicide. Then she found you. A protector in life. She has no right to you! You were my protector first."

Janey started to cry.

"I'm nobody's protector. I threw all of that away. Now I need you and Aerial and this store to prop me up."

"No you don't. You had succeeded in a tough and demanding profession that was all wrong for you. You had one lapse. You didn't try to go back and make the same mistake again. You cut the ties to the past and managed to wind up doing what you really wanted all along. Yes, I know you love it here. You may not be the artist that I am. But you love working at the store. You've been strong enough to put up with me trying to get you away and Arthur trying to shut the place down, trying to make you feel guilty, without blowing up at either one of us."

Randy remained silent. It amazed him that his wife understood him far more than he had thought.

"We don't prop you up," she continued. "Sometimes you prop us up. I've been frantic at the idea of losing you to Laurel. I don't know what I would do without you."

"I thought you blamed me for losing your social status. What gave you that idea I really wanted Laurel?"

"Laurel gave me the idea. I know you have been meeting Laurel here at the store. I guess after helping Aerial every night, you have been having sex with Laurel."

"Janey, I swear, I cannot deny I have had some feelings for her but- but she-"

"She wants you. She told me everything about you and her. She's in head over heels." Janey's composure, so effective she had believed, was about to break down. She knew it but could not do anything about it.

"I don't love her, Janey."

"You've been bedding her right here in the store with Aerial's knowledge, right under Aerial's nose," said Janey, anger spilling over.

"Janey! No! I would never do that here."

"You're in love with her! You want to leave me!" Janey broke down and cried.

"I don't love her, Janey." Randy tried to embrace her.

"Oh, don't lie to me." Janey pulled away.

"I love you, Janey."

Janey feared he was telling her what she wanted to hear.

"Randy, is that really true? It's me you want and not Laurel?"

"I thought you didn't love me anymore. I'm the one who damaged our life together."

Janey was very tired of fearing her husband did not really love her. What if he did? This was a chance not to throw their marriage away.

"If we can accept that we want to remain married, then what do we do now?"

"Go on being married?" Randy suggested. "Like we already are."

Janey had so long been preparing for a change, this

was a new thought to her. It flooded her with comfort.

Not only could she remain Randy's wife, but she could retain her ties to Aerial and Arthur, people she considered family.

She would be spared the sad duty of telling her own parents that her marriage had failed.

She had kept her marriage problems from them, flinching lately every time they prophesied grandchildren someday.

"So there's been no real relationship between you and Laurel?" Janey wanted confirmation one more time.

"No. It was mostly in her head. I admit there were times that I did not discourage her. To my disgrace."

"Let's not use the word disgrace. Laurel knew you were a married man. You cannot blame yourself for her weakness."

"Like my father blames himself for my weakness?"

"You and your father are more alike than you realize!"

"If I have a son, I hope I am never as cold to him as my father is to me at this moment. He is more distant than ever."

Janey gasped. "Oh my goodness!"

"What is it?" Randy was suddenly concerned for her health. Janey turned a little white. "Are you ill?"

"I'm afraid I may have told your father that you are having an affair with Laurel."

"Janey!" In spite of the repercussions that could cause, Randy could not help but smile a little, envisioning his father's shocked reaction. But he stifled his smile and in a lightly scolding voice said, "It's not like you to accuse without knowing for sure."

"I thought I did know for sure. Aerial told me."

"Aerial?" Randy wondered confusedly how that gossip came about but as Janey was crying again, he let the thought pass.

He took Janey in his arms and tried to console her.

There was a polite knocking on the closet door but the visitor did not wait for an answer before opening the door and peeking in.

"Randy, are you in there? I thought I heard your voice. That police officer wants you and Janey downstairs again. Just give him a few moments to talk with that insurance agent-"

Aerial gave a little start as she saw Janey there, in Randy's embrace.

"My goodness! What does this mean?"

"Well it certainly means that I'm not having an affair with Laurel."

"You're not?" asked Aerial.

"No, Aerial. What made you think that?"

"Laurel told me."

"Laurel has indicated she has feelings for me but in no way have I led her to believe those feelings were any more than appreciated as a gesture of friendship." Randy bit his lip. *Close to the truth,* he thought.

"Oh dear, what was I thinking? Laurel told me how she felt about you, Randy. And I, well, I read too many romance novels. The idea of true love right under my roof, my store. It was so nice when it first happened with you and

Janey. And I guess, well, the idea of it happening again was so nice…it brought back memories of the good times before Marcus died. Oh, I'm sorry, Janey. I thought you were unhappy with Randy and wanted to leave us. Laurel said we should not stand in your way."

"What else did Laurel tell you?" Randy felt less guilty now.

"That the two of you have found true love and Janey was going to go away and you were going to marry Laurel."

"I love Janey. Listen, Aerial," said Randy, embracing the older woman. "Laurel has misunderstood the situation."

"And I'm going to have to correct Arthur's impression about the situation," said Janey, wiping her eyes. "I repeated what you had told me to him."

"Oh heavens! Children! Forgive me! I know you two love each other. I see that now. What a fool I have been! And the situation with Laurel is now- Oh, what are we going to do?" Aerial stepped back, anxiously looking at both of them.

"I don't know," said Randy. But silently he decided he had better have another word about the situation with Plate next time he could get him alone.

Chapter 39

To give Randy and Janey a little more time alone, Aerial came downstairs by herself and talked to Plate.

Daphne had magically appeared as soon as Plate had concluded his interview with Aerial, which was not an interview but merely an exercise in reassuring her she was not going to be held responsible for the deaths in her store.

Unless, of course, she was the killer.

As he saw Daphne and Aerial standing side by side in front of him, he had another thought.

He sent Aerial back up to fetch Randy and Janey again and told her to tell them to come back down one more time, after giving him about 20 minutes to finish his interview with Daphne.

Plate really had nothing more to ask Daphne but she had recalled the piece of information she had wanted to tell him, but had forgotten in the chaos.

"When we had all converged on Monica's body, I noticed that Eileen had been wearing different clothes," said Daphne. "A formal gown, but it came from the costume rack. I had seen it there earlier."

"Why on earth would she change into a costume?" wondered Plate.

Daphne related how Eileen had then disappeared with the congressman after Monica's body was discovered. Plate filed that information away for the moment, wondering why he had ever had the notion to trust a congressman.

He didn't care anything about the congressman's sex life but he didn't want knowledge that could compromise his judgment later.

There was just too much information and not enough knowledge.

He felt the weight of fatigue and his injury very much.

Daphne had then sat with him in silence, having procured more ice, helping to hold the ice on his head while he leaned back and closed his eyes, letting him have a much needed silent and dark recovery session before continuing the questioning.

Upon feeling better, he then sent Daphne back upstairs as the Harrimans came back down, having asked her to make sure no one else came down until after he had spoken to Randy and Janey alone.

He postponed interviewing the others, feeling the situation with Randy and Janey was crucial. He could not afford to let them become entangled in their marriage problems right now.

He needed Randy.

And he might need Janey.

"Have you a safe or lockbox in the store?"

"Of course, we have a safe, Lieutenant Plate," said Janey. "And there are the small lockers in the manager's office where the employees can lock up their purses."

"That might be best. Is there one that is empty?"

"Sure," said Janey.

Janey led Plate to the manager's office. Randy followed.

"What are you going to put in there? If I may ask?"

"The victim had substantial amount of cash on her. It was in her purse that had fallen down to the side. I went ahead and took the purse away because there's the possibility that somebody here knows she has that kind of cash and may attempt to go back for it. You won't be held responsible for it. The responsibility is mine."

Janey caught a glimpse of the money as Plate opened Monica's purse and took it out.

"There should be room in the locker for the entire purse," said Randy.

"That's even better," said Plate. "I'm going to leave her briefcase and umbrella at the counter, sort of as bait to see who's really interested in it. There's nothing in the briefcase. Somebody got to it before I did."

"Here is a blank locker. To set the combination, code it in and press the numbers you want," said Randy.

"Is there any way I could see that money?" said Janey. "It looks like the money, some of it at least, that we took in yesterday. I remember a couple of old bills passing by. I intended to go back to the register and replace them with new bills so I can add them to my collection. But I forgot all about it."

"Why don't you just go to the register and see if the money is there?" Plate suggested.

Janey went over to the register, beat on it a little bit and it popped open. It was empty. She lifted the drawer where the larger bills were supposed to be after they were slipped underneath. There was no money there.

"The money is all gone. The register is empty."

"Why would anyone take the checks and the credit card receipts?" asked Randy. "Only a master forger would want them. Nobody else can do anything with them."

"That's true," said Plate. "Most thieves don't even take them because getting caught with them is so incriminating and not worth the risk."

"This makes no sense." Janey voiced the obvious.

"Let me let you look at this money. See if you can recognize any of it," Plate instructed Janey.

Plate spread the money out so that Janey could get a good look without having to touch it.

"Yes, I recall those two one dollar silver certificates, I was going to go back and redeem them. I don't have those years in my collection. I even remember who spent it. It was one of our regular customers, a little old lady who lives in one of the higher end subdivisions. She frequently comes in here with silver coins and old money. I think her adult children have got her on an allowance and this is money she squirreled away years ago and they don't know she's got it."

After sending Janey and Randy back upstairs with instructions to send Eileen down, Plate went over to the costume rack and searched it for a formal pink evening dress.

He found the dress and could tell it had been recently worn. Matching gloves had been carelessly stuffed into its bodice.

"I suppose someone saw me in that and mentioned it," said Eileen, as she came down for her interview and saw Plate had the dress beside him.

She felt humiliation like she had never known when explaining where she had been and why she had been dressed that way.

Plate did not comment on her morals, merely assured her no mention would be made of the situation unless absolutely necessary.

He gave the same assurances to the congressman, who surprisingly did not use his office to make any veiled threats.

His interviews with JW, and then Deidre Smith, were completely unproductive. They both said they knew nothing, heard nothing, had seen nothing.

He didn't believe them.

Laurel and Misha both begged off being interviewed, each claiming separate ailments.

He didn't believe them either but had little hope of learning anything from them, so he allowed them both to postpone having a session with him.

Upon finishing with the Smiths, he felt like the only concrete result of talking to any of them individually was learning Eileen's full name.

Chapter 40

Although they had been permitted to come downstairs at will after Plate finished his interviews, few came down and nobody stayed down very long.

In addition to the police officer, only the minister and the life insurance agent had some tolerance of the presence of death.

Arthur sensed this. And to relieve some of the crowding upstairs, he voluntarily stayed downstairs for a long time, sitting on the bench where he and Monica had loitered when they first came in the store, reading the Bible he had extracted from his briefcase.

Daphne also came downstairs and stayed a while, still getting the impression she was in the way upstairs. Mark and Eileen remained in the general storage room.

Daphne lingered back in an aisle on the side of the store opposite from the Sleeping Beauty Display. She could see Arthur on the bench and Plate, reading a paperback novel, sitting near the display that held Monica's body.

She decided to approach Arthur first.

"Am I intruding?" she asked the preacher, with an indication that she would like to sit beside him.

"No, not at all my dear." Arthur enjoyed looking at Daphne. She looked very young and pure to him.

Unaware of Arthur's feelings about the store and having been trained that most small business owners loved to talk about their company, Daphne tried to make small talk about Innovations.

She asked a few questions as to how the store came into existence and what its operating procedures were and how, with so few employees, anyone ever got a vacation.

Arthur patiently explained the store's history as he knew it, concluding, "it got to where it only closed only briefly between New Year's Day and Valentine's Day for employees to have vacations.

"Then it reopens February 1st with displays for Valentine's Day and St. Patrick's Day. Then Easter, the Fourth of July, a brief clearance sale, then promotes Halloween, Thanksgiving, Christmas and New Year's."

"And then the cycle repeats?"

"Yes," said Arthur, turning back to his Bible.

Daphne sat there a few minutes.

This isn't working, she thought.

"Where is your church?" she asked, after a moment.

Arthur closed the Bible and turned to face her. He gave her not only the location but directions.

Okay, this is what he wants to talk about, she reflected.

It was a new approach but maybe she could make it work.

"Who actually owns your church building? It's nondenominational correct?"

"Well, the board, church board, actually owns it. I'm part of that board."

"I see. Is there a mortgage?"

Arthur laughed as he saw the point of her questions at last.

"We are completely insured," he said, not unkindly.

"I only sell life insurance," said Daphne. "Have you thought of providing that the mortgage be paid off in case of your death?"

Arthur looked at her with some contemplation. "No, as a matter fact I haven't."

"Perhaps I could come by and talk to you about it sometime?"

"How would you like to visit our church one Sunday?"

"Well."

Here Daphne had to decide whether or not to keep pretending she didn't know where the church was or tell a different kind of lie.

"Actually to come clean, Reverend, I have been to your church. I visited there several months ago. Once."

"Well," said Arthur, pleased. "And have you had a chance to think about coming back?"

Here Daphne again debated with her conscience. To tell the truth might cost her the appointment which it looked like she already had sewn up.

Daphne briefly calculated her finances. She had grossed over $7000 the previous month. She had a few things on the horizon that she thought might come to fruition before the end of the year. Even though this month she had only made $900 so far, that was enough to pay her bills. This season was that time of year when buying life insurance was not uppermost in most people's minds. She normally took the entire month of December off as her annual vacation.

So things were going well. In addition to the extra large check of last month her average monthly commission hadn't fallen below $3500 since the beginning of 1982.

"I don't plan to return to your church, Reverend."

That statement would have normally produced a hostile reaction from Arthur. However, the last couple of days he felt different as if something had a strange effect on him. He marveled that he felt no hostility at all towards this beautiful young girl who had just rejected his life's work.

"Why not?" he asked simply.

"I didn't feel welcomed there."

This truly astonished Arthur and the astonishment showed on his face.

"I see that you wonder why," said Daphne. And that he did wonder why impressed her favorably.

"Yes, I most certainly do. Were you not greeted with friendliness?"

"Oh yes. I was greeted with friendliness. No less than twelve different people asked me where my husband was. And I would say only six or seven of them overtly dropped the friendliness when I said I wasn't married. Overtly."

Arthur mentally went over the picture that Daphne had just presented to him.

"Didn't anyone mention to you that we have a wonderfully active group for singles?"

"Oh yes, several people did. I think it was that I said I wasn't interested, that I was happy being a single woman, that's when the friendliness vanished completely."

"I see."

"Maybe," said Daphne. "See, I used to go to church every Sunday. I went with my parents when I lived with them. They live in Katy. You know, really West Houston these days, but it is incorporated. When I was in college I went with college friends. But I've been out of college several years and working as an insurance agent since then. I live alone and quite frankly, socializing is part of my job. I really don't care to go to church to socialize, I feel like I'm at work if I do. I go to church to worship God."

Arthur was silent.

Daphne was undeterred.

"The problem is most churches I have been to push the socialization and consider me unsociable if I don't dive right into it. If I do dive into it, then questions about my personal life, what they're interested in is my romantic life, or my sex life as they imagine it, just explode. I have some single women friends who do go to church. I had wondered why they didn't experience this alienation like I did. But when I visited their churches with them at their invitations I saw the problem."

"What do you see the problem as being?" Arthur managed to ask.

"My friends, both of them, when they were asked about the status of their romantic lives, both replied as to how they were praying and hoping for a husband to come any day, and emphasized how miserable they are being single working women."

"I see," Arthur repeated. And he was seeing a picture he had never seen before.

"So I came to the conclusion that the modern day churches, at least the mainstream Protestant churches that interest me, only want single career women who are unhappy."

"And you are happy being single?"

Daphne was beyond deception now.

"No, I didn't say that. I am not happy BECAUSE I am single. But I am not an unhappy person. I am not leading a miserable life. I am not spending my days pining away for the man who might or might not ever come. I'm enjoying my life right now, every day, every minute, every new experience, even this experience here, tragic as it may be. I find all aspects of life interesting."

"Well," said Arthur.

"It's not that I'm enjoying the experience so much." Daphne backtracked a little. "But I don't see why I shouldn't use it to gain clients if I can."

Her voice was defiant.

"Talking to you has given me some things to think about," said Arthur diplomatically, but truthfully.

"One of the reasons I had visited your church," Daphne continued, thinking he might actually be listening to her, "because I heard you were a single pastor, the only one in Sand Waves as far as I know, other than the Catholic priest, of course. I had hoped single people, happy well-adjusted single people, not just people looking for a husband or wife, would be welcome there."

"I am single, not by choice," he said. "And looking back there has sometimes been negative reaction."

"If in light of what I have said, if you want to forgo the appointment, I'll understand," said Daphne, thinking expressing her feelings for a change was almost worth losing the appointment.

"No, no, you go ahead and give me a call in a week or so. I might need some life insurance. And I would hope you would give my church another chance. But give me little time to work on the congregation, okay?"

"Okay, it's a deal."

Daphne and Arthur stood up and shook hands.

Plate looked up from his paperback, too far away to hear what they had said, but he could see them.

And he wondered about the handshake.

"I tell you what," said Arthur to Daphne. "I'm going upstairs for a little while. Why don't you go over there and talk to that nice looking young policeman? He may need life insurance."

"I was just headed that way."

Chapter 41

"So what are you reading, Officer?" Daphne asked.

Plate recalled his official interview with her as she pulled up a chair and sat down. It had not been lacking in formality, with no mention of any of the interaction between them when she had found him in the sleigh. Nor had she said anything about the gun. And he had not learned anything else about her either.

Except that for some reason her presence was a great comfort.

Now having interviewed the Smiths, after talking to her, he now wanted to ask her a couple more questions.

Here was the chance.

He put the book away.

"Just popular sci-fi, I found it over where it had fallen when I was assaulted," he said, turning his attention to her. "It's about a different world where humans and aliens frequently get caught together in dangerous situations. The only insurance they have against trouble is trusting each other. Which reminds me, I need to ask you what you may know about an insurance matter."

Uninterested in science fiction, Daphne perked up. But his inquiry did not lead to the discussion of life insurance in the way she desired.

"It is actually illegal for me to discuss any aspect of any financial status of any insurance company," she said in reply to his question about the West Texas Ranchers Life Insurance Company.

"What?" Plate had only begun his questions about the company with a general inquiry. He was not expecting a stonewall at once. "You're kidding."

"It is against the rules for me to tell you anything I might know about how stable or unstable any insurance company is. You should know the law. Seriously, I was told there is really a rule forbidding me, as an agent, to reveal anything I might know about the monetary health of an insurance company."

"That's incredible."

"The insurance board insures all policies. They prefer that if a company goes into receivership-"

"What does that mean? Receivership?"

"Oh. Er- bankruptcy. The board prefers that policyholders not be alarmed. If there's no way of knowing, they won't worry. They're not going to incur any type of loss anyway. Why are you asking me questions about this specific insurance company? "

Not too long ago her general manager had given her a tip, via a confidential memo, to cease writing any policies with West Texas Ranchers. Of course, he had not stated why, but there was only one reason besides commission reductions.

And West Texas Ranchers still paid standard fare. But commissions could be affected when companies went into receivership. Usually they were not, but they could be. Agents quietly took their best customers out, if they could covertly manage to.

"What do I need to tell you to get beyond the canned spiel about legalities?"

"I don't know." Daphne had never considered that any situation might be worth risking her license just to discuss the finances of an insurance company.

"Maybe if I tell you it might have some bearing on these murders?"

"Maybe."

"It does. The Smiths are heavily involved as co-owners of this life insurance company."

"I see. Well, I don't see. So what?"

"They are representing themselves as extremely wealthy people with no financial concerns and it has come to my attention that there is some money that is not where it's supposed to be in the middle of all this."

"That's all you can tell me?"

"That's all I can tell you."

"Well, problem is I don't have access to the information you ask."

"So you can't tell me if Deidre and JW's insurance company is solvent?"

"In a nutshell, no. First of all I have no access to that information, as I said. Secondly, if I did hear rumors not only can I lose my license, I could be fined for repeating them. A lot."

"Well, I now know more about insurance," said Plate. "Anything you CAN tell me."

Daphne thought long and hard.

"My general manager doesn't like the company," she finally said.

"What does that mean?"

"Just what I said. He does not like the company anymore."

"He used to like the company previously?"

"Yes."

"When did he stop liking the company?"

"About two weeks ago."

"Okay, thank you. I'm going to have to ask you to ask Mr. and Mrs. Smith come down and talk to me again."

"But I wanted to talk to you about-"

"Later," said Plate brusquely. "Please go get the Smiths and ask them to come and see me. Thank you."

Exasperated, Daphne went back up the stairs.

On her way to find the Smiths, she was surprised to see Eileen weeping and Arthur sitting with her with his arm around her shoulders. They were now occupying the living room but the door to the furniture storage room was not completely shut.

Daphne caught sight of Laurel who was standing in the open doorway obviously listening to what they were saying, tears on her cheeks as well.

Daphne did not make eye contact with Laurel and did not linger but still heard part of the conversation between Arthur and Eileen as she passed by.

"I think, my dear, that while love in any form can be used for good, it is not always good in and of itself. We are forbidden to love evil, to love idols, to covet our neighbor's spouses."

"Love is the word. Not covet. Pastor, I do not expect Mark to leave his wife for me."

"Yes, perhaps, it is, but do you truly in your heart love the congressman unselfishly. Is the word covet not addressed?"

"He is all I have," Eileen sobbed.

"No, my dear, he is not all you have. You have Christ," said Arthur.

Eileen stopped crying suddenly.

"And while your present position may seem enviable to some," said Arthur, "do you not know in your heart that you are better than that?"

Chapter 42

While Daphne had been talking with Arthur, Laurel had confronted Randy and Janey in the clothing storage room.

Overhearing Janey and Randy's indiscreet sounds as they made love in the small room had been too much for her to bear.

She knocked on the door and demanded they let her in. The Harrimans dressed hastily and complied.

Laurel had dreamed Randy, forced to choose, would reject his wife for her.

But with Janey at his side, Randy had told Laurel there was nothing between them and never would be.

Janey had tried to mediate with understanding but this only made the scene worse. Laurel became abusive. Then submissive. Then detached.

She wanted to be alone, she told them.

Randy and Janey had gone downstairs after their confrontation with Laurel but had gone around to the left side of the store, past the Cowboy Display, not wanting to interact with anyone else for a while. They went to the Santa Display and sat between it and the exterior window, sitting together on the floor holding each other and watching the rain through the huge window.

Back upstairs, Laurel stood in shock, still in the clothing storage space.

Randy had rejected her once and for all.

She had figured out what was going on with Eileen and had formed a mental bond with her, although they had not spoken about their similar situations.

So after Randy had told her there was no hope she had gone to find Eileen but instead had overheard her conversation with Arthur.

"You are young and lovely. Do you not truly believe there will be another man for you?" Arthur had asked Eileen.

Laurel had turned away stunned.

She did not remain to hear how Eileen answered that question. She knew what her answer was. No.

There would never be any other man for her than Randy.

She would live her life alone.

But the idea of being alone, with nothing but a cat, working in a retail store and selling cosmetics to make ends meet, was no life.

Like Randy and Janey, Eileen had also gone downstairs.

Like Laurel, she wanted to be alone.

She was not sure why her conversation with the pastor had occurred at just that interval.

Maybe because she had abruptly realized the boy in the warehouse had been dead while she and Mark had made love on a nearby display, stored for the Fourth of July holiday.

A backyard scene with a hammock, they had gleefully temporarily displaced the mannequin that slept there.

The covering tarp had masked everything while they were beneath it.

Eileen went the opposite way from the Harrimans

and quietly slipped into the dressing room where privacy was assured.

She locked the mirrored door behind her.

Upstairs, Daphne slipped through the empty dinette and knocked on the Smiths' door and relayed Plate's message.

By the time she had turned and come back into the section where Arthur had been counseling Eileen, they were gone.

But standing in the living room was Laurel, her face still wet with tears.

Daphne wasn't sure where she should go.

She didn't feel like comforting anybody right now. She had enough paying clients who required company and comfort at regular intervals.

She turned around and went through the door to her space in the general storage room, which she expected to be empty since Eileen must have gone downstairs.

She had forgotten about the congressman. She found herself in the room with Mark.

She backed out of that room quickly.

The congressman was sitting in there, weeping as well.

The Smiths passed by on their way down to Plate. Deidre had needed time to fix her makeup and perfect her hairstyle, while JW had put on his coat. Lack of adequate toiletry facilities had not fazed them at all. Deidre had extracted a fully lighted makeup mirror from her luggage.

Daphne noticed her perfect facial composure.

Daphne touched her own face. Her makeup needed

repair. It had been far too long since she had enjoyed a change of clothes.

She followed the Smiths downstairs but turned off to the costume rack as they went on to see Plate up front.

Laurel sat on the couch with Aerial's cat and made a decision. Daphne had gone downstairs, after the Smiths, and all three had passed her. She had barely noticed them.

She wondered now if she would lose her job as well as everything else. Surely Janey would not want her around anymore. Probably Randy would fire her.

It seemed only hours ago she had nourished high hopes of getting back into Sand Waves and living a good life. She blamed these murders for spoiling that cherished dream forever.

Life did not seem worth living now.

But now that she had decided to end her life, she was alert again.

Trying to be nonchalant, she slipped downstairs.

Watching to make sure no one saw her, she went straight to where she had spotted the ideal hiding place for a gun. It was still there.

She had never considered owning a gun, knew how to use one only because her brother had shown her once.

Problem was, knowing where the gun was located no longer was enough. She retrieved the gun and put it in her shirt pocket. But this gun was heavy. The pirate shirt was light silk, the .38 weighed it down visibly.

She fetched her cosmetics case. She opened it and looked around.

If someone saw her she would just pretend she had

found the gun and was eventually going to turn it over to the cop. She had found it. That was true. Naturally, she could say, she was thinking about keeping it to herself, considering the danger they were in. She wanted it upstairs with her until she made a final decision. That was true also.

She put the gun in the case and carried it upstairs.

Where to put the gun where it would be easily and quickly retrievable but not in sight?

The premises would surely be searched sooner or later.

With two roommates, especially the snoopy Misha, she dared not hide it where she was staying. She wandered about looking for an obvious spot.

Ah ha, she thought, as she realized the perfect place and hid the gun there.

It was ideal.

A chest of drawers sat in the clothing storage room just under the uncovered vent through which Randy had run the electrical cords. She pulled out the drawers and, stepping inside them, used them as stair steps to reach high enough to slip the .38 in the vent, nudging it next to the wiring.

Hopping down, she closed the drawers, forcing back inside some of the clothing her feet had disturbed.

All the better if the gun were found in a space which implicated Randy and Janey.

She looked at the entangled bedding on the floor where they had made love in the opposite corner and kicked at it as she left the room.

Chapter 43

When he heard the shrill sound of the telephone ringing, Plate almost knocked Deidre and JW down in his dive to get to it.

An amplifier for the telephone bell was also sounding upstairs simultaneously.

Randy had rigged it up so that Aerial would know when the phone rang downstairs.

He and Janey got up from their retreat by the window.

Eileen came quietly out of the dressing room.

Moments earlier, Daphne had tried the dressing room door and found it locked so she had taken the two-piece costume she had selected from the rack to the restroom to change. That worked out well as she wanted to wash out her clothes in the sink. But this caused her not to be able to hear the phone when it rang.

Upstairs, Aerial and Misha woke up with a start.

The congressman bounded downstairs eager to communicate once more with the outside world.

Laurel knew at once she had made a mistake in bringing the gun upstairs. She had begun to think she was a fool to remove it from its hiding place downstairs and decided to put it back.

As Aerial and Misha came out to go downstairs she ducked into the clothing storage room, climbed up and got the gun. She put it inside her case and trailed her coworkers down.

Laurel had just come through the staircase door when she saw Misha turn around and head back towards her. She had been unsure if she wanted to keep the gun in her cosmetics case or back in its hiding place.

Now she had no choice.

She could not get it to the hiding place.

"The phones are on," said Misha, unnecessarily as she passed Laurel and turned off towards the restrooms.

Nodding to Misha, Laurel turned left and went around the luggage promotion, dropping off the case there. She locked the case, making sure to hide it towards the back of the display.

Aerial suddenly remembered that one of the toy ensembles, aimed at little girls, contained bags of unpopped popcorn. A rush to the aisle this priceless commodity occupied produced a quantity of six. These boxes were immediately ripped open and the popcorn carried upstairs to Aerial's microwave.

Also discovered, on the same aisle, were two packaged toy ovens, each containing a dry vanilla flavored cake mix. The attempt to bake the first package of dry cake mix, water added, in the microwave failed miserably and resulted in something inedible that those who did not possess a microwave had never experienced before. Therefore, the second package of cake mix was simply stirred with water and served like a pudding.

Everyone partook of the popcorn and cake mix. No one complained. Despite their culinary inferiority, neither food was candy. And both were surprisingly filling.

The phone lines were jammed and the busy signal prevailed most of the time. Yet calls were getting through sporadically. The first caller to get through had been from the congressman's office staff, which had continuously been ringing his last known location.

Impatiently, Plate waited for the congressman to assure his staff that he was okay and explain that there was a law enforcement officer that needed the telephone line urgently (nothing to do with him, please reassure his wife), and get his secretary off the phone.

It began ringing again immediately but Plate held the receiver up and pushed the button up and down until he got a dial tone. Whoever was calling could get mad about it later. He had to get through to his police chief and relay the situation at the store.

The police chief did little more than confirm that Plate had acted acceptably and in accordance with procedures as much as he possibly could, considering the situation.

Rescue was still several hours away. Live people were still in danger from the floodwaters and while the situation at Innovations was technically an emergency, the murder victims were beyond help and could not take up valuable rescue resources at this time.

The chief did have one suggestion that nobody had thought about.

Plate was a bit chagrined that it had escaped him, although the chief said it was perfectly understandable considering his having been hit on the head, in addition to everything else going on.

"Randy, find any cameras y'all have here at the store, load them with film and batteries for me would you?" Plate directed.

The store did not carry cameras but by accident had six 110 instamatics in stock and two rolls of film with two packages of flashcubes for each thin camera. Being displaced by the 35 millimeter film cameras, the 110 camera was now being marketed for children and was found in a toy set that the store had six in stock. Film was included as were the flashcubes.

Plate passed out cameras and asked everyone available to assist in photographing the entire interior of the store especially the displays. Plate himself stepped behind the curtain and photographed the Sleeping Beauty Display with Monica's body on it.

Soon flashcubes were going off everywhere.

Plate debated on removing the barricades across the warehouse door to photograph the Witch's Display. But he decided against it. He felt the strain of dealing with the reality of the decomposing body would be too much for the group.

If anyone did take a peek at Monica Moon, she still looked very close to what she had looked like in life. Her sprawled position notwithstanding, the blood on the back of her head had dried. Her eyes were closed. Her skin was still white and taut. She was not unattractive in death. She had not been dead long enough to impose the gruesome facts of decomposition on anyone that viewed her surreptitiously.

Chapter 44

Daphne distracted everyone when she emerged from the restroom. She had on a semiformal simple black dress with a fake white fur stole.

Combined with her natural blonde hair, the 1960s style costume gave her a classic Hollywood movie star look.

"I could not stand wearing those clothes any longer," she said. "I hope no one minds that I have them drying, draped over the stall doors in the restroom. I'm hoping they will dry and I can change back as soon as possible before we are rescued. Although it seems like we are never going to get out of here."

"It does appear to be a lost cause," Mark said lightly. "The phones are back, however."

"Misha told me," said Daphne. "She helped me wash out my clothes in the restroom. She knew just how to do it. I'll call my folks shortly."

A note of hope was sounded when Aerial got through to the Sand Waves 24 Hours Delivery Pizza Parlor. Located in a high section of the area, it was open for business, hampered only by floodwaters too deep for its delivery vehicles to traverse.

A large order was placed. The pizza people promised delivery as soon as possible.

By boat if necessary.

Nobody seemed to know quite when that would be.

Plate requested that the photographing continue until they ran out of film.

As most of the others were busy snapping pictures

and calling family and friends in turn on the phone, Laurel went back upstairs. She had called her mother. It had been a vague and confusing conversation, not unusual anymore. She had no one else to call.

She was now unsure she wanted to take her life. Contact with the outside world, the prospect of rescue put a different light on the situation.

It had been a long time since she had any pizza. Normally, she could not afford it.

Again Laurel thought seriously about how she could put the gun back where she had found it. But she decided that was a bad idea, better leave it in her case downstairs. She might want to use it. Why was she unsure? She went into the furniture storage room, her assigned space.

Aerial's cat was now curled on the bedding, asleep. She stretched out by the cat, waking it, and the kitty crawled into her arms. She had thought she would cry. But she didn't cry this time. She just curled up, petting the cat and staring into space.

Arthur came back upstairs and saw Laurel's detached demeanor as she went in without closing her door. He knocked on the doorframe, not waiting for a reply, and entered the room with her. Although she was not weeping, he sensed her distress and saw her isolation.

"Can I speak to you my dear?" he asked.

"I am not interested in what you have to say, Reverend," said Laurel, turning her back to him and clutching the cat tightly. It meowed.

"Let me know if I can be of any help," Arthur said, backing out and shutting the door.

He turned to find Misha directly behind him.

"I was looking for the cat," said Misha.

"The kitty is occupied right now," said Arthur, preventing her from going in with Laurel. "Have you finished your phone calls letting your family and friends know that you are okay?"

"My friends don't have phones. They are too poor. Poor Vietnamese who came to this country with nothing. Phone bills have doubled in the last two years and my friends all had theirs disconnected. If you cared about people you would know these things."

Arthur was used to these appeals. He reached into his pocket and drew a ten dollar bill from his wallet.

"And your parents?"

"We're estranged." Misha said the word as if she had deliberately learned it to describe the situation. She stared at the money in his hand.

"Don't you think, still, they would want to know you are safe? I'm a little at odds with my son, sometimes, but I never would want to be in doubt about his well-being."

"I have no desire to talk to them. They don't care anything about me."

"Let me tell you about Someone who cares about you no matter what you do," said Arthur.

"I know all about the Christian faith. My parents converted to Catholicism. They thought it would get them out of Vietnam faster. But I wasn't going to give up my heritage."

"I see. And is that the cause of your estrangement?"

"Yes. Now leave me alone, Preacher. I'm not

interested in anything you have to say."

She took off down the stairs.

Arthur stood in contemplation and put the bill back in his pocket. It had been years since anyone had rejected him and his message so brutally. He was used to rejection from Randy but that was personal. Still he did not feel insulted or discouraged or even angry. The latter emotion would have been his reaction a few days ago. Instead surprisingly, for the first time in a long time, he felt like he was on the right path.

He fingered the outline of the cross he wore under his shirt.

Chapter 45

The approaching darkness seemed gloomier this night, despite the restored communications and prospect for rescue early Sunday morning.

There was no food of any type left except candy. After remembering the popcorn and finding the cake mix, Aerial and Randy had searched all the other merchandise on the aisles. But there were no more goodies encased with any toys or Christmas decorations.

Cassius did have an adequate supply of cat food still left. A few glances had been directed at it but no one had touched it yet.

Janey had thought about the cookies in the Santa Display. They were real but somebody had already got them. Just the empty boxes were left. She scoured the downstairs office space for the box of cookies that was used to replenish the real cookies on the plate when hungry customers swiped them. That happened so frequently the cookies never got stale.

Aerial had stocked up on cookies last fall but they had gone rapidly as soon as the display had been unveiled. Still there should have been one box left. That box of cookies was gone too.

Plate feared nobody was going to sleep well this night.

Throwing inventory records and profit concerns to the wind, Aerial pulled the expensive board games off the shelves and several people teamed up to play.

"I need to make another phone call," said Randy to

Plate. "One I don't want anyone but Janey to know about."

"And who will you be calling?"

"My mother."

"Your mother?"

Plate had known the story of how Randy's mother had abandoned him as a small child from back when they had worked together.

Randy had expressed such resentment towards his mother that Plate was surprised he would even consider ever talking to her for any reason.

"I need to let her know that I am okay. It will be a long distance call so you'll have a record of it for your investigation."

Most of Sand Waves residents paid a fee to have unlimited calling privileges to the Houston area without incurring long distance charges and also, they thought, avoiding records of who they called on their bills.

It was an accepted myth that only long distance call records were maintained by the phone company.

This fiction was promoted by TV and movies but in reality, if need be, the phone company could pull records of any call made anywhere anytime.

Aerial, in her cost cutting since her financial troubles, had done away with that feature so all calls put from the store to any area outside of Sand Waves were toll calls.

"Your mother's in Houston?"

"She's at the Houston Cancer Center."

"Oh, I'm sorry," said Plate.

"It's okay," said Randy. "She had been trying to contact me ever since I turned 18. After my grandfather died, I decided to return her call. And found that she was ill."

"Serious I presume. I have heard HCC is not the sentence of death that it used to be."

"No it's not. People go home now sometimes. The verdict is not in for her yet."

"Well, go ahead and let her know you're okay."

"Thanks," said Randy.

Randy made his call which was received with joy and when he hung up the phone he found Arthur standing near him.

"You know who I was talking to?" asked Randy.

"Yes, she contacted me a few months ago also. I did not respond well, I'm afraid. Could you tell me how she is doing?"

"As well as can be expected."

"Would you ask her for me if I can do anything?"

Randy looked surprised.

"Also," Arthur continued. "Janey has set me straight about you and your employee."

"That's a relief."

"I caught her crying upstairs but she was not interested in speaking to me. What do you intend to do about her employment here?"

"I don't know."

"I have some contacts. I might can get her a job that will pay at least as much as this."

"I do know she wants to be in Sand Waves."

"I hardly know anybody outside of Sand Waves anymore. Any job I could find her would be here."

"Okay, thanks for the offer, Dad. I'll let you know."

This night no one protested when Plate insisted they all retire to their assigned space upstairs around 7 PM.

Most were already in their space.

Plate had let the comforting thought that Mack Moore had been the sole culprit go unchallenged for most of the day.

But he didn't believe it.

He didn't believe, if Mack Moore was one of the Detached Robbers, that Moore would risk assaulting a lone police officer, taking his gun, all before making his escape.

If he thought his vehicle would make it, or he had some other plan no one had imagined for escape, why not just slip away when he got the chance and go?

He would surely have had his own gun hidden somewhere.

And if he had felt the need to assault a sleeping, dozing police officer, having killed already, why didn't he hit hard enough to kill again?

Plate was sure these questions were going to keep him awake tonight.

Not to mention he had confiscated what little was left of the coffee and had loaded up a plastic bag full of candy, the combination of which, when ingested, should keep him awake for a week.

Or so he hoped.

Chapter 46

About midnight Plate decided staying in the living room upstairs had been the wrong decision.

A vote had been taken. Everyone needed sleep. Everyone had made all their phone calls. Chatting casually was not an option as the phone lines needed to remain open. Calls were still coming in, wrong numbers, newspaper reporters, and concerned inquiries, legitimate and illegitimate.

The phone bell extension had been switched off so the ringing phone would not disturb anyone's sleep.

The result was that Plate decided he was too far away from communications.

Aerial's cat followed him as he slipped quietly down the stairs. He carried a couple of couch cushions, intending to lie down behind the counter, where he could easily reach the phone with one swift motion if necessary.

He decided against telling anyone of his change of plans.

He didn't feel like any conversation right now anyway.

Settling in, he must have only been dozing a moment when he heard a noise that indicated someone was creeping down an aisle.

The lights been turned down low again.

That had been a mistake, he realized, a little late.

He got up quietly, his hand on the .32 revolver.

He went down a parallel aisle and circled around.

As he was going back up the aisle towards the noise the staircase door came open.

"Hush," he whispered to Janey as she came through the staircase doorway.

Janey made a warning motion. "I heard two different people come down just a few minutes apart," she whispered. "I don't know who."

"I know. Stay back."

"Randy's getting dressed. He fell asleep."

"Hide and watch for anyone else coming down. Let me know if they do," Plate instructed.

Janey hid in the Carolers' Display.

The .32 still in his pocket, Plate came up behind Misha just as she was pulling the money from the pockets of Little Red Riding Hood's cloak on the Cowboy Display.

He caught her by the shoulders.

"It's my money," she whimpered. "It's all I've got left. That bitch Monica Moon took the rest."

"Where else do you have money hidden in this store?" asked Plate.

"Just some in my locker. I've been getting it out of all the displays and putting it in my locker so I could get to it easily when we are rescued," said Misha. "But somebody had been taking it. Finding it. I don't know how."

"Let's go get it," said Plate. "What's left- you need to give it back to Mrs. Harriman."

Without losing sight of the younger girl, Plate stepped back and motioned for Janey to remain hidden.

Then he took Misha's arm and walked her over to the manager's office. Inside the cubicle, beside the set of lockers stood a lantern. Misha had to move the lantern to get her locker opened for Plate.

Aerial's cat watched from on top of the time clock.

The lock fell off at Misha's touch. She looked genuinely surprised.

Startled, the cat jumped down and vanished around the corner.

Inside Misha's locker were the money, credit receipts, and checks as she had said, but also on top of the register contents was a pair of gloves with dried blood all over them.

Chapter 47

"These gloves have blood on them," said Plate, as he examined them.

"I've never seen them before," Misha protested. "It's not my gloves. They don't fit me."

But it was the next object, also with blood stains visible even in the dim light, which startled him as Plate retrieved it from the very back of the locker.

It was unlikely that this was the weapon that knocked him out.

But the dagger had to be the weapon that killed Monica Moon.

Before Plate could demand an explanation, Misha went on the offensive.

"That's not my gloves! The dagger is mine, but I don't know how it got blood on it," said Misha. "It's my only protection. It came from Vietnam with my family. Somebody smeared it with blood to make me look bad. You cannot do anything to me. You don't have a gun anymore. If you take my dagger from me you are stealing my property and I will sue you-"

A shot and a scream interrupted them.

The cat scrambled across the lobby.

Plate pushed Misha down behind the unfinished display, desperately trying to ascertain where the shot came from.

The bright lights came on.

Randy ran into view.

"WHAT'S HAPPENED?" he yelled.

313

"I don't know," said Plate. He pulled the .32 from his shirt pocket. "Where is your wife? You must've passed her."

"You have gun, Honorable Policeman Sir?" said Misha, rising a little, her eyes widening. "Honorable Officer, whatever is your wishes-"

"Hush," said Plate, pushing her further down.

Randy stood without protection in the lobby listening as the .38 fired again.

Then they heard Janey scream again.

"BACK HERE!" yelled Mark, from across the store. "Between the trees and the Christmas singers."

Plate and Randy dashed all the way to the back of the store.

Janey had blood on her sleeve. She was holding her arm, as she crumpled over against the song leader in the Carolers' Display.

Randy grabbed her, and pulled the dress from her shoulder.

"I think I'm all right," Janey sobbed. "Must've just grazed me. I'm trying not to get blood on the display."

By this time everyone was downstairs, Plate was watching them all as they came up to Randy and Janey.

Janey started to pass out. Aerial rushed to Janey's aid first.

Everyone followed as she and Randy managed to help Janey get to the front of the store, placing her on the table by the counter.

"Look! The gun!" Daphne shouted.

When Plate looked at Daphne, it registered in his mind that she was carrying her enormous briefcase, holding it in front of her like a shield.

The gun was on the floor in the center of the lobby.

"NOBODY touch it!" yelled Plate, raising the .32 he held in his hand.

At the same time the phone rang.

The shrill bell distracted them all.

Plate made a move to grab the phone without taking his eyes off the gun but suddenly as he did, the lights went out again.

Completely out.

The store was pitched into darkness and the phone kept on ringing.

More than one of the women screamed loud as or louder than the ringing bell.

Randy left Janey to Aerial and raced to the breaker box. He flipped the main breaker and the lights came on again. So did the music and animation until Randy was able once more to manipulate the switches so only the lights stayed on.

Plate grabbed the phone with his left hand and cursed as he spoke into the receiver, surprising the pizza parlor night manager who was calling to see if water had receded enough there so the store was able to get deliveries yet.

Slamming the phone down, Plate looked at the spot on the floor where the gun had been, mentally willing it to still be there.

It was not.

He held tightly to the .32 in his possession.

"Damn," he said again. He looked at the startled people surrounding him.

Some were looking at the floor.

Others stared at the gun in his hand.

Everyone was present.

"People, one of you fired that gun. When we get out of here there are tests that will show who did it. Meanwhile, no one wash their hands-"

He was contemplating the inadequacy of that statement and the impossibility of his situation when Daphne approached him.

"Officer Plate, I need to talk to you," said Daphne.

Plate looked at Daphne as if she were mad.

"Not right now," he said, teeth clenching.

"Yes, indeed. Absolutely right now," said Daphne. "Remember our conversation earlier, the one about my briefcase after I found you in the sleigh. That conversation?"

Plate looked at her. She was smiling but her eyes were deadly serious.

"Ladies and gentlemen, I am going to ask you to remain here, completely in one another's sight, as I speak with Miss Martin and then I will give you instructions. Again, do not move from where you are standing. I will be right back. Anyone moves, I will detain them with handcuffs," he threatened.

He lowered the .32 but still gripped it tightly in his hand.

With his other hand Plate took Daphne by the arm, pinching her and dragged her down an aisle far enough away so the others could not hear.

She was going willingly but his legs were much

longer and he had to pull her beside him for her to keep up.

"What?" he hissed at her when they stopped, still grabbing her arm.

"Look in my briefcase," she whispered confidently, smiling a little.

He let go of her.

She rubbed her arm.

He opened the briefcase and pulled out an object wrapped in a fuzzy piece of cloth with sparkles on it.

"It was right near me and when the lights went out I just popped my case open and made a grab for the gun. There was someone else grabbing for it. But I got there first." Her voice was triumphant but low.

Sure enough inside the wrapping was a gun.

"But this is the fake gun from the Cowboy Display," said Plate in disbelief.

"Right, that's what was on the floor. I'll bet your gun is still in the display. Whoever fired it must have hidden it there in plain sight and threw this on the floor. These cloth Christmas tree skirts were on the shelf right next to me where I was standing. So I grabbed one, and dove for the spot where I had seen the gun. I grabbed it with the cloth so fingerprints are still intact."

"Did you know who else was near you when you dived for it? Are you sure they were grabbing for it? Or putting it there?"

Daphne bit her lip, thinking, but she shook her head disappointedly. "I don't know."

"That's okay," he said, glancing around.

Plate could not see the holster in the Cowboy Display

from where they were standing.

"Go over there quickly and tell me what you see in the cowboy's holster. But don't touch anything."

"I'll have to climb up there. I'm too short to see from the ground."

"I'll distract them while you do," he said.

She paused, wondering if she dared speak. Wondering if he would take her seriously. "Listen, don't you think it is time to set a little trap?"

Plate listened to Daphne's idea, relieved her of her briefcase, then went with a grim face back to the group of people waiting for him while she went towards the Cowboy Display.

Chapter 48

"We have the gun," Plate announced, loudly, although there was no reason to shout except for effect. "With fingerprints intact. We are sure. So not to worry, as soon as rescue gets here in the morning, fingerprints will be taken and we will know who fired it."

As they were all looking at him, out of the corner of his eye, over the top of the short aisles, he saw the top of Daphne's blonde head as she jumped up on the Cowboy Display.

She was back with them all in a moment, and with a slight nod of her head, silently confirmed to him their theory was correct.

Plate hesitated only a moment before putting the idea, they had so briefly discussed, into action.

He told them then, with high praises for her, about Daphne's retrieval of the gun in the dark and concluded his speech by holding up the white bundle, the gloves, and the dagger that had been found in front of Misha's locker.

"Here it is. This wraps up everything. I won't say where I found these, as that is confidential. But this is the murder weapon for Miss Moon. The gloves have blood on them. I'm really just a traffic cop. My responsibility is only to get this to my superiors intact as soon as we are rescued. I am really exhausted. I am not even going to unwrap it. I am going to lock it up in the employee lockers and just sit here all night watching it and Miss Moon's body. So all of you just go back upstairs. I have confirmation we will be taken out of here, by boat if necessary, as soon as it is dawn. So don't worry about washing your hands, the gunpowder

319

residue will have faded by then anyway."

Everyone digested this information in silence. Plate locked up the bundle as he had indicated he would. The others were slowly filing toward the stairs.

Aerial came down, moving faster than usual.

"Everyone go on upstairs. Mrs. Janey Harriman's wound was not serious. She is bandaged and will be okay," Plate repeated, adding what Aerial had just reported.

"I will speak with you tomorrow," said Plate to Misha, as she passed by. She cast her eyes down but did not speak. "Mrs. Harriman will watch you tonight."

Aerial agreed emphatically. "I'll see to it she behaves. Come on, Misha."

She took Misha by the hand and led her away.

Daphne was the next to last to go. She went to Plate and kissed him on the cheek. "Good luck, Officer Plate," she said.

He grunted in reply and whispered to Randy.

Lastly, on Plate's orders, without questioning why, Randy dimmed the lights again, and otherwise fixed the electricity before going upstairs.

As soon as he saw that everyone else was settled, Randy positioned himself to watch surreptitiously and stealthily follow anyone who went down the staircase.

Also without questioning why.

Also as per Plate's instructions.

Chapter 49

Downstairs, after one last chore, Plate settled in on the chairs, propping his feet up. He figured he did not have long to wait.

And he was right.

He could not position himself at the staircase door. That would foil the trap.

So he was too far away to see the figure slip from the doorway and make her way directly to the Cowboy Display at the far back left of the store.

But he went running in that direction when the lights came on full speed and *Home on the Range* blared over the loudspeakers.

Randy had seen to it that the Cowboy Display was the only one with any power.

Randy had already cornered the figure who had climbed the display and taken the real gun, Plate's police gun, out of the cowboy's holster.

"Put the gun down, Miss Moore. You cannot do yourself any harm with it," Plate called to her.

"This is the real gun. All you have is a toy. I just want it back to kill myself," Laurel screamed, holding it to her temple.

"Miss Moore, please believe me, I do have a real gun. Your shell game with my police gun has been in vain. I have been armed all this time."

"Then kill me with it. I don't want to live anymore. I have nothing left to live for. My mother is dying. My brother was all I had left and he is dead."

"Your brother? The deliveryman? Mack Moore was

your brother?"

"No," she sobbed. "The boy in the witch's cauldron was my brother. Half-brother. My mother left Texas when she got pregnant with him after my father died. We lived in Ohio until I came home to Texas for college. He followed me. He got into trouble here. I tried to send him away. Now he is dead. My mother's lost her mind. I still had Randy, I thought but- I shot that bastard deliveryman that killed my brother. I killed him and pushed him out into the water."

Randy and Plate started towards her. Arthur came up behind them.

Daphne came through the staircase doorway with Eileen and Mark close on her heels.

"Stop," Laurel screamed, "All of you! Go back! I'll shoot."

"I took the bullets OUT of that gun!" Plate yelled at her.

"My child, listen-" Arthur began.

Laurel screamed and threw the gun at Arthur. He ducked but the action was enough to distract the other men and allow Laurel to jump the short distance from the Cowboy Display to the lift.

She quickly activated the controls riding all the way to the ceiling.

"Laurel!" commanded Randy. "Come down!"

"No," she screamed. "I am going to jump."

"Miss Moore, you killed Monica Moon? And Mack Brown? Surely in self-defense," said Plate.

"My dear, God can forgive you. Don't take your life!" said Arthur.

"NO!" Laurel yelled. "I killed the delivery man in cold blood and I killed Monica Moon in cold blood. She threatened to blackmail me and Randy. She said Randy would be humiliated because of me. She said she knew about us. And she would ruin the career of the man I loved."

"There's no way she could have known anything. There was nothing to know," said Randy.

"She did know! Somebody told her. Somebody gossiped. I got a note from her saying she knew about my affair with a married man and I had better convince him to pay the price. I did not know what she wanted. I had to kill her!" Laurel caught her breath. "I don't want forgiveness."

"How did you get that note?" Plate called. "Who delivered it?"

"She handed it to me herself! When I witnessed her life insurance beneficiary change."

Oh, no! Eileen thought quietly in despair. *That note was meant for me.*

As Laurel had been talking, Randy began climbing the Cowboy Display beside her.

Plate and Arthur began advancing towards her from the opposite direction.

Daphne went a different way completely.

"STOP! I'm going to jump!" Laurel yelled down at them.

"Child, you will surely not die from such a height. Only injure yourself, possibly grievously!" Arthur called out.

"Don't be a fool!" said Plate. "You could break your neck and be paralyzed for life."

Randy was as high as he could get on the Cowboy Display, standing on the cowboy's shoulders. But still it was not quite high enough.

He eyed two of the empty hooks mounted on the ceiling to hang the floor-to-ceiling curtains. He hoped they were strong enough to hold him.

At that moment Daphne reached the counter, picked up the microphone, and turned the PA system on. She didn't have to say anything.

The loud pop it made when activated distracted Laurel.

Randy grabbed the hooks and jumped at her.

Chapter 50

A few moments later Randy had gotten the lift to the ground and gone back upstairs to see about Janey. He let her, Aerial, and the Smiths know what had happened.

Plate and Arthur were guarding Laurel in the small manager's office by the front of the store.

She was trembling and hostile but no longer violent.

"Put me in the warehouse, let me sit with my brother," she said.

"I am sorry. I cannot do that," said Plate. He had mirandized her and placed her under arrest but then had nowhere to go with her until help arrived.

"Let me call my mother. She doesn't even know my brother is dead."

"I'm sorry. I cannot do that either."

"I should have shot you dead when I had the chance," Laurel said. "I thought you weren't any threat to me because I thought you didn't have a gun."

Plate was still carrying Daphne's .32. His own was now evidence. Laurel had admitted to using it to kill Mack Moore.

Randy came down to report Janey was asleep. Aerial was with her. The congressman had some sleeping medication on him and had lent it, against federal law, to the injured woman.

"It's going to be a long night." Plate indicated his sullen prisoner.

"Just let me go somewhere I can lie down. I promise not to do anything else," said Laurel.

"I can't-"

"There is a place," said Randy.

"Please, Randy. Somewhere I can rest?"

"The safe."

"I can't do that," said Plate. "She'll suffocate!"

"There's ventilation. It has a system built in. We just have to plug it in and turn it on. And it's big enough for her to lie down in. It's about 9 feet by 3 feet and 8 feet tall. And it is totally empty, just a steel vault."

"Suppose she beats her head against the wall or something?"

"Is there a viewer on the outside?" asked Arthur.

"Oh yes," said Randy to Arthur, then he spoke to Plate. "There is a little window. We used it as a courtesy booth when we cashed checks for customers. It originally was located against the back wall. Where the empty space is. You know, where we pushed the Carolers' Display when we had to move it from in front of the staircase door. It was also where employees kept their valuables while at work. After Marcus died, we stopped cashing two party checks so there was no need for it to take up space that could be used for merchandise. We moved it into his office, put in the lockers for the employees, and got an ordinary small safe for the cash."

"Please, Officer. If you will let me go in there so I can be alone, I promise not to cause any trouble. I just want to lie down."

"We can take turns watching her," said Arthur. "I'll take the first shift so you two can get some rest."

"I have to talk with her first, if she's willing to talk without a lawyer," said Plate. "But afterwards that's what we'll do."

"I am willing," said Laurel. "I don't need a lawyer. I'll tell you anything you want to know."

Arthur watched Laurel in the back office.

No one else was downstairs after Plate's interview with Laurel.

Plate had decided to remain downstairs permanently and had stretched out across the chairs near the counter from where he could still see the curtains hiding the Sleeping Beauty Display.

While lightly napping, he was still on guard and vaguely aware when Mark and Eileen came down the stairs an hour later. He pretended not to notice.

They crept by him and sat on the bench near the front door, now cracked but still an effective barrier against the rain.

"It's time to say goodbye, Eileen." Mark could not quite look her in the eyes. "If we see each other again-"

"We won't be seeing each other again, Mark," said Eileen. "I know it's more complicated than the fact that you realize you are married. And that you really don't love me."

"It is more complicated than that. You can't say that I don't love you," said Mark.

"When I volunteered to work on your campaign, our relationship never should have gone past friendship," said Eileen. "I see that now."

"You were the only person I knew who wasn't trying to use my position for their own advantage," said Mark. "I felt like you were my only friend. And our society has no social structure in which we safely can be friends, a married man and a single woman. Maybe someday society will provide some kind of structure, something we can't even imagine right now, that will allow people of all kinds to be friends with each other in a socially acceptable manner."

"I cannot imagine that ever happening. But if it does," said Eileen.

"If it does," said Mark.

"We'll still be friends?" Eileen asked.

"We will still be friends," Mark confirmed. "And I'll continue the allowance as long as you need it."

"No, that will not be necessary. I'm going to sell the condominium and move back to Georgia. I'll find a job there. There's no need for you to continue to support me."

"Well, if you ever need anything-"

"Goodbye, Mark. Good luck on your next campaign. I will follow you on television and in the newspapers. Tomorrow when they come get us, I will go back to pretending I don't know you. God bless you."

"Goodbye, Eileen. Don't think too badly of me when I cross your mind in the future."

They embraced stiffly but yet softly and walked away in different directions although they were going to eventually wind up at the same temporary destination, each with a slight smile, each already putting the other in the past and looking to the future.

Chapter 51

As he stood watch over Laurel, Arthur contemplated his statement to Daphne that he was single not by choice. He began to question its veracity.

Everyone told him he should be lonely and unhappy being single. He had accepted society's verdict on face value. But to tell the truth, he was not lonely or unhappy.

He thought back over the years since his wife had left him. Yes, it had often been expedient to leave Randy with Marcus and Aerial, but essentially he had raised the boy and could take full credit as a father, for better or worse.

It had been hard work raising a single child but many congregation members had lent a helping hand and, difficult to see at the time, he now realized Aerial had served as a mother figure to the boy.

Randy, while not conforming to his idea of a perfect son, was a fine man, who like everyone else, occasionally made mistakes, but without a doubt was a good, decent human being.

He knew many children of intact marriages, even the children of ministers and their wives, who had turned to criminality in the 1970s or worse.

He knew many married people who were miserable.

Was it possible he had been confusing society's definition of a happy life with the Lord's will for him?

The years as a single father and pastor of a growing congregation had been very fulfilling. He had many opportunities to keep company with eligible women. But he had always been too busy, too engrossed in promoting the church.

What social contacts he had with the opposite sex was usually with the goal in mind to bring his woman companion closer to the faith. Then secure in her faith, she could go ahead and find happiness with the mate the Lord had in mind for her.

Much as the insurance agent reserved her social activities for selling policies, he thought wryly, his social life had been reserved for evangelical pursuits.

And a single celibate life had been the simplest way to accomplish that. At least for him, he concluded. A little loneliness occasionally was a small price to pay. He had counseled many lonely married people.

Yes, that was what had been happening all these years, without him really knowing it.

Remarriage, always planned on someday, was for him, something he subconsciously had put in the category of sailing, traveling, fishing- something to do in retirement when he had time.

A perk, which if it happened, would be a great treat, but if not, would not be essential to his life's work.

He felt refreshed. Life would be easier now that he did not have feel so guilty for being happy with the circumstances life had dealt him.

He looked at the girl imprisoned in the steel box he stood before. She had fallen asleep on a Christmas blanket.

He started to pray for her.

Chapter 52

Not only had the rain stopped, the sun was shining and there were innumerable rainbows all over the greater Houston area.

Plate knew he wouldn't be leaving anytime soon.

In Marcus Harriman's office, Daphne Martin was beginning a turn watching Laurel, who had done nothing but sleep since being isolated in the courtesy booth safe.

Plate sat at a desk, in that same office, that had been crammed up against the wall to make room for the courtesy booth safe.

He had a notebook and pencil before him.

Just before dawn he had planted himself at Marcus Harriman's old desk, regardless of who was on duty watching Laurel. This was expedient. He could be on hand and yet sit at the same time, and doze occasionally. Not exactly rest, but better than standing. Volunteers keeping an eye on the prisoner had to remain standing to see inside the window.

When he let Plate know he was just too sleepy to continue, Arthur had finally been relieved by Mark about 5 AM. Daphne came on duty at 7 AM.

The paper before him was still mostly blank. However, Plate had the sequence of events somewhat arranged out in his mind, although he wasn't clear on everything.

To help clarify the situation, and in anticipation of writing reports for the next six months, he started writing down the sequence of events in first person, using the facts he knew and common sense speculation.

And above all, discretion.

Dated: November   , 1982

Location: Luxuries and Innovations, a specialty store located in the colony of Sand Waves, an unincorporated Command Design Colony collection of neighborhoods located south of Houston.

This store specializes in holiday displays, some of which figured in the crimes and are mentioned herein by titles they are commonly referred to.

Exceptional circumstances- the following crimes were committed while several persons were confined at the above mentioned store due to a massive flooding situation.

Most persons trapped in the store were uninvolved bystanders.

"Why did you leave the date blank?" asked Daphne, standing over him.

Plate stopped writing and looked up at her with some exasperation as she peered at his words.

"Because I cannot remember what the date is," he admitted.

"It's-" She stopped. "I can't either."

"What was the date of your appointment with Aerial? We'll figure it from that."

"Oh, I didn't really have an appointment with her. I usually take Fridays off. It was taking forever for her to finalize the application and pay. She was waffling. I had turned in her application without payment, arranged for the physical, we got the results and they were good. But she was hesitating. It's not unusual."

"So you just dropped in?"

"Fraid so. I could go get my calendar book or my checkbook calendar from my briefcase."

"I'll fill it in later," Plate said, and went back to writing. "I need one of those watches that shows the date and the time together."

"I almost bought one of those not too long ago," said Daphne. "But they are so unattractive."

She turned back to watching Laurel.

"Does this make sense?"

Plate began reading what he had just written aloud to Daphne.

"Prior to the flooding situation trapping people at the store, I had been assigned to keep the store under surveillance in a clandestine fashion as it was a possible target for the Detached Robbers, two criminals who had been operating in the greater Houston area for the past several months.

On this day, for the first time, they had committed murder in the act of committing robbery.

"So I was placed at the Innovations location to keep an eye out for any suspicious activity.

It was there that I was trapped by the floodwaters as was everyone else mentioned in this report."

"Sounds good," said Daphne.

"Great," said Plate. "I always have trouble explaining exactly how I come to be in these situations."

He started writing again.

Daphne stepped back over near him where she could

see.

Plate was more aware of her watching him this time.

This report contains a summary of events as I currently understand them and is subject to change later.

When he had first arrived at the store, robbery suspect Mack Moore, a white male, had put the body of his partner in the robberies in the Witch's Display cauldron and gone back to his truck, probably intending to flee but had thought better of it for two possible reasons.

One, he didn't have the papers that he anticipated would help him get into Mexico.

Two, he probably didn't know whether or not his partner's accomplice knew anything about him. He returned to the store. Fearing to be found with a gun, he hid the gun in a holster worn by a mannequin in the display known as the Cowboy Display. He hid his briefcase containing gloves, with the victim's blood on them, among the luggage promotion where Laurel Moore also hid a cosmetic case, resembling a large briefcase.

"I put my briefcase there also," said Daphne. "Not because I was trying to hide it. It is so heavy, especially with the gun in it. I just got so tired of carrying it all over the place."

Plate stopped writing.

"I'm going to have to give you some lessons about caring for and maintaining a firearm," said Plate. "Especially about just leaving it lying about anywhere you please."

"The briefcase was locked!" said Daphne. "There were no children anywhere around. How was I supposed to know there were criminals about the place? I was in a high end luxury store in Sand Waves, for heaven sakes. Supposedly one of the safest places in the world."

"Ha!" said Plate, picking up the pencil again.

"The briefcase was locked!" Daphne repeated.

"Oh, the briefcase was locked and that meant nobody could have ever gotten it open," said Plate facetiously.

"Go back to your writing," said Daphne.

"And about Sand Waves being one of the safest places in the world," said Plate.

"Yes?"

"Never mind." He turned his back to her.

Suspect Laurel Moore, a Caucasian female, had been the contact for the Detached Robbers, planning to aid her half-brother, an African-American, and his partner Mack Moore to escape to Mexico.

For clarification- suspect Laurel Moore and suspect Mack Moore share a common last name, but are not related. In fact, did not even know each other before these events. The third suspect, Mack Moore's partner and Laurel Moore's half-brother, had a different surname.

"What was it?" asked Daphne, glancing quickly at his words, then returning to her post. Her arms folded, she leaned against the booth, staring through the window at the sleeping woman inside.

"I'm not sure," Plate said. "She told me, but it was some long French name and I didn't quite catch it. It'll be in the records when I get back to my office."

"You have to admit, despite the commonality of the name, that Laurel and Mack having the same last name was quite a coincidence. And then Monica's married name, as well, being Moore."

"That might not have been Mack's real name. We don't know yet," said Plate.

"I'm sure it was though," said Daphne.

"Why?"

Daphne thought a moment.

"Because when he first said his name, he was proud of it. Made sure we all knew how to spell it, when there was no reason. No one was writing it down."

"Hmm, maybe. I'm writing it down now," said Plate, and resumed writing.

Chapter 53

The robbery at the Houston boutique resulted in the murders of three people by suspects, Mack Moore and his partner. Then they had quarreled and Mack had killed his partner somewhere on the way to the Innovations store.

"I have a question."

"Do you have to interrupt me?"

"Why didn't he get rid of the van?"

"Well, he didn't have time before the flood hit. Plus there was probably little blood in the van. The boy's body shows little blood in the cauldron. He was most likely killed with a blow to the head."

"But Mack had to get rid of the body."

"Right. And be quiet so I can finish this."

Evidence indicates the Detached Robbers had been coworkers, not friends, and neither had trusted the other so they knew little about each other. Forged birth certificates and driver's licenses found in Laurel Moore's cosmetic case indicated that Laurel Moore's brother had failed to indicate any information about his partner and the papers she had procured for Mack Moore were incomplete.

"Is it that hard to get into Mexico?"

"Haven't you ever been there?"

"No. I get free trips every year on convention. Mexico has not been one of the destinations. Otherwise, I don't care that much for travel. It's a waste of money."

"It's fairly easy to cross the border. All you need is routine identification, a driver's license and a birth certificate will do. They really just do random checks of those. But all of these people coming to Texas from all of these other states don't realize that. They think you need a passport."

Plate resumed writing.

Circumstances indicate not knowing this, and not knowing anything about their contact other than it was his partner's sister, Mack Moore had mistaken an innocent African-American woman for his partner's sister, feared she knew about him, and tried to kill her with a heavy lantern.

Plate put his pencil down. Then he erased the last paragraph.

"Why did you do that?" asked Daphne, looking over his shoulder again.

"We still don't really know Mack tried to kill Eileen. If he did toss that lantern at her, it was possibly just to get her attention. Or maybe he did think she knew too much. Either way it is a moot point. The Powers-That-Be may want to know Eileen's name and I'd like to keep her out of it. And after all, Mack is dead. His probable attempt on her life has no real bearing on the other crimes."

"Couldn't that show that he was dangerous and Laurel had reason to fear him?"

"She killed him in cold blood. She said so. For heaven sakes! She made an appointment to meet him with the intention of killing him. That her chances of success were minimal, until she got my gun, is also a moot point. In the end, she did succeed."

"If she realized he had tried to kill Eileen and that it was because he thought Eileen was his partner's sister, and

Laurel knew if he found out SHE was the partner's sister, he would try to kill her. Well, what was she supposed to do?"

"Go to the police. That would have been me." He picked up the pencil and began writing over the erased words.

"Oh. But you weren't in uniform. You were still wearing that theatrical costume."

"I was on the scene. She knew who I was by then. Even if I had not been here-"

He stood up, faced Daphne and put both his hands on her shoulders and looked straight into her eyes.

"Try to understand this. Planning and carrying out a cold blooded murder is illegal under any circumstances. Try to keep that in mind in the future."

"So," said Daphne, ignoring his sarcasm and moving closer to him. "Getting back to what you wrote here instead- *'evidence suggests failing to get any recognition from her'*- meaning Eileen- *'even after trying to kill her, he was at a loss as to who might be able to identify him, it never occurring to him that his partner's sister was white.'* "

"That's right," said Plate. As his hands fell away from her shoulders, he resisted the temptation to put his arms around her. He sat back down.

"Likewise Laurel had not known Mack must be her brother's cohort for she was expecting her brother's partner to be black," said Daphne.

"I know. That is what I wrote and that's true. But she was actually anticipating seeing her brother himself so she hadn't really thought about the partner much. She said she thought if she helped her brother get away to Mexico their mother might never learn about his activities and he might even reform."

"That sounds unrealistic."

"Very. After hearing about the killings in Houston, she did not know what to expect. She panicked and tried to leave but was flooded out. The congressman played Good Samaritan and brought her back. She was not sure whether her brother and his partner had made it through the flood to the store. She told me all that."

"But she must've seen the delivery van in the parking lot," said Daphne.

"She didn't say if she saw the delivery van in the parking lot or whether she even knew her brother and his partner used a delivery van. I didn't think to ask her that. She claims her connection to the robberies did not go beyond securing the fake travel papers. And providing them with clothing stolen from the store."

"That's why you and Randy and JW had such a hard time finding any clothes that fit. Laurel took most all the male costumes that looked like normal clothes. She just left a few so the racks wouldn't be empty."

"Yes, the boxes on the unfinished display were full of the men's costumes that Aerial assumed had been sold."

"Mack was supposed to carry them out to his truck?"

"Her brother was supposed to come for them. Mack had no idea about that," Plate said.

"She was expecting her brother to show up as the delivery man. Plate, that shows she knew about the van, knew details about the robberies."

"You know. You're right. She must have left the back

door unlocked for him," said Plate. He was amazed.

"Okay, what happened after it was not her brother that came in with deliveries? She didn't know if maybe he and his partner had just fled town, right?"

"Right. Then she noticed the substitution of the gun in the Cowboy Display which told her that probably her brother and/or his partner had made it to the store at some point in time."

"Are you going to put all the switching and moving of the guns in your report?"

"I'm just going to try to give a synopsis," said Plate.

"What did Laurel say about the guns?"

"This is the ironic part. While hiding his real gun Mack Moore had failed to hide the fake gun and left it lying on the platform. That's what caught Laurel's attention. She looked up at the holster expecting to see it empty, thinking some kid had been on the display, but there was a real gun in the holster. Laurel then pushed the toy gun out of sight. Not knowing where her brother was, or what to do, she had kept quiet. But she was now alert. And at that time, only she was on alert.

"I was still just following routine clandestine stake out procedure with no reason to suspect Innovations was really the next target of the Detached Robbers. Hey, that sounds good for my narrative."

He started writing again.

"Would you have ever revealed who you really were if they had not found the body in the cauldron?"

"Depends. Maybe. Randy and Janey knew who I was. Look I need to write some more of this, while it still fresh in my mind."

Daphne became silent, watching and reading as Plate continued to write, occasionally going over to the steel enclosure, glancing at Laurel, who slept on.

"The owners of the store discovered a body in the warehouse area. I secured the area, explained to everyone that there had been an accident and began to investigate the crime. The announcement of the discovery of the body caused Laurel Moore to suspect it might be her brother."

"Is that clear?" asked Plate, after he read it to her.

"Yes. I'll bet she noticed Mack's case. Found it, opened it, and saw the bloody gloves, probably confirming her suspicions that Mack was her brother's accomplice and had possibly killed him," said Daphne. "But she wanted to be sure and made attempts to get into the warehouse and see the body, finally succeeding, ironically because Mack's attempt on the life of Eileen distracted us."

"Us?" Plate asked as he wrote more.

Then, having slipped into the warehouse to see the body when everyone was distracted, she became sure, at that point, the victim was her brother.

"Yes," said Daphne, as she silently read the next part. "I did say 'us'."

Plate smiled.

"For your information, I had come to the conclusion that if one of the Detached Robbers was trapped with us, it had to be the deliveryman. Laurel must have come to that same conclusion," said Plate, thoughtfully. "She had realized Mack must have killed her brother, came to dump the body, meet her for the papers and mistook Eileen for her."

"Now you know he really did try to kill Eileen. You've got to put that back in," Daphne insisted.

"I do not," said Plate. "Leave me alone. I know how to write these reports."

Chapter 54

Evidence suggests suspect Mack Moore got his .357 from the Cowboy Display and hid it upstairs in the vent, where it left traces of gun oil, which adhered to the fur of the store cat, who climbs routinely in the vent.

Suspect hid his gun when he realized we were all going to be trapped here and the body was discovered so he didn't want to be found with it.

"Why did you never think to check the cowboy's holster?"

"I did. My gun was never in the Cowboy Display when I checked. Laurel was always careful to put the plastic gun back in the holster. Likewise, when I looked in the attic vent, all I found was gun oil. And not the type I use."

"You can tell?" asked Daphne.

"Yes, some are thicker and have a different smell. Depends on the brand. Anyway, Mack had retrieved his gun from the vent by then. Laurel had not put mine there yet."

"So, you just missed the guns," Daphne concluded.

"Bad timing," agreed Plate.

"When you took up guard at the door, Mack decided nothing was going to keep him from meeting Laurel and getting his papers," Daphne further surmised.

"Right. He hit me over the head, probably with the heavy lantern, took my gun and dragged me over to the sleigh. He probably thought I was dead or dying. The rolling chair caused it to be just a glancing blow and probably saved my life."

"Did Laurel know he was going to try to kill you?"

"She says she didn't. She said when she came down she just happened to see him putting me in the sleigh and saw what he did with the gun. She had been planning to kill him with Misha's dagger. She'd never been able to get her hands on Misha's weapon but she knew where it was. And those lockers were easily broken into, like those briefcases you all carry. That's why Laurel asked Mack to wait in the manager's office where she knew the dagger was accessible."

"Did she really think, as big as he was, she would be able to get the dagger and kill him with it?"

"I don't know. But when she saw him put my gun in the cowboy's holster she saw an opportunity to have a more effective weapon."

Daphne was silent again, contemplating what might have happened if Plate had not been sitting in a rolling chair.

He resumed writing.

Although she denies it, evidence suggests suspect Laurel Moore must have known suspect Mack Moore planned to assault or kill me. She states she followed him downstairs, watched him assault me and put me in a place where it would be hard to find my body. Then she saw him take my gun and hide it in the cowboy's holster. Although she was aware I was a police officer, she made no attempt to help me or alert anyone that I was injured or possibly dead.

"That adds several years to any wimpy sentence some bleeding heart jury may give her," said Plate, with satisfaction.

"Laurel then took your gun from the display, again being careful to replace the toy gun in the holster," said Daphne.

"Correct," said Plate. "That shows she is in her right mind, if you ask me."

Having illegally obtained a police officer's gun, she lured Mack Moore to the front door and shot him with my gun. His own gun went out the door with his body.

"Now comes the tricky part," said Plate.

"What?"

"I have to decide how much to reveal about Randy and Janey, the congressman and Eileen."

"Won't it all come out anyway?"

"Maybe. But Laurel's wanting to plead guilty. She's feeling a lot of remorse. There may not be a trial."

"Why did she kill Monica? Of all of them, she didn't seem to have a motive."

"You didn't have a motive."

"I didn't kill her, either."

"Monica wrote a blackmail note that was meant for Eileen."

"Oh. I thought the relationship between Mark and Eileen was obvious. How could they be blackmailed?"

"It was not obvious."

"You saw it, didn't you?"

"Eventually. Monica's blackmail note was given to Laurel by mistake, and she came to the conclusion that Monica was targeting her and Randy. But the note was about the congressman and Eileen."

346

"Laurel and Randy? But Randy so obviously loves Janey."

"Yes, that is obvious to you. And me. But not to Laurel. She took Monica's note as meant for her."

"So Monica didn't just stumble onto the situation?"

"No. Laurel had intended to kill both Mack and Monica and take the consequences. She had appointments with both of them, one after the other. She didn't really give herself enough time. But Monica was late. Laurel was able to shoot Mack, force the doors open, and push him out into the water. Thunder covered the sound of the shot, she said.

"She forced open Mack's briefcase, pulled out the gloves with her brother's blood on them, and left them to implicate Misha. Then she did get the dagger from Misha's mini-locker. She killed Monica, stabbing her in the back of the neck, placed her clumsily on the Sleeping Beauty Display, replaced Misha's dagger in the locker, and replaced my .38 back in the cowboy's holster.

"It was easier for her to hide the fake gun in the clothing she was wearing," Plate continued. "Her shirt was not only too light, but was still wet from pushing Mack out into the flood. She dried out, as much as she could, in the bathroom with the hand dryer. It was just bad luck that nobody noticed she was damp. Some of those expensive theatrical Halloween costumes repel water very well."

"Before she shot at Janey, the gun was in her case, after the attack, she got it back to the holster?"

"Right," said Plate.

"She had really learned from Mack's mistake of just leaving the fake gun lying on the display," said Daphne thoughtfully.

"That is what had alerted her in the first place or she might never have figured out who he was, never contacted him and killed him."

"She never touched Mack's gun? She just left it alone when she first saw it?"

"Right. That was an error on her part. She learned from that mistake also. She got my gun when she saw it. But after she shot at Janey and put it back, she had nowhere to go with the toy gun when everyone converged downstairs upon hearing the shot."

"No one who was innocent would have reason to be holding the toy gun."

"Right. She feared I would search her," said Plate. "After she fired at Janey, finding the fake gun on her would have been just as damaging as finding the real one."

"I'm glad you didn't suspect me," said Daphne.

"So she took the opportunity of the power surge to toss the plastic gun onto the floor," Plate continued, ignoring Daphne's comment. "When you snatched it up, having the presence of mind to grab a Christmas tree skirt to protect fingerprints, Laurel was suddenly faced with ultimate exposure."

"What chances she took," said Daphne. "It was all so entangled. Again, tell me, why did she kill Monica?"

"Killing Monica was the result of the note Monica had given Laurel when Laurel and Eileen witnessed Monica's beneficiary change. Eileen got a generic thank you note meant for Laurel."

"I remember that! I thought it was such a good idea."

348

"Monica thought it was Eileen that sent a note back arranging to meet with her," said Plate.

"But it was Laurel?"

"That's right. Here's the note from Monica," said Plate, opening up his file folder. "Just read, don't touch it."

Do not think what you are doing is going to be kept quiet. Men never leave their wives for their mistresses whether they love them or not. Attempting to break up a marriage will cause you nothing but grief and your lover is going to have to pay. This is to let you know that you had better cooperate and convince him to pay the price that I demand or I will see to it that he is totally ruined and will never be able to face the residents of this colony again.

I'll be happy to speak with you about this at your convenience.

Cordially yours,
Monica Moon

Chapter 55

"She SIGNED such a blackmail note?" Daphne was amazed again. "With a business letter complimentary close! But no salutation! That might have saved her."

"She was an arrogant woman. She boldly delivered it right in front of you. But to the wrong woman."

"It is so easy to mix up papers. What did Laurel's reply to Monica say? No signature there, I presume."

"No. Laurel says it just requested a meeting with the promise that Monica's blackmail would be paid. Laurel says she wrote to Monica that she did not understand what Monica wanted and would need to meet with her."

"Well, she really would not have understood."

"Regardless, that note has not been found. I only have Laurel's recitation of it."

Plate resumed his written narration. Daphne sat with him, reading silently as he wrote.

For some unknown reason, Laurel Moore replaced my gun in the holster on the Cowboy Display and armed herself with a dagger belonging to another store employee who kept it as a collectible. Ms. Monica Moon, a Sand Waves real estate agent, unfortunately came upon Laurel Moore right after the crime of killing Mack Moore. Ms. Moore then killed Ms. Moon with the dagger.

Daphne read this and smirked. "I notice you say Miss but write down Ms."

Plate looked at her and suppressed a smile and wrote-

After I recovered from being struck on the head, and

found myself without a weapon, Ms. Daphne Martin, an insurance agent, revealed she had a permitted gun on the premises. She thoughtfully allowed me to carry her gun during the duration of these events. Although I had cause to draw the gun, I had no cause to fire it at any time and returned it to her unfired. She is willing to produce it if necessary or required.

"That's J. Daphne Martin."

"I can look into that gun permit, you know."

"Go ahead," said Daphne. "You won't find anything. You better be nice to me. You might have to borrow my gun again someday."

"Can you shoot it at all?"

"A little."

Plate shook his head and resumed writing.

Next, suspect Laurel Moore attempted to kill Janey Harriman, wife of one of the owners of the store, again for unknown reasons.

Daphne smirked again. Plate glared at her and continued writing.

"You're supposed to be watching the suspect."

Daphne rose, leaned over a little, and peered through the small window again. "She is asleep still," said Daphne. "Murder is tiring, I guess. She is exhausted."

"You can see her breathing?"

"She's breathing. She's alive. Don't be so paranoid."

"She's my responsibility," said Plate, but he did not get up from his writings.

Again Ms. Moore was able to switch the toy and real

guns in the display. She was stuck with the toy gun, now as incriminating as the real one, as others, including myself, came on the scene.

At this point, during a power surge that temporarily killed the lights in the store, she threw the toy gun on the floor where it was retrieved in a quick thinking action by Ms. Martin, who wrapped it in a concealing cloth.

In cooperation with Ms. Martin, I pretended I did not know the fake gun was not real. Fortunately by this time the suspect, Ms. Moore, was in a highly agitated state and accepted this deception without question. She had become suicidal, (attach evidence of previous suicide attempt).

"You won't find any," said Daphne, back beside him again. "She would have told me about it. She told me about her drug addiction. And 'stuck' is not the right word to use. Find a better verb."

"Shut up," said Plate.

"If I just had a little more time with her, she would've told me everything." said Daphne, thoughtfully.

At this time, although I highly suspected Laurel Moore as the perpetrator of the crimes described herein and attributed to her, I did not know for sure it was her.

"You suspected her?" said Daphne. "Really?"

"Really," said Plate. "Could you let me finish this?"

After everyone went upstairs, ostensibly to retire for the night, I removed the bullets from the real gun, replaced it in the cowboy's holster, and waited downstairs.

Ms. Moore returned downstairs to get the real gun in order to end her own life, she claims. Her effort to do so was thwarted by myself and Randy Harriman, a former police officer, now part owner of the store, at considerable physical risk to himself.

"I owe a lot to the Harrimans that I won't be able to report," said Plate. "Janey came down to warn me after she heard first one person, then another, on the stairs. She did not wait for Randy to get dressed. That was brave."

"Laurel and Misha did not know each other had come down, obviously. Which one came down first?"

"Laurel. She got the gun out of her case while Misha went to get money out of the Little Red Riding Hood cloak. I got to the back of the store as Janey emerged and I told Janey to hide in the Caroler's Display, since she said Randy was on his way down. Thinking she was alone, Misha was not even trying to be quiet so I heard her. While Janey was hiding and I was distracted with Misha, by then we were in the manager's office, Laurel shot at Janey."

"And you cannot write all that down because?"

"Cause Aerial does not want to get Misha in trouble."

Daphne laughed at the indescribable expression on Plate's face.

It was at this point in time that it became clear that Laurel Moore was the killer of Monica Moon and behind the attempt on Janey Harriman's life. She admitted such before witnesses and also confessed to the killing of Mack Moore.

Chapter 56

"Is that all?" asked Daphne, when Plate folded his papers. "You know your grammar is terrible."

"It's just a rough draft. It's not going to be graded on grammar anyway. I have not had to answer to school teachers about my grammar for many years," said Plate. "I'm going to be rewriting and writing and rewriting reports about this for months, especially if it does go to trial. This is just something I can refer to when it gets to that, if it does."

"It would be nice to know that we actually are going to be rescued someday."

"They're coming. It's been a bad bad flood. But rescue shouldn't be more than 20 minutes away."

Plate was right. The first rescue boat showed up about 15 minutes later, manned by civilian volunteer rescuers. That it was little more than a canoe and could only take two people was far less important than what it brought.

Breakfast! Donated biscuit sandwiches and coffee.

Everyone cheered. Even Laurel smiled when she was awakened to receive her share. Plate oversaw as Daphne, Aerial, and Eileen went with her to the restroom. Then he escorted her back, let her eat, and watched her fall right back to sleep. Aerial took over watching her.

It had already been decided who was going first as the only boats able to get through the flooded roads were john boats and small speedboats.

Janey hid her injury from the rescuers, not wanting to go to a hospital. She promised her family she would have the scrape examined at an emergency clinic and told Plate she would give a statement as soon as it was feasible. Her injury had been bloody and painful, but minor.

So the congressman and the Smiths were the first to go.

They went to separate boats. The congressman, with only a briefcase, fit into a small john boat with another passenger from a nearby gas station.

JW and Deidre needed a large boat to accommodate their entire set of luggage. A volunteer who owned a 24-foot sailboat with a retractable keel, and fitted with an outboard motor, obliged. Already full of people who had been stranded in other locations, the owner strapped JW and Deidre's luggage to the deck and showed them where to hold on so they wouldn't get hit by the mast if it accidentally broke loose.

The congressman tossed a small roll of undeveloped 110 film into the water as soon as he was sure his boat was in a deep area. Monica's 110 camera remained in his coat pocket, where it had been since shortly after she died. No one could prove it had not always been his own.

Both JW and Deidre, their boat on a parallel course, saw him toss the film away but said nothing, not even to each other. They were attempting to be as inconspicuous as possible lest anyone noticed they were making off with the costumes belonging to Innovations, which they were still wearing.

There had been a last minute tiff between them. Deidre had told JW not to both wear a hat and carry one, to leave one behind. Randy, Janey, or Aerial would surely realize they were making off with the clothing. He had refused and said he would chivalrously take the blame alone if they got caught.

But no one noticed. As the boat puttered out of sight of Innovations, they relaxed and Deidre moved close to JW and he put his arm around her and they smiled at each other with love.

JW pulled out a box of cookies from his inside coat pocket and opened it.

Still parallel, the congressman saw them and wiped his eyes. No one in either boat paid any attention, everyone preoccupied with their own individual results from the flooding.

Then county officers in a small police boat came for Laurel. She was awoken again, handcuffed, and taken from the store still half asleep. A separate pontoon police boat, crewed by forensic technicians, carrying a deputy county coroner, came for the bodies. Routine procedures were completed. Plate turned over 12 rolls of film to the forensics department of the county, as Sand Waves Police Department had no forensics section or even a morgue. There would have been room on that boat for Plate but for a lifeless body that had just been found in the water on the way to the store.

Plate said that was no problem. He didn't mind waiting. In fact, thinking it over, he and his fellow law enforcement officials agreed it might be best if he waited until everyone else had been rescued.

Then an emergency on the freeway caused non-emergency rescues to be suspended again in the area. But a canoe manned by a volunteer came with room for one more person. Eileen went that time.

"Hey," said the volunteer to Aerial. "I haven't forgotten I owe you for that Christmas tree."

"Don't worry about it," Aerial told him.

"Sorry I cannot come back again," said the Christmas tree customer. "But they told me this is the last trip because they found a man's body floating near here and he had been shot. Only the police boats are coming in this area to pick up people from now on."

"That is okay," said Randy. "More police will be back here soon. We had one officer here with us all the time."

"You sure saved my life when you helped me load that tree," said the tree customer. "If I hadn't left when I did, if I had waited to pay for that tree, or had loaded it by myself, I would have drowned. Or been stuck here all that time and then my wife would have killed me."

"I hope the tree got home okay, so you can have a good Christmas. There is nothing like a great tree to make Christmas perfect," Aerial called to him, as he paddled away with Eileen waving.

Arthur sighed and held his head in his hands.

More sirens sounded from the direction of the freeway.

So Plate, Randy, Janey, Arthur, Misha, and Daphne had to wait a little longer to get home. Aerial, of course, was already at home.

Misha announced she was going to refuse to be rescued.

"It's my constitutional right not to be rescued. Plus, I have no place to go." she said. "I'll just stay here."

Plate thought about the comforts of modern jails.

"If it weren't for the fact that the Harrimans are not going to press charges, you would definitely have a place to go," said Plate.

"You can't do anything to me. I'm a juvenile," said Misha, smugly.

"Just how old are you?" asked Plate.

"You told us you are 18 but that's not true is it?" said Aerial.

"Okay, I admit it. I'm 16."

"Really?" said Plate. "We can find out, you know. The phones work now. I can get immigration records in a snap."

"Okay, maybe not quite 16."

"How much not quite 16?" Plate persisted.

"Like, maybe 14. I have Houston bus pass. I'm legal."

"Oh my God! You're 14 years old?" said Randy.

"I'm a very mature 14," said Misha. "Almost 15. And I really was evicted from an apartment. I rented it under some of my cousin's documents and they thought I was 18."

"Tell us about your experience at these apartments," said Randy, skeptically. He recalled Monica's words that Misha could not have gotten a lease in Sand Waves.

"It was in Houston," she admitted. "I may not have paid the rent. But I didn't have the money. I make too little here. We had to send money back to Vietnam to my relatives who got caught there. For them the money is life and death. They could be executed if they cannot pay bribes. I didn't want my parents to know. I will have to go live with them in West Houston. I kind of like it in Sand

Waves actually."

"My dear, I had no idea. You mean you've been living out there! Out there with those people, those homeless people under the bridge?" said Aerial.

"Yes. And they're not bad people, just caught in this economy. Nobody can buy a house unless they're rich or have a high paying job. Nobody can get a loan. They're just people like all of us down on their luck, and some of them are my friends, and had to drown in this flood!"

"My dear, my dear. You are so bright for a 14-year-old!" Aerial exclaimed.

"No one had to drown," said Plate. "Before the flood got too bad the Salvation Army and the Red Cross helped the police departments evacuate all the homeless willing to leave to safe shelters. The whole area has flooding but it's not a hurricane. As long as they're on higher ground everybody's going to be okay."

"You can come and live with me," said Aerial.

"Aerial!" warned Randy.

"Oh, I forgot. Ha ha. I may not have anywhere to go myself."

"I'm sure our friend the congressman can look into the situation and something can be worked out with the colony federation," said Arthur.

"I wouldn't bet money on that," said Plate.

"Having me here would just make it harder for you to get permission to stay," said Misha. "And I have already stolen from you. Not knowing you needed the money yourself! I thought you were rich. I tell you what. You get the police to give you my dagger. It is valuable."

"My church can find someplace for this child. The members of my congregation can take her in."

"No. I will not be coerced into changing my religion."

"I will guarantee no one will try to force you," said Arthur. "We will respect your wishes. If you come to the Christian faith it will be through the work of the Lord, not as the result of coercion."

"What about us?" asked Janey. "We could take her."

"Janey," said Arthur. "You and Randy need some time to yourselves to work out your problems."

"Everybody is forgetting about her parents," said Plate.

"My job is here at the store, here in Sand Waves," Misha sniffled. "I love the holiday store. I love working here. I didn't want to admit it. I was ashamed I was stealing. I wanted to hate the place. I wanted to hate everybody."

"Suppose all of you let me handle Misha's living arrangements," said Arthur. "Misha, you cannot stay with me, I'm a single man. But, I promise, I know people in my congregation who will let you stay with them."

"I'll have to go to church?"

"No one will force you."

"And on Sunday morning when they are in church they are going to leave me at their house and not worry that I will steal? I doubt that. You must have inhuman congregational people."

"That is not a problem that cannot be solved. We can work around it. All I am asking is for a chance to help you. No strings attached. And perhaps I can speak with your parents when the time comes."

Cassius took that moment to pounce on top of the unfinished display, causing boxes and loose ornaments to go flying.

"GET down from there," yelled Janey.

For a moment all eyes were on the cat. But then everyone focused on two objects revealed by the feline's action.

From underneath the clutter disturbed by the cat, Laurel's box cutter and hairbrush had become exposed on the platform.

"Good thing she forgot about that box cutter," said Misha.

"Yes," said Daphne. "Think of what she might have done with it. She must have become so focused on the gun and dagger, she never thought of that as a weapon."

"Praise the Lord for that," said Arthur.

"Amen," said Plate.

"I'll go get the cat food," said Aerial, walking away. "Here Kitty Kitty."

Chapter 57

So when the next police boat came with room only for four, Misha asked to go with Arthur. Daphne refused to go, insisting ladies first was antiquity, and Randy needed to be with his wife. They said a tearful goodbye to Aerial, who was determined to wait out the inevitable subsidence of the water and stay in her home.

"I won't starve," she told them. "I have plenty of candy. When the pizza parlor delivers, I'll have lots of pizza."

Plate recalled his words when the pizza place called earlier. Hopefully, they would forget that phone call.

Aerial did, however, beg off to go upstairs, taking Cassius, leaving Police Lieutenant Sinclair Plate and Insurance Agent Daphne Martin alone among a lot of still beautiful but slightly disarrayed Christmas decorations and displays.

After getting her clothes sufficiently dry enough to change out of the movie star costume, Daphne sat down beside Plate on the bench in the lobby. He was reading his science fiction book again. Daphne looked over his shoulder and read along for a few paragraphs. There seemed to be some romance in this science fiction book. At least the female character named Sophia seemed aware that romance was possible. But the hero seemed to be preoccupied with battling the bad guys and talking to his cat.

Daphne sighed loudly. Plate ignored her and kept his eyes on the book.

Daphne began to think of questions to interrupt Plate's reading. She started with-

"So do you think Misha really lived under the bridge with the homeless?"

"Yes, apparently she's a runaway." Plate answered that one without looking away from the book.

"I don't understand how that could be happening. We have such prosperity all around us. Whatever do you think the outcome of the homeless situation will be?" said Daphne, her voice somewhat demure.

Success! Plate put the book down and gave Daphne all his attention.

"I don't really know but something has to be done. There's a lot of homeless people right now, especially near here," he said, "who are not completely without means, just without anywhere to live. Formerly upper class, refugees from the latest financial downturn."

"Well, I guess I just don't understand it all," said Daphne, whose BBA major had been economics. "I suppose those type of homeless people might not do her any harm."

"From my experiences with them, they probably tried to help her," said Plate. "She probably picked up her knowledge of the economy from them."

Daphne relaxed. She had his full attention now. The unfinished paperback was now in his pocket.

"I suppose Misha will not really be able to return to her job here."

"Of course not," said Plate. "She is too young to work. She won't be staying in Sand Waves either. Whatever plans the good reverend may have for her, she will have to be returned to her parents. I don't think she told the truth anywhere along the line here. I doubt her parents escaped from Vietnam. She might not even be Vietnamese. Is Misha a Vietnamese name?"

"I don't know," said Daphne. "I don't have any Vietnamese clients."

"Doesn't sound Vietnamese to me," Plate judged, without having any idea either. "She had no type of ID. The last name she gave me was unpronounceable, just a bunch of consonants. I think she made it up."

"Misha could just be a nickname," suggested Daphne.

"Yeah, right. HPD will deal with her. She is probably just a standard runaway, turned thief to survive, who happens to be of Asian descent. She probably stole the dagger from some elderly senile person that lives under the bridge."

"You are destroying my faith in my fellow human beings!" Daphne protested.

"Yeah?" Plate said. "Well, I could be wrong." His tone of voice indicated he thought no such thing.

"And we are to assume the floating body the Christmas tree customer talked about was Mack the deliveryman?"

"Yes, that's been confirmed as much as possible under the circumstances. The man fits Mack's description and was wearing the same type of clothes. His gun was still in a concealed inside pocket in his shirt."

"Why do you think he was stupid enough to trust Laurel?"

"He had no reason not to trust her once she contacted him. Because Laurel admitted that once they had connected, she let him believe she cared nothing about her brother's death and was willing to go away with him because of all the money he had from the previous robberies."

"Oh, so she let him think she thought he was attractive." Daphne squirmed a little bit. "Men do fall for that. Was he really a deliveryman?"

"Apparently so. I am sure we will find he made deliveries to all of the places that have been robbed. I suspect that when Laurel's brother decided to quit, Mack decided to kill him."

"And he never considered that his partner's sister was white," Daphne repeated, wonderingly.

"And, at first, she didn't think about the possibility her brother's partner wasn't black."

"Mack lied about never going into parts of Houston with very many blacks?"

"Of course he did. That lie, like different stories about where he lived, was obvious from the start. But it was not conclusive. It could have just been a vanity lie."

"A vanity lie?"

"You know, a lie to impress or, more complicated, to both impress and generate approval of those listening at the same time. Vanity lies tend to change frequently depending upon the audience targeted."

"How could Laurel know her brother was dead in that cauldron and not show any emotion?"

"But she did show emotion. When she heard the description of the boy, she was distraught. But so was Aerial Harriman. They were distraught for different reasons. A death in the display was going to taint this business, Aerial feared. Everyone thought Laurel's emotion was just paralleling Aerial's."

"What's going to happen to Laurel's cat? She kept talking about it."

"Animal control will take it from her apartment if she really has a cat. Her supposed affair with Randy Harriman was not exactly real. The cat might not be either. Most apartment complexes don't allow pets, so it is probably a cat that hangs out in the facility, mooching scraps, sheltered here and there by sympathetic dwellers, but not too long by any one person so as not to get caught with it. We have an apartment cat where I live. It spends the night with me about once a month. I put out a little cat food beneath the shrubbery whenever I think about it."

"I have a real cat," said Daphne. "She is a wonderful companion. When I go out I leave her in my garage and she is fine for several days without me so long as I put out food and water. Which she has plenty."

"And you have a real business, I presume?" Plate laughed.

"Of course."

"Apparently all Laurel's cosmetic business ever consisted of was her buying the starter kit. It was all intact when we opened it. She had never sold any cosmetics."

"Poor woman," said Daphne.

"I don't have any sympathy for her. She killed two people and attempted to kill one other. She thought she might as well kill Janey Harriman, the one person she really hated, after having killed Mack, a stranger, and Monica Moon, also a stranger."

"Are you really going to keep it quiet between the congressman and Eileen in the long run?"

"It's better if we don't talk about that."

"There's just you and me here. Nobody can hear. I was here during it all, you know."

"Yes, they are probably going to call you to be a witness."

"I'll bet there's never even a trial. They'll take one look at Laurel and say 'poor single sexually repressed female, terrified of the biological clock. Must be a mental case. If only she had found the right man and gotten married and had some children, all this tragedy could have been averted'. "

Plate shrugged his shoulders. "Whatever it takes to lock her up for good. If she doesn't get the death penalty. It's coming back, thank goodness. Lethal injection. First one in six years scheduled next month. Don't forget what I told you about making an appointment with someone and then killing them."

Daphne threw a plastic Christmas ornament at him.

Chapter 58

Daphne glared at Plate. "If I write my version of these events, I could probably get you in trouble," she threatened.

"Let's talk about something that will get you in trouble," said Plate, smirking at her bluff. "Apparently Deidre and JW's insurance company is on the skids. So much for being rich."

"Oh, they'll come out of it all right. They've got layers of liability insurance somewhere. All the policyholders will be okay too. The taxpayers will bail them out."

"I hope that idea doesn't spread."

"I'm sure it won't. Insurance is a unique field. People pay money for something they hope they never use but if they find out it's not available, they run to the government and complain and yell 'illegal, criminals at work!'. Then government steps in, passes meaningless regulation and my paperwork load goes up again."

"Complaints about illegalities and criminals are the forces that generate my paychecks. They tend to be more concrete complaints. But the paperwork is there too."

"How long have you been a cop?"

"Oh, since I was 21. I was drafted as soon as I got out of high school in 1973. I would have been an MP in Nam but never got out of the states as the war was winding down by then. When my two years in the army was up I went right to the police academy. I never thought of doing anything else. It was all I ever wanted."

"Aren't you a little young to be a lieutenant? Aren't you supposed to be at least a chief to wear a white hat like that?"

"Our police force is only seven people. There is a chief. He also wears a white hat. There's no deputy chief or captain. There's just him, me, and the other officers."

"So you're second in line? Are the other five all younger than you?"

"No, it doesn't work that way. I have a degree. After the police academy, I started going to night school."

"I have a BBA. You don't have to have a degree to be an insurance agent but they would not have hired me if I had not had my degree. The unofficial rules are different for women," said Daphne. "I suppose your degree's in criminology?"

"Yes. I have a bachelor's degree, earned a couple years ago. And now I'm working on my master's."

"Really? So you are able to get into a master's program in college and you still want to remain a policeman?"

"Oh, it's family tradition, sort of. My great-grandfather was a famous lawman in the 1900s. And most of us have been police ever since."

"Really? What was his name?"

"Dell Plate."

"Never heard of him."

"Well, he was famous in his own time."

"What did he do?"

"It is hard to explain exactly. He got mixed up with a beautiful woman who was the daughter of a famous politician and involved with a musician who was celebrated throughout the world in the early 1900s. It's complicated.

Somebody wrote a book about it."

"What was the title?"

"*Murder as the Organist Plays*," recalled Plate, with a little difficulty.

"That's a strange name for a book about a Texas policeman," said Daphne.

"You just have to read it."

"Still in print?"

"Probably not. I've got a family copy somewhere."

"I'd like to borrow it sometime. I love old books like that. It sure is hard to find books out of print. You have to just hit the exact right little used bookstore at the exact right moment. Someday there's going to be an easy way to buy and sell used books. Where it is not so hard to find exactly what you want."

"Yeah, okay. Let's be real. Maybe in some sci-fi fantasy future. Not in our lifetimes. That sounds like some of the stuff I read."

"You like to read detective novels?"

"Sometimes. I mostly read science fiction."

"I would think you would be a big fan of say, *Colombo*."

"I am. That's TV. Reading books is different."

"So is that why you go by your last name? To be like the TV detective?"

"No, that has nothing to do with it."

"Then, what is your first name? Is it a secret?"

"No, of course not. It is Sinclair."

"Really? Sinclair?"

"Yes, really. I'm not in the habit of lying to people

about my name."

"I would not blame you."

"I told everyone what it was when I introduced myself after the first body was found."

"I forgot. So why were you not named for your famous ancestor? Dell. Nice. Unusual but dignified."

"Oh, my brother got that name. He's older."

"Does sound like some company name to me. Like Southwestern Bell. Do people call him Dell?"

"My mother does. I don't know what he tells people outside the family to call him. Probably just Plate, like me. I don't stop people from calling me Sinclair. Just nobody ever calls me that, not even my mother. And I'm not going to be called Clair or Sin. You can understand my objections to both of those. So you see why I just go by Plate."

"What about a middle name?"

"I have one."

"What is it?"

"Now that, I'd rather not say, let's just leave it at that," said Plate. "I will tell you, however, it is an old, traditional name."

"So it must be outrageous. Hezekiah, Josephus, Methuselah?"

"I can assure you it is a perfectly normal name."

"Not from the Bible, eh?"

"Actually it is in the Bible. Quite prominently, actually."

"So what is it?"

"I'll have to swear you to secrecy."

"It's a common normal biblical name. But it is a

secret?"

"Yes."

"Okay, I swear. Tell me."

"Peter."

"Peter, why that's a nice name- oh!" Daphne burst out laughing.

"You see?"

"Sinclair Peter Plate."

"Yes, my mother has a perverse sense of humor. Peter by itself, perfectly fine. Plate by itself, okay. But together? So I just say Sinclair, in an unfriendly tone of voice and scowl. Usually nobody asks for more. I do have a gun."

Daphne collapsed in laughter. "Your secret is safe with me."

"It's a shame in a way. If I had my preference, Peter is the name I would use. Or I would just follow the modern trend of going by initials but SP doesn't work. It doesn't have that ring to it like JW or JR."

"Yeah, and it stands for 'misspelled word' or 'salt and pepper'."

"Reversing it to PS doesn't work either. And of course, the initials P and P…" He grinned.

When Daphne had recovered from near hysterical laughter she asked, "if your mother does not call you Sinclair, what does she call you?"

Still grinning, he hesitated again. *Might as well tell her everything.*

"Petey."

Daphne continued laughing, but regained control. "What did you ever do to your mother?"

"She really doesn't hate me. Petey, that was her little brother's name. He was lost in Korea."

"Oh, I'm sorry." She stopped laughing.

"I never knew him. It's okay."

Daphne coughed to try to hide excess joy that was fighting to be let out.

"My mother forgot men don't change their names when they marry." He laughed, trying to recapture the levity. "And so what is your full name? What does the J stand for?"

"Jeanne Daphne Martin."

"And why Daphne, not Jeanne?"

"Well, I love my name. I love Jeanne. But you know there's that program from when we were kids, still in reruns every day. *I Dream of Jeannie.*"

"One of my favorite shows, one of my favorite characters, beautiful bright perky bubbly. Sparkling and funny and sunny."

"Yes, that's just it. I am trying to be taken seriously in a man's profession. I am one of the first female insurance agents ever hired by my company. They didn't want to do it. Jimmy Carter made them, to make a long story short, and most of the others have already failed. They put a lot of obstacles in our path. They don't really want us."

"How do you fail, other than just not making enough money, at a job like yours?"

"In the beginning during the training period, you are under a contract, there is a quota. And it's easy to make the quota. In fact, it's so easy that in the beginning, most people go way over the quota. But in the fine print it says that for every time you go over the quota, the quota for the next month goes up. So the trick is to only meet the quota, never exceed it. That way it remains realistic. But most people are trying to do as good as possible as soon as possible. Family members and friends step up to buy policies to help you out. So what happens usually is, in the middle of it all, the quota suddenly becomes mathematically impossible to meet. This gives the company complete control over who they really want to keep as agents. Most of the men get excused several times if they don't meet their quotas, but the first time a woman doesn't make her quota, she's out."

"I wouldn't think they could get away with that. Isn't that discrimination? That contract sounds like communism."

"Oh, but they do get away with it. All the women they dismissed as agents were given nice jobs as secretaries or clerks or policy service providers. Deep down, we are told, we women who have to work really want the security that comes with a daily routine and guaranteed paycheck. The salary this company pays is quite generous, no matter what your position. The failed women agents all got good jobs so nobody complains."

"But that didn't happen to you?"

"No. I met my exact quota every month for 18 months. Never less and never much more. Then I was free and clear. I went on full commission. Everything I make now is mine except for a small cut that my general agent gets for providing me an office. I am my own boss. I call my own time. As long as I can make enough money to pay my bills, I'm okay."

"You have to come up with your own customers?"

"Clients. Yes, and there is keen competition."

"The name you go by matters," he concluded.

"Yes. So I went with Daphne, somewhat less serious than Jeanne actually, but without the connotation. Don't get me wrong. I love the actress. I like the show. But it's just that it is still what comes to people's minds when they hear the name, like Samantha is a witch and Lucy is a red headed housewife."

"What about that cartoon character?"

"What cartoon character?"

"Don't you watch cartoons?"

"Certainly not, what an insulting thing to say! I'm 27 years old. I don't watch cartoons. I haven't watched cartoons since I was 6. That was 1960!"

"Sorry, never mind."

"Cartoons indeed!" She moved away from him just as he was being tempted to put his arm around her.

"I'm sorry! Anyway you could not be less like-"

"Less like what?"

"Less like anyone I've ever known," he said seriously.

"Oh, well, okay. Thanks, I guess." She was mollified a little.

"So can I call you Jeanne? If I promise not to think of you living in a bottle, not that you don't look- Don't look at me like that! Hey! You are more beautiful than she is, in my opinion."

"Very funny. I don't really look like her if you study us both. And she is beautiful. I don't compare, but in an ordinary crowd, well I do stand out."

"How does that affect your being a sales agent?"

"Well, I could downplay my looks, wear glasses or something. But why should I? I know that there is a certain percentage of my clients who maybe chose me over some other insurance agent because of my looks. After all, the policies are all pretty much the same. There are just as many that turn me away. Women who don't want me around their husbands. I could dress down for them. Leave off my makeup. But I am not going to. I am going to look my best always."

Daphne turned away. She was a little embarrassed to have revealed all this. After all, he was really a stranger.

"We're like people on a ship, stranded here," he said, as if reading her mind. "I have told you a few things I usually would never mention."

"Ships passing in the night?" asked Daphne, hoping the catch in her voice was not noticeable.

"Maybe," said Plate. "So can I call you Jeanne?"

"When I can call you Peter, you can call me Jeanne," she said, trying to strike a light tone, but inwardly quite serious about that declaration.

He laughed, "Now you're talking about ships colliding in the night."

Chapter 59

Another forensic team arrived to continue the work, in the store and its warehouse, collecting evidence left behind after the removal of the bodies.

Hearing there were still a few people left to be rescued, they considerately brought some extra sandwiches that would have supplemented their own lunches, but they offered to share.

Plate had chicken salad. Daphne ate the pimento and took the ham and cheese upstairs to Aerial, who was back in her own bedroom. Aerial interrupted her sleep long enough to wolf down the sandwich. Daphne returned to Plate.

"I don't think I'll ever feel the same about Sleeping Beauty," said Daphne, as the display was dismantled and torn apart for evidence. "Just goes to show what can happen if Prince Charming does show up. You can get the life crushed out of you."

"Well, what actually killed Monica was the stab to the neck. It just looked like she was crushed between the two animatronic figures. There was actually a safety mechanism that caused both mannequins to bounce back when they detected an object caught between them. Monica was already dead from the dagger wound."

"Was her jewelry ever found? She had a Rolex didn't she? And not a few diamonds on her fingers and wrists?"

"Yes. Laurel had taken it all upstairs and planted it in Misha's bedding. She expected everyone's personal belongings to be searched but I didn't have the authority to do that, not clear authority anyway. Everybody watches too many movies."

"One of my favorite new shows this season is about a detective who solves the cases by knowing all the movie plots."

Plate pulled out his science fiction novel. "That's ridiculous," he said, opening it and beginning to read.

"The actor's really good looking. He doesn't have that unkempt long hair. His hair is cut nice, like yours."

While Daphne failed to distract Plate from his book, a forensics team member managed to get Plate to put down the book by requesting that he point out all the locations involved in the activities of the last few days.

"We're going to be here all night!" said one of them to a coworker, after surveying all that Plate indicated.

"With these flood waters no one can still get very far. The police boat had to bring me all the way in from my area where water is lapping at West Houston," said another.

They forgot all their logistical troubles when they discovered the bloodstained dolly. Hungrily they started taking it apart.

Phone conversations with civil defense authorities had informed Plate and Daphne that both of them would be able to get to their homes due to the locations of their respective dwellings in Sand Waves.

Once another rescue boat became available.

Daphne's house had not taken in water, being in the lower echelon colony, price wise, which was farthermost from the Gulf and thus on the highest ground.

Plate lived in the third floor of the apartment complex which had just enough water to flood the parking lot basement. His personal car was ruined there, as was

Daphne's car in the Innovations parking lot. He had a 1977 Impala and she drove a 1981 Pontiac Bonneville.

His patrol car, parked a block away, like most of the cars in most of Sand Waves that had not been driven onto higher ground before the floods, was flooded as well.

Inside the warehouse, the off season displays had to be uncovered and searched, just in case something had been hidden there. But none of the displays, either in the store proper or behind the warehouse wall, needed to be destroyed, and only the Sleeping Beauty Display was dismantled. It was the only casualty inside the store, besides the victims.

Plate abandoned his book long enough to stand with Daphne as they observed the forensics people unveil the last of the displays that had been stored behind the witch and her cauldron. All others, including a large Fourth of July Display, had been quickly gone over and dismissed by the scientists.

"Will you get special consideration from the car insurance companies?" asked Plate, as the patriotic scene was recovered and the technicians started climbing on the one beside it.

"No, when it comes to casualty insurance I'm just like any other policy holder," said Daphne. "I don't even get a discount on premiums."

Watching from the warehouse doorway, Daphne and Plate were distracted from their vehicular losses by the unzipping of the tarp of the final display, the large impressive Valentine's Day Display.

The display consisted of two lovers holding each

other as they sat in a wooden and metal swing. Dressed in 1950s spring clothing, the female mannequin dropped her head on the shoulder of the male who had his arm around her. Both figures had been facially repainted so that their eyes appeared closed. In his hand, the male mannequin held a diamond ring. When turned on, the swing gently rocked back and forth. Rounding out the display were spring flowers, birds and butterflies.

The display was so simple that it was striking compared to the other complicated elaborate scenarios Plate and Daphne had become used to during their confinement in the store.

For a short time both Plate and Daphne were silent.

"And what about you, Lieutenant Plate? Do you have a girlfriend?" asked Daphne, trying to strike a light tone in her voice as the sound of an outboard engine coming towards the store became louder than the sound of the motor that powered the Valentine's Day lovers' swing.

Plate paused before answering. "Yes, I do." Both his voice and his look were somber.

Daphne became somber too. Turning away from the Valentine's Day Display, they began walking towards the front of the store.

They soon spotted the red and blue lights of a police boat approaching, causing a disco effect for a moment as the rotating lights hit the glass windows of the store just the right way.

"Oh, I see. You are spoken for." Daphne spoke again as they arrived back in the lobby.

"I uh- she is recently divorced. So our relationship is

on the slow track."

"But serious."

"I- yes it has become serious. For me at least."

"So, then I guess I will not be seeing you again. Unless of course I need the police and you show up at my house?"

"I work behind the scenes most of the time. I don't do routine reports, but- possibly." He stopped and she stopped and he took a long look at Daphne as if trying to commit her face to memory.

"Possibly?" She looked unexpectedly bright and pretty.

"I might could use some life insurance in the near future. Do you write policies on police officers?"

Daphne struggled to control the happiness she felt at this request. "Are you in good health?"

"Excellent!" He was not looking at her, but watching the boat out the front windows.

"Smoke?"

"Certainly not."

"Exact age? You have to tell me. The premiums depend on your age."

"I'm 29. I usually say 30. That won't be true until later next year."

Two years older than me, thought Daphne. "If you get a policy before you turn 30, you'll save a substantial amount of money. So how much money do you make? I have to ask that question to everybody so that you don't take out a policy out of proportion to your regular income."

"Really? Well, my salary is public record."

"Yes, a face value policy more than four times your salary is a red flag for suicide risk. Policies don't pay off for two years for a suicide no matter what. But there are the questionable deaths and some people are more patient with plans to do away with themselves than generally acknowledged."

"$14,000 a year, I get $3,000 extra because of my rank," he said proudly, turning back to her. "What about you?"

Signals from the boat indicated it was as close as it could get since the flood waters had receded a little. They were going to have to go out the door and wade in the parking lot water.

Plate automatically took Daphne's briefcase for her as she retrieved her umbrella from the still substantial pile by the front door.

"Oh, uh, you know I work on commission. So it varies."

Daphne had actually made almost $51,000 so far in 1982. While she didn't make $7,000 every month, she had made almost $48,000 the previous year and that was with taking part of November and all of December off. Plus in the summer, she had earned convention travel to Hawaii, having been to Delaware the previous year, Canada before that. All expenses paid.

"And I get two weeks vacation a year," he continued as they exited the front doors of the store. "Also I have a pension. All this is for working about 60 hours a week though. I work most weekends and holidays. I earn it all."

"Wow," she said, as she realized she could not walk

in the water with her heels. She stopped and took them off.

Daphne had a pension, profit sharing plan and stock options. She aimed at working 20 hours a week, definitely no more than 25. If clients demanded more of her time she compensated by taking a week off here and there throughout the year in addition to five or six weeks during the holidays. She never worked a weekend or any holiday and usually took off on Fridays.

Plate picked her up then, saying quickly that she couldn't walk barefooted in water filled with debris. Her shoes, the briefcase and the umbrella were sandwiched between them as he carried her to the boat.

The boat operator helped her aboard. The briefcase sat across her lap like a table as Plate climbed in. Facing her in the small boat, he signaled to the driver when they were both safely settled in.

Both she and Plate were still completely dry above the knees. She slipped her dry heels back on over wet hose. Plate squeezed the water out of the bottom of his trousers. The temperature was soaring into the 90s so they would soon dry out.

"Well then," said Daphne, still examining how it had felt to be in his arms.

"So you have no objection to having a client in law enforcement?" Plate asked, picking up the conversation from where it had been interrupted by the boat's arrival. "I've been told some companies don't like us."

"Despite your high risk profession, I can get you a good rate, Lieutenant. My card." She pulled a business card from her jacket pocket. "Shall I call you? Or? Or wait for you to call me?"

That was the least desirable option. He might never call.

"Tell you what." He took the card and put it in his pocket. "If I haven't called you by, say, oh-" he pictured the Valentine's Day Display in his mind, "by say, Valentine's Day, you call me at the station and we will set up an appointment."

They both had to speak a little louder as the boat engine revved. The ride was slow and smooth though. The driver had to carefully manipulate the boat around stop signs, telephone posts, and the rooftops of drowned cars.

On either side of them water lapped at the roof eaves of one story houses, remaining below the upper floors of most second story houses. Despite its murky brown color, the sunlight caused the water around them to glisten as the boat proceeded.

Plate pulled his paperback book from his pocket and opened it near the end and started to read.

Daphne slowly opened her briefcase and carefully extracted her appointment book, closed the case and set the book on top. She then popped the book open with what she hoped would be a causal gesture.

"Will do, Lieutenant," she said loudly, but lightly with a smile.

He glanced up from the book and returned her smile briefly. Then resumed reading.

She flipped her appointment book to mid-February 1983. The section was blank, without any scheduled encounters, as it was months away and furthermore contained a holiday. She tilted the book towards her so he could not see the pages if he looked up from his paperback.

On the page containing the Valentine's Day date she wrote in big letters covering the entire sheet-

Lieutenant Sinclair Peter Plate, single male, age 29.

Beside those words she drew a big Valentine Heart.

She slapped the book shut and dropped it back into the briefcase and they rode together in comfortable silence as the little motorboat taking both of them home glided on down the streets of Sand Waves.

Also by Deborah DR Kralich-
Historical Fiction
    The Mystery of the Missing Persons

Historical Mystery Fiction
    Murder as the Organist Plays
    The Mystique Woven in Our Land
    Interlude of Carelessness

Lt. Sinclair Plate Mystery Series
    An Innovative Murder for the Season
    The Ruler of the Toys
    A Kaleidoscope of Masquerades
    The Unknown Puppeteer

Short Stories
    Show Up
    Poised Like a Knife

The Ruler of the Toys- second in the series

"An in depth mystery that explores social change in the 1980s while being highly entertaining. Part of a series but not necessary to read them in sequence. More serious and thought provoking than the first, still enjoyable in the tradition of old fashioned mysteries." 1983 spin says the days of racial hatred are over. Yet prejudice leads to murder in a mystery which reaches back a century, finding the age old motives devaluing lives of some, while enhancing others are the same as ever. Innocents are the victims when sin becomes legal. The world is changing in the 1980s and the new generation is having to cope with the legacy of the old. Elites would like to forget the social ills of the past and proclaim the new social order has arrived. But the boast is premature. Intolerance and prejudice are major factors in the murder of an innocent woman who should have been without an enemy in the world. Tamica was a threat to no one and would have little claim to notoriety if not for being the granddaughter of a living legend. Amelia Mattworks is 94 and beloved as an entertainer of color who withstood the bigotry of the early 20th century, though numerous tragedies cost her most of her family. In the eyes of her fans, even if her soap opera life did make good drama, Amelia did not deserve the heartbreaks of the past, and much less this compelling new tragedy in the winter of her days. But rather than compensate for the appalling treatment that the high society of the first half of the century meted out to her and her family, those in power in the second half are oblivious to Amelia's latest suffering, or patronizing at best, when she suddenly loses her only granddaughter to a murderer. Lt. Sinclair Plate, second ranking officer in the tiny police force in the community where Amelia lives, is shouldered with the responsibility of protecting the only surviving blood relative the famous diva apparently has left- the 16-year-old daughter of the victim, also the seemingly inexplicable target of the murderer. Surrounded by in-laws who are strangers, jealous competitors from the past, contemporary fortune hunters, and disloyal employees, the vulnerable Amelia, and her pregnant great-granddaughter, are encompassed in danger from all sides. The absence of motive for the murder and continuing threat is balanced with a plethora of suspects for the detective to choose from. They range from the famous- politicians, rights activists, sports figures, movie stars- to the ordinary- servants, security guards, medical and security personnel, even apparent drifters. Before he can expose the masquerade of the killer, Lt. Plate has to uncover and understand deep dark secrets of long vanished eras. Eager to delve into history with Lt. Plate, exploring superstitions and evils of ages gone by, is insurance agent Daphne Martin who has a secret agenda of her own. Plate and Daphne find sins of the past have long tentacles that reach far into their own times of the 1980s, and threaten to multiply in their future which, for the reader, is now. Before the end, this 1980s couple must make life and death choices in a world where good and evil have blurred and a wrong decision is fatal. Second in a series with the descendant of a 1900s law man and his insurance agent girlfriend. 350 pages in 12 Pt Times New Roman Font, 6 by 9 paperback.

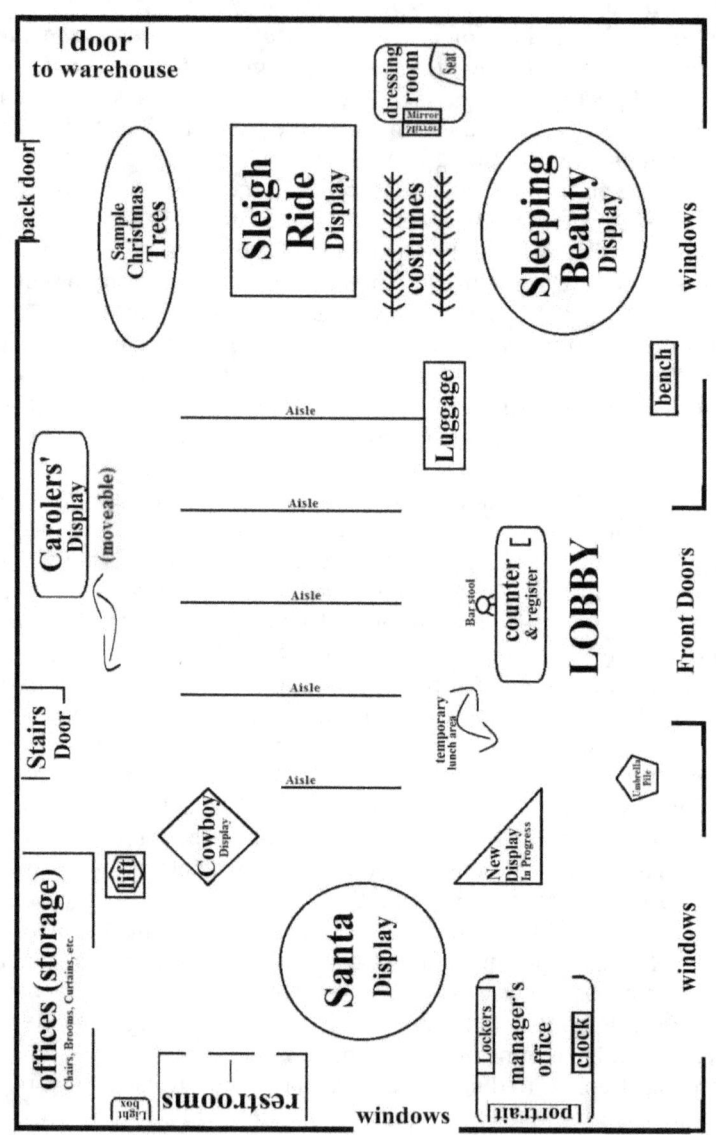

Enjoy the sci-fi book Lt. Plate was reading! Also published by Ruskras Corner

3748 A.D. The Return of the Cat
by Carl S. Kralich

"Humorous young adult science fiction with Christian values."
It's the year 3748. Humans have long been separated from Earth and cats have long been thought extinct. But Christianity endures and a young history student gets caught up in enthralling events when his evangelical-minded sister gets in trouble and he has to travel the universe to find and help her, meeting princesses and pirates along the way. Plus he finds the demise of the feline has been greatly exaggerated. 180 pages in 12 Pt Times New Roman Font, 6 by 9 paperback.

Visit Ruskras Corner Facebook Page for tips on our next giveaway.
All books available on Kindle.
Other Mysteries-
Murder as the Organist Plays-
"A mystery set in 1904 in old East Texas with many twist and turns." As the wedding music starts, the bride begins her long walk to the arms of her groom. But she will not finish the journey. The beautiful bride emerges stunned, blood on her dress. She stands alone, blood dripping from a dagger at her fingertips. Unknowing, his back to this scenario, the organist plays on... The processional music is the soundtrack for the murder that shatters the wedding day. The celebrated socialite goes from bride to victim to suspect in a matter of hours. Only one man, flamboyant and mysterious, stands between her and a noose or an asylum in this 1900s high society mystery thriller where political intrigue complicates all efforts to discern the truth. Turn of the Century picturesque East Texas is the setting for this mystery thriller with historical aspects. What happens next takes the reader on an exciting journey of mystery, love, and suspense with a completely twisted ending. 248 pages in 12 Pt Times New Roman Font, 6 by 9 paperback.

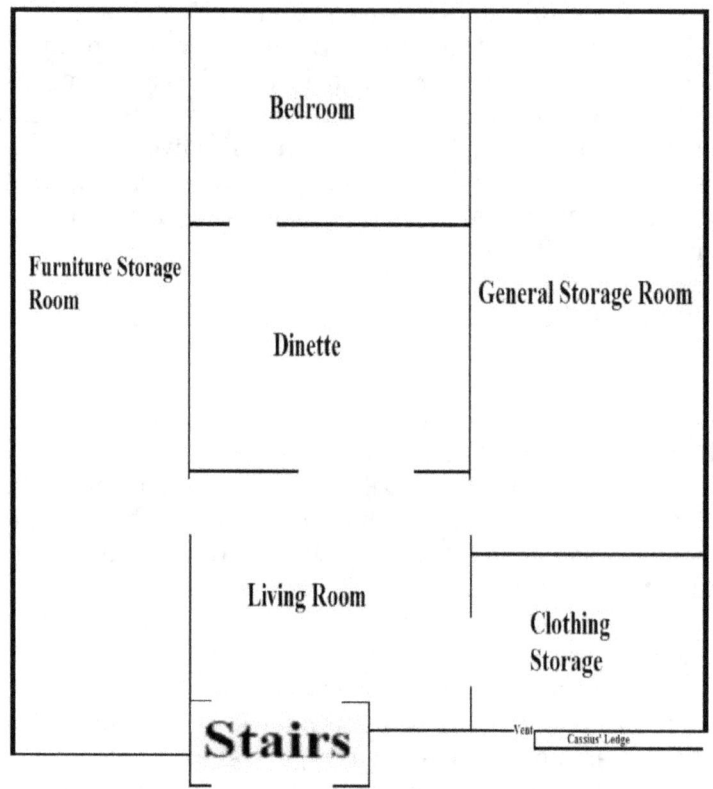

Second Floor